The Dead Among Us

Tracy L. Ward

Willow Hill House

Ontario, Canada

ISBN: 978-0-9881334-7-1

Cover Art Copyright © 2013 by Claudia McKinney
@ phatpuppyart.com
Cover image by shutterstock.com

Edited by Lourdes Vernard, Comma Sense Editing

Chapter Headings are linear excerpts from the poem
"Chorus of Eden Spirits"
by Elizabeth Barrett Browning (1806-1861)

This is a work of fiction. Any names, characters, places
and incidents are either the product of the author's
imagination or are used fictiously, and any resemblance
to actual persons, living or dead, business establishments,
events or locales is entirely coincidental.

For my Nanny

Chapter 1

HEARKEN, oh hearken! let your souls behind you

London, 1868—Ainsley unwittingly held his breath, and would have turned away from the horrid sight were he not being closely watched by Inspector Simms. They stood in a yard behind a butcher shop, somewhere in the labyrinth of East London, the body of a boy, no more than fifteen, cradled in a damaged, weatherworn cart between them. The stone that made up the rear yard was swathed in a deep red blood, mostly pooled, although some trickled to the nearby gutters, where it would remain stagnant until a heavy rain would wash it further down the cobbles. The boy's limbs were splayed outward from his torso, his face hidden behind one of his arms. So mangled was the corpse that Ainsley could not tell where the blood of the victim ended and the blood of the butchered animals began.

"Saving all the easy cases for me, I see?" Ainsley said, trying to hold back a sickness that churned inside him.

"I trust no other," Inspector Simms answered.

Ainsley looked up, surprised at the detective's words. Trust had been a hard-won battle that commanded a steep price. Of all the surgeons in London, Ainsley was certainly not the most experienced, nor could he claim to be the best. He had the misfortune of crossing paths with Simms at one of the worst times of the young doctor's life and it was during that time that Ainsley proved his loyalty to the job, even above his own family.

A smile and nod passed between surgeon and detective.

"This is the fourth body, you say?" Ainsley asked, studying the cart and immediate area around the scene.

"Yes," Simms confirmed. "I'll have the others sent to St. Thomas so you can have a look at them."

Ainsley internally winced at the thought of others but outwardly he nodded.

"And no one has moved him?" the surgeon asked, glancing to the constables who barred pedestrian entry to the yard.

"Correct."

During the carriage ride over Ainsley had been told this was the third body found in such a way, limbs contorted, torso gutted, and organs missing. All the victims were children, homeless street rats, and none had been identified or claimed. This victim was the first boy and, judging by what Simms had already told him, he was the oldest.

"Do we have a name at least?" Ainsley asked.

Simms shook his head, an answer that only added to Ainsley's work.

Ainsley's survey of the scene expanded beyond the cart, the blood and the mud-smeared cobblestones, and he looked to the fences, the four-storey high buildings that surrounded them, and the myriad of curious faces peering down at them from above.

Despite the heavy presence of officers and detectives alike, local residents had scaled the rickety wood fences that circled the yard to peer keenly over the weatherworn wood to see the body. With great effort, Ainsley had for the most part ignored them, though his insides burned with anger at their insensitivity. So monotonous and dreary were their lives that they could not help but find some measure of enjoyment from the suffering of others.

Raising his gaze to the onlookers, Ainsley shook his head in disgust.

"Nothing can be done about that, I'm afraid," Simms said, as if aware of Ainsley's anger.

"Can we not cover the body?" Ainsley was indignant, his patience quickly running thin.

Simms pointed a finger to a nearby constable and instructed him to retrieve a blanket or canvas, something to shield the child from view. As they waited, Ainsley knelt down, bending his knees and resting his backside on his heels at the base of the cart where it had collapsed on the ground. His attention focused on the body, Ainsley fingered the boy's torn clothes, threadbare and shredded at his midsection.

"Was this all he wore?" Ainsley asked without looking from the clothes. "Seems odd for March."

On a hunch, Ainsley looked to the boy's bare feet, blackened by the filth of the streets, and also saw signs of severe frostbite. The boy's smallest toes on both feet were a deep black and did not clean when Ainsley ran his thumb on them.

"Where are his shoes?" he asked, shifting to look around the yard.

Simms shrugged. "He did not have any when Cooper responded to the call."

"His shoes must be around somewhere," Ainsley answered. "He'd have either pilfered some or been given some at the workhouse."

Simms signalled for two constables to canvass the area for possible leads on the boy's shoes.

Ainsley reached for the lad's hands and carefully turned them over to study his palms. The boy had cuts running the length of his hands but they were not recent. Healed over and reopened repeatedly, most likely due to some repetitive task he had been assigned to perform. The nature of his work Ainsley could not guess, as street children were known to be hired as casual labourers, often changing tasks daily.

Two constables positioned themselves on either side of Ainsley, draping the blanket behind him, shielding him from those gathered at the fences and the tenement windows that faced into the courtyard. A homogenous moan rose from the onlookers, followed by a few shouts of protest.

"Give us a look-see!"

"Have a heart, Inspector!"

"Off with ye!" one of the constables shouted, raising a fist into the air.

Simms knelt down on the opposite side of the body and together Ainsley and the inspector moved to look over the boy's face and head.

The boy's hair had been cut haphazardly, and some patches to the scalp left red blotches on the otherwise white skin. Gingerly, Ainsley raised the boy's lip to look at his teeth and noticed the front two were missing and his gums were red with blood.

"He was struck in the mouth," Ainsley said, indicating the wound.

Simms nodded and wrote down something in his book.

"Send him to St. Thomas," Ainsley said at last, and gestured toward the mess that was the boy's torso. "I can tell you what's missing, but I need my tools."

Simms nodded.

Ainsley stepped out from under the blanket and motioned for the officers to lay it on the body. Simms took a step closer to Ainsley's side, his eyes reviewing his handwriting, but Ainsley could tell there was more.

"There's something else I should tell you," Simms said, folding up his notebook and avoiding Ainsley's gaze. "Have you read the papers this morning?"

Ainsley shook his head. He had been so firmly entrenched in his grief over the loss of his mother he had nearly forgotten a world outside Marshall House even existed.

Just then a man broke from the throng waiting at the main street. Pushing past the uniformed constables, he jogged between the buildings, heading straight for Simms. Unsure of the man's intentions, Ainsley stepped forward, placing himself between the charging man and the inspector.

"No one is permitted back here," Ainsley said, trying to be gentle as he pushed the man away. He noticed a small notebook in the man's hands, a pencil in the other, and for a moment Ainsley thought him to be another inspector. However, the man bore no likeness to the other officers of the law Ainsley had come to know. Small and lanky, the man had excitability about him, unlike the strong, stoic stance of Simms.

With the man insistently trying to push past him, Ainsley curled his hands into fists and readied himself for a confrontation.

"Ainsley, no!" He felt Simms's hand on his upper arm, pulling him back. "He's known to us."

"Theodore Fenton, Daily Telegraph and Courier." The man presented a slender hand to Ainsley and when Ainsley didn't respond in kind he grabbed for Ainsley's hand anyway.

"A reporter?" Ainsley looked to Simms.

Simms exhaled and adjusted his jacket. "Theodore and I have known each other for some time."

"Don't be modest now. We're kin, we are," Theodore said with a jubilant smile.

Ainsley could not help but dislike him. Considering where they stood, there was nothing to be so joyous about.

"Theodore married my sister," Simms explained, "Lord rest her soul."

Ainsley saw a disparaging look on Simms's face as he explained their connection. Such a contrast existed between these two men. Simms looked stern and ill-amused while Theodore Fenton had the look of a simpleton, unaffected and most likely unaware of the emotions happening all around him.

"We've got another one, have we?" Theodore asked, stepping past Ainsley to look at the scene. The boy had been covered and Theodore started to crouch down, as if to raise the sheet, when Ainsley grabbed his arm.

"Should I escort you out?" Ainsley asked. Kin or no kin, this man had no right to traipse all over their crime scene.

Theodore looked from Ainsley's hand and then to

Ainsley's face. "I haven't seen you before," he said, shaking off Ainsley's hand. "Are you a transfer from another division?"

"He's a specialist," Simms answered quickly. "Go on now, Theodore. I'll give you what you need in a little while." Simms waved in a nearby constable and pointed to Theodore. Instantly, the constable knew what was asked and went to Theodore's side.

"Don't mean to intrude," he said as the constable grabbed him by the underarm. "You and your men have much work to do to catch our *Surgeon*." Theodore's voice grew fainter as he was escorted from the scene.

"Surgeon?" Ainsley looked to Simms.

"That's what I was trying to tell you," Simms explained. "The papers have taken to calling him *The Surgeon* on account of what's being done to the bodies."

"That's horrendous. No self-respecting surgeon would ever perform such acts!"

Simms shrugged. "You and I share a commonality; our professions are equally untrusted."

Ainsley grimaced at the thought and rubbed his forehead. The public's mistrust of the medical profession held fast, it seemed. Judged as labourer and therefore less respectable than a physician, Ainsley's position at the hospital offered him neither glory nor riches and now he might well be lumped in with the worst kind of criminal.

THWACK!

Ainsley glanced up; the sound of the butcher's cleaver meeting the wood block at the back door of the shop stole his concentration. The resounding chop, chop, chop of the knife making quick work of the hunk of meat on his butcher's block held Ainsley in a trance.

Four victims, all children. Murdered, mutilated, and discarded. To what end?

Unblinking, Ainsley stared at the cleaver's movements and then watched as the discarded bones were slipped into a bucket alongside the table. And that's when Ainsley saw two eyes, crouched in the shadows just beyond the butcher's table, staring at him.

It was a boy, no more than twelve, with the ruddiness of the streets smeared into his red, cracked cheeks. No, not staring at him, Ainsley realized. The boy was mesmerized by the body and was not aware he was being watched by anyone. Ainsley saw a steady stream of tears trailing down the boy's face.

"Doctor?" Inspector Simms asked.

The boy's eyes grew wide and shifted, finally seeing Ainsley and knowing his position had been discovered. Jumping to his feet, the boy turned and ran, slipping through a hole in the fence boards.

"He knows him!" Ainsley yelled, pointing in the direction the boy had fled. And then, realizing he was the only one who had seen the child, Ainsley took after him. Slipping through the fence, he was just able to see the boy running full hilt down an alley and into the main thoroughfare, already bustling with morning traffic.

Ainsley had to turn his shoulders to slip through the two brick walls on either side and this slowed him down considerably. Once on the kerb Ainsley thought he had lost him, a large coal cart rolling by and narrowly missing his toes, until he caught sight of the boy farther down, turning a corner.

"What is it?" Simms appeared beside the young doctor, out of breath but determined to keep pace.

Ainsley pointed but kept moving in the direction of the fleeing child. "He knows our John Doe."

The boy weaved skillfully through the mass of pedestrians while Ainsley struggled against the current, unable to manoeuvre as easily as the child.

"Wait!" Ainsley called, realizing he could not catch the boy on foot.

The boy looked back but did not alter his speed and everyone in the vicinity looked disinclined to help a bobby catch their equal.

"Better pick up yer feet!" a man yelled at Ainsley from a stoop. "He hasn't much mind to wait for ye." His joke incited laughter from many around but it lit a fire under Ainsley, who dug his heels in and began pushing his way through the crowd.

"Wait!" he called again fruitlessly.

At the corner, Ainsley narrowly missed being tromped by an approaching team of horses hitched to a carriage. The team's driver shouted obscenities as he rolled passed. Through breaks in the carriage traffic, Ainsley was able to see the boy turning left into an alley. A few paces away from him, Ainsley could see a gateway into a courtyard and reasoned the alley must lead to the same row of yards.

Running across the street, Ainsley pushed through the gate and ran through backyards of mud, discarded waste, and cesspits. He crept through holes in rickety fences or scaled them easily since they were dilapidated so badly.

There was no sign of the boy and just as Ainsley slowed his pace, he looked to the closest alley and saw him, leaning against the bricks and panting heavily. Their eyes met at the same time and though the boy turned to run again, Ainsley was within a few paces of him and was able to grab the boy's shoulder.

Struggling against Ainsley's strong hand, the boy tried hitting him and wriggled against his captor. His desperation to get away was so pronounced Ainsley was almost knocked off his feet.

"Stop fighting me!" Ainsley said through gritted teeth.

"Let go of me!" the boy yelled. He tried to plough forward but Ainsley caught him at his midsection, hoisting him in the air with his arm. When Simms arrived, out of breath and chagrined, Ainsley was grateful for the secondary presence.

A groan escaped the boy's lips as he flailed. "Don't you know who my father is?"

"Who is he then?" Simms asked, through tight inhales of breath.

"A man of business!" the boy yelled, nearly spitting in Simms's face as he crouched before him. "And when he comes back—"

Simms waved a dismissive hand and straightened his stance. "Ah," he said turning.

"It's true!" the boy yelled, pulling against Ainsley's tight grip.

"You knew that boy," Ainsley said, moving the boy to the brick wall behind them so he and Simms could question him at the same time. "The one killed behind the butcher's."

The boy stopped his struggling and Ainsley eased up on his grip, realizing both of them were weary and out of breath. He kept a steady hand on the boy's shoulder, pressing him into the wall.

"You knew that boy," Ainsley said again with increased force.

The boy just turned his head, refusing to look Ainsley in the eye, his desire for storytelling suddenly nonexistent.

"Why were you running?" Ainsley asked, his annoyance evident in his tone.

Just then, a uniformed constable entered the mouth of the alley and jogged his way to them. He waited to the side, blocking the exit from the alley.

The boy folded his arms over his chest and refused to look at Ainsley, no matter how the young doctor moved in front of him to keep eye contact. After a few moments of this, Ainsley turned to Simms. "Take him back to the workhouse," he said.

"I ain't at no workhouse!" the boy yelled.

"Cooper." Simms took hold of the boy, seizing him under the arm, and passed him along to the assisting constable.

Cooper held him as Ainsley crouched down in front of him. With threadbare clothes and oversized boots, the boy looked in no better circumstances than the boy they had just found dead.

"Give us the address then," Ainsley demanded. "Your father can clear this up."

The boy hesitated and Ainsley smiled.

"Thought so." Ainsley stood straight, aware of how he towered over the child, and slipped his hands into the pockets of his trousers. "Mind telling me why you took off?" he asked.

The boy just looked away.

"What's his name?"

The boy's lips pinched into a thin line and his jaw tightened.

"Who is he? Your brother? A friend to pilfer with?"

"We ain't no pickpockets."

Ainsley laughed. "Then what is it?" he asked. "It is in this gentleman's right to arrest you for impeding an investigation but if you can prove you weren't involved, we can let you go." Ainsley shrugged at the simplicity of it. "Unless you had something to do with this."

"He was my friend." The boy began to struggle but the constable tightened his grip.

"From where?"

Again the boy hesitated.

"Tell him!" The constable pulled the boy's arms tighter at his back and the boy winced from the pain of it. The brutality of the act did not sit well with Ainsley. When tears began to streak the boy's face in silent protest Ainsley raised his hand.

"Ease off a bit," he said. Ainsley tried to look into the boy's eyes but he just turned away, this time down, as if trying to wipe the tears on the remaining threads of his shirt.

Ainsley turned to Simms. "Where is the nearest workhouse?" he asked. "The boy must be known to them."

The constable cocked his head to the south. "One down on Harbinger."

"I told you I don't belong to no workhouse!" the boy protested.

"Then where do you lay your head, son?" Ainsley asked.

The boy swallowed and turned his head to look down the alley. "Limehouse Foundling Home," he said quietly.

With those three words Ainsley's bravado was extinguished. He knew the home and its head matron well. His mother, Lady Charlotte Marshall, had been particularly fond of the orphans there and regularly assisted by hosting events to raise money. She visited regularly and often took Ainsley, his sister Margaret, and their brother Daniel there to assist. With her grave so recently dug and the loss still fresh, Ainsley heard the words as if they were a stab to his nearly broken heart.

Chapter 2

Turn, gently moved!

The foundling home was a grey brick building with three floors of matching rectangular windows and limestone sills. The building's adornments ended there save for black iron grates bolted on the outside of the windows and a long fence that ran the length of the wall, protecting pedestrians from falling into the concrete trench that had been constructed to allow some light into the basement windows.

It looked smaller than Ainsley remembered. He hadn't laid eyes on it in some years, long before medical school and even some years before when his mother retreated permanently to The Briar, their family's country home. As if standing before a ghost from the past Ainsley took in the sight, awed by its persistence and dreading the forthcoming memories. He had returned to work in the hopes it would busy his mind and distract him from the pain caused by his mother's death. Instead, his occupation had led him right to the most injured portion of his heart.

"You look as if you've returned home," Simms said from his side, his grip firm on the boy they had brought back.

Ainsley swallowed nervously, looked to the boy and then back to Simms. "This was my mother's charity," he confessed.

Simms nodded, realizing the connection. "Will they recognize you then?" he asked. "As Lord and Lady Marshall's son."

"Undoubtedly."

Confined to a mortuary in the basement of St. Thomas Hospital, Ainsley had never needed to worry about the two lives he led. Amongst the dead, he was Dr. Peter Ainsley, morgue surgeon. But when he walked amongst the living he slipped seamlessly into the role of Peter Marshall, second son and heir to the Montcliff earldom. Never before had the contrast been so abrupt.

"After you, Mr. Marshall."

The connotations did not sit well with Ainsley and he scowled at the detective's words. He hated his family's fortune and titles more so than the expectations that came with it. His father and brother accepted their roles amongst society without protest. Ainsley, however, abhorred his.

With resignation, Ainsley ascended the stairs to the front door, and opened it wide to allow Simms enough room to escort the boy in. With the door closed, the temperature remained the same as it was outside, cool and damp, but the darkness of the place highlighted the conditions even more so. As a pungent smell of sick filled his nose, Ainsley cringed internally at the dank conditions and marked chill.

At the far end of the hall a woman came into view, swishing a rag mop side to side in a haphazard pattern, showing little care or interest in her task.

"Excuse me!" Simms called. The woman stopped moving the mop but did not look up. Instead, she leaned into the wooden handle, her long, greasy hair reaching for the floor. "Miss?" The detective gave Ainsley an unsure look.

Together they walked toward her, the boy being led with little force. As they drew closer the woman looked slightly to the side as if peering at them through her strands of hair and then turned her back to them.

"Ma'am?" Ainsley asked as he drew close. By the time they reached her, Ainsley realized there would be nothing to gain from a conversation with her. Touched by the faeries, her family must have said before depositing her at the foundling home. Her gaze was vacant and her features contorted in an unrelenting twitch.

They looked around the corner from whence she had come. A set of double, wooden doors, propped open by rusted iron doorstops, led into a large dining hall, lined with rough wooden tables and benches to match. Ainsley cocked his head toward the door and led the way.

Muted sunlight to guide them, Ainsley walked into the room and panned the expansive place. A few girls, no more than six years old, were hurriedly wiping tables and straightening benches. Then Ainsley's gaze found Mrs. Glendora Holliwell, somewhat greyer since the last time they'd met, but then again Ainsley would have been about fourteen years old at the time.

"Mrs. Holliwell," he called out, surprised at the reverberation of his voice. "Ma'am?" They began to walk toward her.

The woman turned, raising a hand to sweep some strands of hair from her cheek. She gave Ainsley and Simms the briefest of looks before her eyes fell on the boy. "Benjamin Catch!" she admonished. She placed her hands on her hips. "What have ye done now?" She was not angry, not as Ainsley would have expected from such a place. But then he remembered why his mother favoured Limehouse Foundling Home so much.

Mrs. Holliwell was unlike any other sorts who were willing to take such an assignment. Matrons at workhouses and foundling homes were more often brash, crude women, grateful for the meagre pay and free food, but rarely concerning themselves with the well-being of their charges. He was reminded instantly of the warm heart she showed the children and attention she gave them as if they were her own.

Ainsley saw the boy let out a breath, refusing to look at her as he had refused to look at any of them.

"Mr. Marshall?"

Mrs. Holliwell approached him, offering a hand and a warm smile. It was the colour and shape of her eyes that he remembered most and then his mouth salivated for her gingersnap cookies, warm from the oven.

"How have you been, Mrs. Holliwell?" He could not

help but smile despite all the memories he had of her related so closely to those of his mother. Ainsley swallowed back the discomfort and grasped her hand with both of his.

"I was so sorry to hear of your mother's passing," Mrs. Holliwell said, placing her free hand over their grasp. "She was still quite young, was she not?"

Ainsley nodded.

At his father's request, no doubt assisted by a large sum of money, the papers published nothing of Lady Marshall's murder save to say she had passed away at the family's London home. Though everyone in Ainsley's family knew the true turn of events, and Simms as well, no one dared to speak of it.

Ainsley's thoughts fumbled for something to say in response but found nothing. Mrs. Holliwell must have seen the hurt in his eyes for she did not press further and turned her attention to Benjamin and the inspector beside him.

"What is this about?" she asked hesitantly.

"I'm afraid we may have bad news, ma'am," Ainsley explained.

Mrs. Holliwell's gaze dropped to Benjamin and then back to Ainsley, who was still unsure how to explain his involvement with the investigation.

"I believe this boy knows the identity of an unfortunate soul found not far from here," Simms explained. "One of the constables wished to question him. He tried to run and this gentleman was quick to give chase." Simms indicated Ainsley as the bystander.

"That's not—"

Benjamin's protest was quickly hushed by Mrs. Holliwell. "I shan't allow you to waste any more of these gentlemen's time," she said.

"He cried as if he knew the boy," Ainsley said.

Benjamin's face puckered, hard and angry. "I did not cry!" he snapped vehemently. The boy looked angrily at Ainsley but Mrs. Holliwell's stern expression halted any further discord. He dropped his gaze to the floor and drew in a long breath. "It was Jonathon, ma'am."

"Jonathon?" A sudden look of confusion slipped over her features.

Benjamin nodded and was quick to raise his hand to wipe a tear from his lower eyelid before it spilled over on his cheek.

"You are sure then?" Mrs. Holliwell asked, slouching slightly to look Benjamin in the eyes. "It was him, the murdered child?" The boy said nothing as more tears came. Seeing the boy's sadness Mrs. Holliwell raised a hand to her mouth, and grasped at her stomach with the other hand.

"He is a charge here then?" Simms pressed.

She nodded, feebly, and reached for Benjamin as if to console him but he simply pushed her away. With a deep growl, the boy shook off any attempts to contain him and left the parlay. Finding a bare wall, he leaned against it, crossing his arms over his chest, and turned his gaze away.

Ainsley offered Mrs. Holliwell his clean handkerchief. She smiled as she accepted it.

Mrs. Holliwell looked at Benjamin sympathetically before using the delicate cloth to wipe her eyes. "They were close," she explained amidst a slight sniffle. "I cannot imagine how this affects him."

"Jonathon was a charity case here?" Ainsley asked.

Mrs. Holliwell nodded as if unable to speak, as more tears came.

"His last name, ma'am?" Simms asked, his notepad at the ready.

"Most here don't have names until we give them one," she explained. "Master Catch is so called because of his tendency to flee and our need to try to catch him." She looked to Benjamin with a sweet, loving smile. "He's been like that since he was five."

"Five?" Ainsley choked.

She nodded. "Oh, yes. He and Jonathon have been with us so long. Jonathon came to us at two, I believe.

Benjamin was brought in a few years later."

"How did Jonathon come into your care?" Simms asked with a marked air of professionalism. He was neither soft nor hard. It was a manner which Ainsley would describe as neutral, if a bit unsettling.

"I believe he was brought to us by a woman who cares for many babies for their mothers." Suddenly, Mrs. Holliwell appeared uncomfortable. "You understand, mothers of unfortunate circumstances. His mother never returned for him and this woman could not find him a home due to his combative personality."

"Combative?" Ainsley asked, genuinely interested. He could hardly see any child the age of two having a combative personality, certainly not any more than other children his age.

"Jonathon was difficult to please. Abandoned children often experience such emotional discord but he was... less resilient than the others." Her gaze drifted and then snapped back to Ainsley and Simms.

"Could he have quarrelled with someone?" Simms asked. "Did he have any issues with the staff here?"

"The staff?" Mrs. Holliwell looked genuinely put off by the accusation. "Are you saying someone here is responsible?"

Ainsley raised a hand as if to calm her but she turned from him, using her hand to wipe new tears. "I don't think that is what the inspector is implying," he said.

Simms raised his eyebrows when Ainsley looked to him. It appeared that was exactly was what he was implying.

"I cannot say anything was so bad," she said, her voice muffled by the handkerchief.

"Anything you can tell us will help, ma'am," Simms said.

Mrs. Holliwell turned, her composure returned. "Of course." Her shoulders sank as she let out a breath. "There was an incident last week," she began. "We had some carpenters here helping to fix a leak in the roof on the third floor. Jonathon had been out running a message to my son and when he returned Mr. Jarvis was replacing his bed to the corner."

"Mr. Jarvis, the carpenter?" Simms clarified.

Mrs. Holliwell nodded. "Yes. He had to move the bed to get access to the ceiling but Jonathon did not know. He accused Mr. Jarvis of stealing his things. Mind you, I haven't the faintest clue what would have been worth to steal. The children who live here possess very little."

"May we see where he slept?" Simms asked.

Leaving Benjamin in the dining hall with the girls, Mrs. Holliwell led them up two flights of stairs.

The first thing Ainsley noticed was the thin layer of ice clinging to the inside of the window panes, encasing the glass and wood frame completely and distorting the little light that made its way inside. A breathy cloud circled their heads as they walked in.

Jonathon's bed, like all the beds, was rusted metal, painted many times over and chipping away to the black iron beneath. Though unlike the other cots, Jonathon's was placed against the wall at the darkest corner of the room.

As Simms, Ainsley, and Mrs. Holliwell marched down the slim aisle to Jonathon's cot, Ainsley noticed all the beds were neatly made. The sheets were a dingy colour of grey, with thin blue stripes. There were no pillows or extra blankets and Ainsley could not imagine the thin fabric doing much to keep out the chill of a winter night.

"Sometimes the younger children sleep in the same bed to share warmth," Mrs. Holliwell explained, as if obtaining access to Ainsley's thoughts. "The older boys tend to shy away from such things."

Ainsley nodded and Simms looked to a grate in the floor that should have brought heat to the higher rooms from the boiler.

"We have a strict ration of coal," Mrs. Holliwell explained. "We cannot risk running out."

"Do you have the address of that carpenter, ma'am?" Simms asked.

Mrs. Holliwell nodded. "I will be a moment." She excused herself and slipped out of the room, leaving Ainsley and Simms to sift through Jonathon's bedclothes. They pulled the bed from the wall and looked at the floorboards beneath in case the boy had need to hide anything. They examined the plaster walls, cracked and shedding in thin layers, and moved picture frames in search of possible hiding spots. There was but one shirt, not of any thickness, folded over the head of the bed.

"Interesting," Ainsley said after they had exhausted all possibilities.

"What do you notice, Dr. Ainsley?" Simms asked.

"Where's his boots?"

Without warning, Mrs. Holliwell returned, a small piece of paper in her hand on which she had scratched down the name and address of the carpenter. "This was the first time we had used Mr. Jarvis," she explained. "I think Jonathon was caught off guard."

"Do you remember what was said in the altercation?" Simms asked.

Mrs. Holliwell forced a smile and shrugged slightly. "I was helping some girls in the laundry," she explained. "It's in the basement. I only heard the yelling once I came up the stairs with a basket. I had never seen Jonathon such as that. He flew into a rage, he did, and was breathing hard, perspiring. He wouldn't let me touch him."

"What did the carpenter say?" Ainsley asked before realizing he was not supposed to let on he was helping the investigation.

"He told me Jonathon had yelled at him, though he never said what was said. We had to stop the other boys from entering their dormitory to give Jonathon some space."

"Would you say that was typical for this boy?" Simms asked.

"I must admit we've had far worse instances here than that. A nearly grown boy yelling at a tradesman is the least of my worries. He was a good boy; that is why he was allowed to stay here for so long." As if remembering the reason for the inspector's visit, Mrs. Holliwell raised a hand to her cheek and lowered her gaze. "How did he die?" she asked quietly, as if not really wanting the answer.

Simms hesitated, giving a glance to Ainsley.

"He was stabbed," Ainsley answered, not giving any details more than that.

Her breath stopped then and she covered her eyes with her hand. "I don't understand how someone can do such a thing." She choked back tears. "To a child."

Forgoing professionalism, Ainsley stepped forward and wrapped his arm around her shoulders. Her crying intensified and she turned into him slightly.

Mrs. Holliwell was right. There was no justification for killing a child, an innocent. Usually detached from his work as a morgue surgeon, Ainsley could not detach himself when children were involved.

"He was to go to Canada soon," Mrs. Holliwell explained between sobs. "He'd been hired as a farmhand. Him and some of the other older boys. He was looking forward to it. Their Great Canadian Adventure, he called it." Mrs. Holliwell raised her hands to her face and cried with vehemence.

"Mrs. Holliwell, are you missing any other children?" Simms asked, flipping his notepad to a previous page. "Girl, eight, black hair and brown eyes. Girl, maybe seven, blond hair, blue eyes." Before he could get to the description of the third child found, Mrs. Holliwell shook her head and covered her face in the handkerchief Ainsley had given her.

"No," she said suddenly.

"Forgive me, ma'am, but I had to ask."

"Of course," she said with a nod and sniffle. "There are no others. They are all accounted for."

Simms nodded and looked to Ainsley. "I will interview

the carpenter then," he said, placing his notebook in his inside breast pocket. "I trust if you come across anything, you will let us know at the Yard."

Mrs. Holliwell nodded.

The doctor and inspector walked down the aisle between the beds and left the room, but not before seeing Mrs. Holliwell slump down onto a bed and begin crying into her hands.

At the door that would lead them to the street they saw Benjamin Catch standing in the shadows. As the pair of investigators neared, Benjamin looked to them expectantly.

"You lied," he said with a pointed gaze. "Why didn't you tell Mrs. Holliwell you are a bobby like him?"

Ainsley gave a half-smile. "Because I'm not. I'm a doctor."

"Why didn't you tell her the truth?" Ben asked.

Ainsley looked back down the long hallway. "Because I made a promise to someone," he answered earnestly. "I said I would keep it a secret for as long as I could."

"So you lie to everyone to keep one person happy?" Benjamin pressed.

Ainsley heard Simms chuckle quietly behind him.

Ainsley kept his profession a secret for his father. A powerful man appointed to the House of Lords, Lord Abraham Marshall loathed his second son's chosen career path and only conceded when Ainsley offered to use his mother's maiden name. As a student and budding surgeon, the task had remained simple, but as time went on his position in medicine grew more difficult to hide.

"It's more complicated than that," Ainsley answered. He turned to the door, eager to be done with his inquisitor.

"Stay out of trouble," he heard Simms say from behind him.

Outside and walking at a quick pace, Ainsley and Simms weaved between carts, carriages, and pedestrians alike.

"You know that woman?" Simms asked.

"I cannot claim to know her well," Ainsley answered honestly. "My mother had taken a special interest in Mrs. Holliwell's work."

Ainsley could remember a time when the late Lady Charlotte Marshall did nothing else but campaign for the plight of the orphanage amongst her friends. Never afraid of the poorer neighbourhoods, Lady Marshall would often visit with the children, reading to them or bringing cast-off clothing from the houses of her elitist friends. She would sometimes lend the household servants to assist its operations during especially hectic times. Ainsley and his sister, Margaret, had visited regularly as well, until their father expressed his disapproval. Shortly after, Margaret and their mother retreated to the family's country estate on a more permanent basis and Ainsley left for school. In truth, it had been some years since he had seen Mrs. Holliwell, though despite a few more grey hairs, she hardly looked as if she had aged a day.

"A trusted source then?" Simms asked with marked seriousness.

"As trusted as anyone, I suppose," Ainsley conceded. "Her devotion to the charity is rather incredible."

"Has she a husband?"

"Died some years ago, leaving her a widow with a young son, though I never found out what did the husband in, in the end. A barrister, if I remember correctly."

"A woman of means then?"

Ainsley shook his head. "Not from what I recall. He was not all that successful." Ainsley rubbed his brow.

Simms must have noticed. "Sad business this," he said as he looked up to the midmorning sun, squinting.

"This any worse than the others?" Ainsley asked, knowing the seasoned inspector had responded to many similar cases.

"Maybe I am getting too old," Simms said.

"Too sentimental, you mean," Ainsley offered.

"The day I stop feeling pity for the victims I investigate is the day I should put forth my resignation," Simms answered matter-of-factly. "How motivated would I be if I cared nothing for the people behind the bodies?"

Ainsley became silent at this. He had spent years trying to turn off the human part of him while in the morgue. He had idealized an unaffected life where his emotions would never get caught up in a case. Such distance eluded him and yet he chided himself for it, wishing he were more detached and unemotional. Simms had reminded him of why he chose medicine in the first place.

"Get back to your dungeon now," Simms said, teasingly. "I must go speak with this carpenter."

The morgue in the basement of St. Thomas Hospital glowed yellow as the afternoon sun shone into the floor-to-ceiling warehouse windows that lined the farthest wall. No longer as chilly as it was during the coldest winter months, there was even more push to keep the work of the surgeons from piling up. The bodies waiting to be claimed were stored in a neighbouring room, devoid of windows and far more cooler than the examination room. The doctors needed light, however, often as much light as could be garnered from the days' sun. The handful of gas lamps hanging over the exam table were only used if the sun could not penetrate overcast skies.

The door swung in easily when Ainsley pushed it forward and was surprised to find Dr. Crawford, his immediate superior, and a young, though imposing man, standing over Jonathon's body.

"What do you suppose made those marks?" the young man asked.

"Well—"

"Don't touch him!" Ainsley yelled, throwing his hand

out as he rushed toward the examination table.

Both men looked up, startled by Ainsley's sudden arrival. "So nice of you to join us," Dr. Crawford sneered.

"This is my patient," Ainsley said, ignoring his supervisor's remark.

"How could that be?" the young man asked with a slight chuckle. "He's only just arrived. Scotland—"

"Scotland Yard brought him for me," Ainsley answered quickly. He pulled the white sheet that was covering the boy's legs up over his face to prevent them from looking further. "I was just at the scene."

Ainsley unbuttoned his coat, and tugged at the edges of his sleeves to coax them from his arms. He turned and claimed his usual hook along an opposite wall.

"But?" the man turned from Ainsley to Crawford, obviously confused.

"Now wait just a minute," Crawford bellowed, rounding the examination table and following Ainsley to the trough sink. "Are you not *my* employee?"

Hands washed, Ainsley turned to Dr. Crawford, grabbing a towel that was nearby. How he wished he weren't an employee of the hospital, at least this hospital. He enjoyed his work but Dr. Crawford had been a thorn in his side since his first day. There had been a time recently when Ainsley thought he'd never work in the hospital again. Shortly after his mother died, her murderer reaching the same end, Ainsley doubted he could live a life so focused on the vileness of human nature. His interest in medicine was, for the most part, fuelled by his father's disapproval of it.

"Perhaps you should set up an office at The Yard!"

"I will take that into consideration, Dr. Crawford," Ainsley answered with an air of nonchalance, "But for now I ask you to leave this boy and the other victims to me."

Ainsley let out a quick breath, lowering his shoulders as he did so, and then placed his hands at his waist. He couldn't tell if his request was reasonable in the eyes of his superior or if he had just called in his last favour.

"What other victims?" Crawford asked incredulously.

"They are being delivered this afternoon," Ainsley said as he placed his hand at his forehead and began to rub his temples. "I believe the papers are calling him *The Surgeon*." He lowered his hand, preparing for an outburst. Crawford hated the stigma against surgeons even more than Ainsley did.

Ainsley saw the young man raise an eyebrow. "I'm sorry, who are you?" Ainsley asked. He looked to Crawford, who pressed his mouth tight.

"Sidney." The young man put out his hand. "Lionel Sidney."

With hesitation, Ainsley shook his hand in greeting and then looked to Crawford.

The anger in Dr. Crawford's face had melted into annoyance. The seasoned surgeon gave a sideways glance to Sidney beside him and then back to Ainsley.

"I just need some time," Ainsley offered, as if presenting an apology.

The threesome stood over the covered body for some time, regarding each other uneasily until finally Dr. Crawford nodded. "Fine," he answered gruffly. "But after this, you will not be able to claim any of these as yours and yours alone." Dr. Crawford cocked his head into the centre of the room, indicating the other bodies that awaited dissection.

Ainsley nodded, not sure if he could ever make that promise. So much of his work of late had been at the behest of Inspector Simms.

With the room quiet, Ainsley leaned over the corpse of the boy, the yellowed sheet still covering him, and closed his eyes. The children got to him the most. Turning, Ainsley searched inside a drawer beneath his cache of tools and found the Scotch he kept there. He downed a quarter of the bottle before picking up his scalpel.

Chapter 3

Our voices feel along the Dread to find you,

Daniel was exiting Marshall House just as Margaret Marshall was nearing the bottom step. Seeing her approach, he waited at the door as Margaret made her way up to him. She had been out at the shops, though nothing tickled her fancy, and returned home empty-handed and disheartened.

"Hello, brother," she said, without trying to hide her disinterested tone. Their strained relationship was no secret. So infrequent were his visits that when he did come around she knew he had no thought to see her. It was their father he came for. They'd hide away in his study talking money and politics, both subjects emphatically shielded from her. Upon occasion, they tried to bring Peter into their parley but he had no patience for such nonsense, or so he confessed to Margaret.

"We don't often see you so early in the day," she said, hinting at her eldest brother's and father's penchant for drink during such meetings.

"I was summoned," he said, looking past her as if scanning the street for his next business conquest. He adjusted his cuffs and then slipped his hands into his trouser pockets as he looked down at her. "Father has been called away."

"Where is he going?"

Daniel shrugged. "Barbados. I am to look after some business matters while he's gone. Accounts and such."

Margaret stammered. She opened her mouth to say something and closed it again. Father had said nothing to her of such plans. He had said less than a dozen sentences to her in the previous fortnight. He was taking his wife's death quite hard.

"Peter will see to things," Daniel said, as if trying to reassure her that she would not be left alone. As if anyone could truly be alone with a staff nearing twenty, Margaret thought.

Daniel went down the steps to his waiting carriage, his driver opening the door as his employer approached.

"How is Evelyn?" Margaret called out suddenly, feeling as if she should say something more personal to her brother. "Is she well?"

Daniel turned, huffing slightly before settling into a scowl. "As well as can be expected," he replied, "given the circumstances."

Margaret nodded and Daniel stepped up into his carriage. She knew his anger was not directed at her and reasoned that his heart was broken for the life they had been promised. Despite everything, Lady Charlotte's death and the skeletons in Evelyn's family, he married her quickly, not wanting to allow anything else to stand in their way. As Margaret watched the carriage roll down the street, she wondered if he regretted that now.

Margaret entered her father's study and was surprised to find him no longer wearing black, as she did. He stood behind his desk, with an open valise before him, wearing his brown waistcoat and trousers. He looked as if he was packing for an extended trip and the sight of it startled her as much as seeing him no longer in mourning.

"What is it, Margaret?" Lord Marshall asked, a shortness lacing his tone. He pulled the slim cigar from his mouth and held it between his thumb and forefinger.

Hesitantly, Margaret walked further into the room. There was no telling what mood she would find her father in. Already, she felt as if she was intruding, but it was too late to turn around.

"I just met Daniel on the stoop," she said.

Lord Marshall raised an eyebrow.

"He said you were leaving for the island?"

"Yes," he answered, "Lord Bailey and I are seeking more investors for our tobacco. He has some contacts there. He said I could accompany him." He replaced his cigar and narrowed his eyes at her. "My valet tells me a man called on you this morning. A young doctor. Jonas Davies."

Margaret's gaze dropped to the floor. She had done well keeping her attachment a secret and she imagined her mother had not said anything even though she had guessed at their liaison almost from the start. "He called on Peter, actually," Margaret said quickly. She offered a shrug of nonchalance but knew it was not convincing.

"Cutter says he specifically asked for you," Lord Marshall charged.

"Jonas has been a friend of Peter's for some time," she explained. "He was only worried about him since... well, since he hadn't returned to work."

Lord Marshall snickered. No doubt his son's disinterest in continuing medicine pleased him immensely. "Have I a need to worry?" he asked pointedly.

Margaret was quick to shake her head. "No, sir," she answered. "None at all."

Lord Marshall kept his gaze on his desk, scanning the papers and dossiers as if deciding which would be best to take. Margaret wanted to turn and leave, knowing her private room would provide far more warmth despite its loneliness. In truth, she felt homesick for The Briar, their country house, and all her friends in Tunbridge Wells. She wished to see familiar faces and perhaps hide away on the pedestrian bridge that crossed the creek behind the stables. Above all, she missed her mother and The Briar contained more of her mother than any other place on earth.

Margaret bit her lower lip, debating whether to speak when her hasty nature blurted out the question that had been nagging her for weeks. "May I have your permission to stay at The Briar?"

The look on her father's face instantly gave her his answer. "Absolutely not," he answered angrily.

"But I—"

Haven't a friend in the entire city, she wanted to say, but didn't. Peter and her new lady's maid, Julia, were her only regular contacts and both relationships had their own unique limitations.

"I have plans to sell it once I return," Lord Marshall said suddenly. "I have no further need of such a place." He stuffed a ledger in his valise.

Margaret fought back stinging tears and tried to still her quivering chin. "But what about the staff? The horses? All of Mother's things?"

"They shall all be sold"—a chuckle escaped his lips—"except the staff, of course. Whomever I have no need of here will be given a proper reference."

"You can't be serious," Margaret charged. "You can't sell Mother's things. She's not been gone a month."

Clearly exhausted by his daughter's incessant questions, Lord Marshall threw his fist down onto the table. "Enough!" he yelled. "I will not be badgered, especially by you!"

Margaret's gaze shifted to the windows, though her shoulders and back remained rigid. She knew he meant to insult her gender, belittle her achievements, and remind her of her place in the family—the very bottom.

"You need an occupation," he said. "By the time I return I want your mother's rooms empty."

Margaret looked up, panicked.

"See to it, will you?"

"Father, you are only— I couldn't possibly—" Margaret swallowed nervously. Just the thought of going through her mother's things and selling them off one by one made her stomach lurch.

He laughed as if amused by the stress he caused her. "You will think of something. Keep what you like, not all of it, mind. Some must be returned to your mother's people. Cutter can help you crate it up and send it over."

"And then what?" Margaret pressed, angered by the

enjoyment he derived. "Shall I dye my hair a different colour and stuff my face to gain thirty pounds?" She raised an eyebrow when he looked to her. "Since you are determined to erase any sign that she ever existed. Perhaps you are wishing I no long bore her likeness."

It was obvious Margaret had struck a chord with him. There was no denying her close resemblance to the wife who had caused him so much pain. The wife who haunted them still.

"You may go now, Margaret," he said sternly, looking away from her and back to his papers.

Margaret did not move. She stood defiant and even thought to approach his desk if only to see how he should respond. Would he spank her or order a servant to do as he had done when she was much younger?

"How long will you be gone?" Margaret asked.

Lord Marshall paused his packing and gave his only daughter a look of challenge. "As long as it takes." His tone demoted her to that of child, worth no more than a message from a governess or butler. Already presented with her answers, her father expected to offer no more and this infuriated the normally calm Margaret.

"You mean as long as it takes to forget *her*. Well, you can't. She's a part of us forever. She walks these halls and haunts our rooms. She was my mother and your wife. Getting rid of her possessions will not erase the fact that she lived!"

Margaret turned on her heels and threw open the door. She charged up the rounded stairs of the open foyer to the second floor, expecting an angry summons to return. When she reached the second-floor landing she saw her father exiting his study, his face turned up to her.

"May I remind you, there were two I loved and lost," he called calmly from the foyer.

She felt a stab at her heart. Amidst all the chaos that erupted following Lady Marshall's murder, the family butler, Billis, a mainstay in Margaret's childhood, also met an untimely end. It was a deep blow to Margaret and she could only imagine the pain felt by her father, who couldn't have been any closer to Billis than if they were born brothers.

Without giving her father a second glance, Margaret went quickly down the hall and found her room.

Margaret had never enjoyed an easy relationship with her father but she had always revered him as protector and provider, the quintessential head of the home, and never saw need to question him, not even when her mother spoke disparagingly of the man she married. Even now, knowing her mother had broken faith with him and seeing the torment the late Lady Marshall had caused, Margaret did not pity him. He expected, as he had always done, to leave his children under someone else's care and that they would all sit, as if in tableau, awaiting his anticipated return.

Chapter 4

O lost, beloved!

Ainsley pulled a counter-height stool closer to the examination table and there he sat, his vantage point giving him full view over Jonathon's dissected body. The most arduous part of the autopsy had been completed but Ainsley hesitated to stitch the boy up before gaining a further grasp of his final moments. With so much damage done and large pieces of organs missing it was hard to say what the murderer was truly after. Something like this would be considered personal were it not for the other bodies found in similar ways. A crime of opportunity would not explain the true length of time it would take to carry out the entirety of the task. The murder defied logic and Ainsley found it hard to reconcile the act with any possible motive.

The door to the examination room opened and two uniformed constables marched in, a covered stretcher between them as they made their way toward Ainsley. Slipping from his perch, Ainsley placed his hands in his pockets. His eagerness to look at the bodies of the fellow victims was tempered by the fact that they were children; to Ainsley, examining children had always been the most challenging on the soul.

"Two others are in the carriage," one of the constables said. "Where'd you like us to put 'em?"

Ainsley gestured for the room off to the side, reasoning it was the only place where he could lock the door and ensure no other surgeons released the bodies without his knowledge.

One after another the constable brought in the three bodies, laying them where Ainsley asked. Only after their cargo was deposited did Simms walk through the doors, his arms overburdened with dossiers and assorted paperwork. The constables tipped their hats to Simms as they passed but were quick to leave, no doubt choking back the smell that had become so familiar to Ainsley that he barely registered it anymore.

"The police surgeon doesn't know I have these," Simms said, letting the pages and books drop from his grasp to the countertop with a thud.

"Does he know you've commandeered his specimens as well?" Ainsley asked, indicating the bodies of the other victims.

"He might catch on if he allowed himself to sober up enough," Simms said.

Ainsley grimaced. His own penchant for drink had rendered him useless a time or two. Making such a condition a permanent fixture in his life was a recurring nightmare for Ainsley, who struggled, often in vain, to conquer his incessant need for the bottle.

"These are the sketches he had drawn up," Simms explained, opening one of the files. He sifted through the loose-leaf pages.

A glossy corner caught Ainsley's eye and he found himself reaching for it. "What is this?" he asked, slipping the shimmering paper from the pile. "A photograph?"

Simms nodded, and pulled a second photograph from the pile. "There's only a few. Dr. Muller had them taken in his dead room at the Yard."

Ainsley tilted the glossy paper to the light over the table. Never before had he seen a dead body in such a way, poised for the camera, as Dr. Muller, the Yard's surgeon, and his apprentice stood on either end. Like some macabre family portrait, the image wrestled with Ainsley's conscience.

"Faster than sketching," Simms said.

"But not nearly as detailed," Ainsley noted as he squinted over the photograph.

Simms shrugged. "I suppose years from now, when all

is said and done, these photographs will stand as a testament to our investigation."

Ainsley was hesitant to agree. How often were such files revisited?

"I doubt this new science could ever really replace a true-to-life sketch," he said, returning the photograph to the pile so he could grab another one. "You have to stand so far back just to get the cadaver in focus," he explained. "All the detail is lost."

Simms placed the papers on the workbench behind Ainsley and reached to his inside pocket. "Something else for you," he said, revealing the G. & J. Deane pistol that Ainsley recognized too easily.

In his mind, Ainsley had already refused to take it into his hands before Simms offered it to him. An integral part of a previous case, Ainsley hadn't expected to ever see it again.

"We have no more need of it," Simms explained, an apologetic look on his face. "I understand your hesitation."

"Get it out of my morgue, Simms," Ainsley said, reverting his attention to the papers Simms had just given him.

"It's a beautiful piece," Simms offered. "Must have taken the smith many hours to engrave."

Ainsley could not bring himself to look. He knew the pistol. He had studied it closely, admiring its art, never expecting its owner would have any practical use for it. "Throw it in the Thames," Ainsley snapped, turning from the detective.

Behind him, Ainsley could hear the pistol touch the wood of his workbench as Simms placed it down. "Why don't I leave it for you to discard?" he said.

Ainsley drifted into the adjoining room, anything to avoid looking at the pistol.

He heard an audible sigh from Simms and turned to find the detective at the doorway to the room. "You have the bodies now. Tell me what you see and we can catch our man." He placed his hand on the doorframe and turned as if to leave.

"I think I will speak with Lady Brant. Perhaps someone has approached her with some of the organs," Ainsley said, remembering a family friend who was well-versed in the science of anatomy. "For her work, of course."

"Is there a market for bits and pieces?" Simms asked, halting his departure. "I should think the price is better for the entirety of the specimen."

"A market? Yes." Ainsley knew the demand for such parts, amputated legs, aborted foetuses, and the like was high. Lady Gemma Brant, in particular, used her surgical knowledge to create works of anatomical art while other anatomists conducted experiments for their many budding theories. "There are many unscrupulous fellows who see profit in such a trade."

"But why not take the whole of the body?" Simms asked. "Why only a heart and half a lung?"

Ainsley shrugged. "Trying to reason out the thoughts of a madman is enough to send anyone to the asylum."

"You ask Lady Brant," Simms said, "Perhaps she has a friend who has suddenly come into some organs of questionable origins."

"And you keep Muller heavily supplied with drink. I can't risk him barging in here, demanding his notes back. I'm in enough hot water with Dr. Crawford as it is."

Simms snorted. "I don't think he will be a problem."

It was late and the examination room windows were pitch-black by the time Ainsley decided to call it a day. His eyes grew tired as he tried to see in the failing light, the gas lamps above his head a pathetic excuse for luminance. Eventually, he was forced to stop. With the Scotch long gone and his fingers tight, Ainsley would only cause damage if he pressed on.

With only a slight reassurance that his victim would not be disturbed, Ainsley begrudgingly covered the corpse and turned to wash his hands and tools. Given the hour, he knew no porters would be about to do it for him and he would not risk rusting his implements by leaving them soiled overnight.

With the tools making their common racket in the sink, Ainsley did not hear the door to the examination room open. Ainsley heard the approaching footsteps first but did not suspend his work in the sink. Instead, he listened, visualizing the movement of the intruder, knowing each creak of the floorboards. With the water still running, Ainsley gripped one of the saws in his hand and waited until whoever it was stood directly behind him.

His hands raised and pinched into fists, Ainsley felt a fool when he realized it was Sidney.

"You risk your life scaring a man in such a way," Ainsley said, not bothering to hide his annoyance. Ainsley turned back to his tools, ensuring each one was placed in its spot. The surgeon's methodical nature did not just apply to his procedures but to anything relating to his work.

"I heard the Yard brought you the others," Sidney said. "I thought I could help."

"Are you a surgeon?" Ainsley asked over his shoulder. He caught Sidney lifting the sheet Ainsley had placed over Jonathon's body. "Don't touch that!"

At the sound of Ainsley's voice the young man dropped the sheet, which fell back into place. "My apologies," Sidney said, with a near chuckle. "I hadn't realized surgeons were so guarded with their duties."

Ainsley could not rationalize the protectiveness he felt for the bodies he worked on but it grated him immensely to have anyone second-guessing his work and findings. "I am."

Sidney nodded but Ainsley refused to turn his back once more.

"I'm not a surgeon yet," Sidney explained. "I'm completing my final courses at King's College. Doctor Crawford said he would hire me once I have passed. Said he needs a surgeon like me."

Ainsley cocked an eyebrow at the boy's arrogance. "He has plans to replace me then," Ainsley said, trying not to laugh.

"Well, not straightaway, of course," Sidney said. "Though he was not impressed by your absence."

"And what do you know of my absence?" Ainsley asked incredulously. He would still be absent were it not for the children. It was for them that he came back.

"Only that you have been away for some time," Sidney explained as he rounded the examination table. His eyes glanced over Ainsley's cache of tools. "And no one knows why exactly." He lifted the empty bottle of Scotch. "Perhaps you have been... preoccupied."

"My mother died," Ainsley said unapologetically.

"Why did you not tell anyone?" Sidney pressed, replacing the bottle to the counter.

"Because I didn't think it was anyone's damn business, that's why!" Ainsley snapped. "If you aren't a surgeon get out of my morgue!" Ainsley stepped toward Sidney, raising a fist as if he meant to hit the man.

Without flinching, Sidney raised his hands with open palms and nearly laughed at Ainsley's overreaction. "All right," he said, backing away. "I only intended to help."

"Get out," Ainsley growled.

Sidney bowed slightly and retraced his steps to the hallway. Ainsley fought down the undeniable urge to hit something. He cared little for the position he held, especially since his mother, his most ardent supporter, was no longer alive to urge him on. He returned for the children, nothing more. The love he once had for medicine had almost all but vanished.

Ainsley walked down a narrow set of stairs, where the air became markedly staler. At the end of dim hall, he opened a solid wooden door, the rusty iron hinges groaning against the movement. The room was a large gymnasium of sorts, buried under a nondescript building and far from the leering eyes of anyone who would rather they follow the Queensberry Rules. The two men in the boxing ring, shirtless and bare-knuckled, were nearing the end of their bout, their bloodied faces, puffy eyes, and sweaty torsos betraying their status.

No gloves, confines the hands, Ainsley remembered a coach telling him once years ago when he had started training. Reactively, Ainsley flexed his own fingers at his side as if to firmly grasp the memory. The Queensberry Rules, the new regulated way to box, had come into effect the year before, but the questionable legalities only pushed Ainsley to the ring even more.

Nothing angered his well-bred father more than his returning home with a black eye and facial contusion or two. That, coupled with his medical training, only served to complete his rebellious nature. Despite having reached a gentleman's agreement regarding his work as a surgeon, they did not speak of his time in the ring. Perhaps his father had forgotten Ainsley's penchant for self-inflicted suffering.

The air was thick with cigar and cigarette smoke, circling the suspended gas lamps in a whirling dervish of conflicting wind currents. The room, though vast, was suffocating and tight, with most men gathered near the ring, fists raised in encouragement of their desired victor. The sound was loud and steady, with conversations carried out at the highest volume.

During daylight hours the room was available to train and spar. Between dusk and dawn, however, the little known corner of London came alive with wide punches and rambunctious betting. Watching the bout made Ainsley stir with anticipation, wishing it were himself in the ring. A well-placed punch in the ring hit him with a soft spray of sweat where he stood.

"Who would volunteer for such a thing?" Margaret had once asked while cleaning a rather ugly wound.

"Who wouldn't?" was Ainsley's reply.

Scanning the room, Ainsley recognized many regulars, men he had squared against, men he had bet against and, at the opposite side of the ring, he saw his school chum, Jonas. Drink in hand, Jonas was standing not far from the ring, his jacket removed and sleeves rolled up past his elbows. Above the heads of the shouting spectators, his eyes met Ainsley's but before he could walk over to his friend a familiar face stepped into view.

"Nice to see you again, Mr. Specialist." Theodore Fenton smiled wide enough for Ainsley to notice a gap in his teeth where an eyetooth would have once been. "I must apologize for the rudeness of my brother-in-law. He never mentioned your name."

Ainsley swallowed. It had been a long, tiring day and all he really wanted was a drink and perhaps a turn in the ring. The man in front of him prevented him from achieving both. "Dr. Peter Ainsley."

Theodore's eyebrow popped up. "Doctor, is it? Oh my. You must come in handy at the Yard."

Ainsley looked past Theodore and saw Jonas looking on with amusement.

"Mind if I call upon your expertise a time or two?" Theodore asked. "This *Surgeon* fellow has my readership in a right tizzy."

"Thanks to some speculative surmising on your part, no doubt," Ainsley charged, his voice raised against the bout raging in the ring.

"You wound me, sir," Theodore said betraying a smile. "We journalists write nothing but the facts."

"I have never met a newspaper man who was above scandal or creative angling to make a story more enticing. Your entire trade is based on the gossipmongers and storytellers of old." Ainsley did not hide a sneer as he pushed passed Theodore.

"And what of your profession, Doctor?" Theodore called after him. "Are you known to always operate aboveboard?"

Ainsley kept his fists at his side and turned a shoulder

to pass Theodore. Ainsley had no doubt the man would make sure any ill-conceived reaction on Ainsley's part was recounted on a broadsheet by morning.

"Who's your admirer?" Jonas asked as Ainsley approached.

"Theodore Fenton," Ainsley yelled over the rise in the crowd. "Daily Telegraph and Courier."

"What business does he have with you?"

Ainsley snorted. "He doesn't. He's Simms's brother-in-law and we happened into each other at a crime scene."

Jonas gestured to Sidney, who stood smugly beside him. "Sidney says you're working the *Surgeon* case."

Up until that moment Ainsley had not realized Sydney had been standing there. "Chums are you then?" Ainsley asked.

"I met him while working at the university," Jonas explained, leaning in to be sure Ainsley heard him.

"How fortunate for you," Ainsley answered, purposely reverting his eyes on the ring.

The bell sounded, signalling the end of the bout. The victor raised his arms in triumph. The defeated fighter remained on the ground, bloodied and dazed. The noise swelled with unanimous excitement and groans as the crowd rushed in, surrounding the bookmakers with outstretched hands, searching for their winnings. Jonas pinched his slender cigar between his teeth and clapped.

A whistle and whoop came from Sidney and suddenly Ainsley felt himself becoming incensed. His sanctuary had been violated not only by the upstart surgeon, but also the man responsible for running his profession through the mud. Sidney's eager cheers and active participation only deepened Ainsley's resentment.

Ainsley slid his arms from the sleeves of his jacket and then loosened his collar, pulling his silk tie from his neck before thrusting it to Jonas.

Jonas groaned as Ainsley pulled his shirttails from his trousers. Unbuttoning his shirt, Ainsley just smiled at

Sidney.

"Peter, you haven't trained in months!" Jonas called out to him, but Ainsley was already through the ropes. The crowd cheered as Ainsley turned in the ring, smiling broadly. He was not the best fighter, Ainsley knew that, but whenever he entered the ring people seemed to love him.

Peter. Peter. Peter. A steady roar came from men who pounded the floor of the ring with their open palms as they chanted his familiar name.

When he turned he saw his opponent, the shock of it causing him to stop suddenly. Sidney was opposite him, pulling at his shoes.

Ainsley shook his head. "No," he said, sternly. "This is a man's sport. Go home to Mother." Ainsley waved him off and looked to Jonas indignantly. Jonas laughed, his cigar pinched between his teeth, and pulled out a bank note from his inside pocket and handed it to the bookmaker nearest him. Ainsley could not see who he was betting on and, for the first time, Ainsley worried it might not be him.

"Can I have a *real* challenger?" Ainsley shouted into the crowd. Men in the front laughed but when Ainsley turned to Sidney he saw the man was serious. The arrogance frustrated Ainsley all the more and by the time the starting bell rang Ainsley had decided he would offer no mercy. The kid should have known better than get into a bare-knuckle fight with him.

Ainsley found Sidney's face first, and rushed him into the ropes, stepping firmly and driving his opponent back with the determination of his steps. Three, four, five punches hit Sidney in the face and then he fell back on the ropes.

Ainsley felt the skin on his knuckles burn, and thought he had split one open before Sidney swung wide. It was luck and Ainsley's distraction that helped the punch land on Ainsley's shoulder but the blow did not faze him. The bout continued like this for some time, Sidney only making contact once for every five or more of Ainsley's blows.

"Lay off him, Peter," Jonas yelled from ringside, hanging over the coarse rope that made up the square ring and trying to get Ainsley's attention. "He's never done this before."

A punch landed on Ainsley's eye and immediately he could feel it run warm with blood. Angered at both Jonas and Sidney, Ainsley threw two concise fists into Sidney's face, sending him backward into the ropes.

Taking a minute to observe his opponent, Ainsley backed off, and saw Sidney had a cut on his brow above his eye and already his cheek was swelling.

"Should have listened to me," Ainsley said, when Sidney opened his eyes.

"Why?" Sidney asked as he pulled himself from the ropes.

Ainsley could see Sidney was barely able to open his left eye and he wondered how much longer the kid would hold out before conceding defeat. Ainsley shrugged. "Face it, kid," he said, matching the boy's arrogance, "you didn't stand a chance."

Sidney stood, fists raised in a defensive posture. Ainsley stood back another second, surveying his options. He could back out, save the boy the embarrassment or continue no doubt knocking the kid out with a handful of blows.

His opponent answered his question for him and charged sloppily. With a swift upper cut to the jaw, Sidney fell back, landing harshly on the ground.

Jerry, the proprietor and Ainsley's first coach, slid into the ring, signalling the end. After checking on Sidney, Jerry raised Ainsley's arm in the air in triumph. Unable to take his eyes from Sidney, Ainsley's win was bittersweet. He did not win many fights but the regret he felt for accepting such a mismatched pairing sucked away all the happiness he should have felt for his victory. He should have backed out. He should have accepted the disgrace and saved himself the stigma of beating an untrained man on his first time out.

Jonas rushed the ring, but did not go to Ainsley. Instead, he slid beside Sidney and placed an ear to his mouth. Panic rose in Ainsley's chest, stopping at his throat. Staring at the kid's chest, Ainsley waited, unable to move, hoping he had not killed him.

"He's breathing," Jonas said after what felt like a decade.

Ainsley rushed to the opposite side of Jonas, his medical instinct kicking in.

"Crawford will never forgive you," Jonas said, as he pulled back Sidney's eyelids.

"Crawford?"

Jonas looked up. "Sidney's his nephew."

Chapter 5

*Through the thick-shielded
and strong-marshalled angels,*

Sidney opened his eyes, one slightly more than the other, but it was enough to allow Ainsley to breathe again. "Oh, thank God," he said.

Together, Jonas and Ainsley lifted the man to his feet and quickly but gingerly took him out of the ring. The crowd was anxious for another bout and lollygaggers were never tolerated. Each with one of Sidney's arm around them to hold him upright, Jonas and Ainsley pulled him through the crowd to a chair placed against the wall.

Sidney fell into the chair easily and would have slumped over completely had Jonas not placed his hand squarely on the man's chest. Ainsley slapped at the side of Sidney's face in an effort to coax him awake. "Sidney. Sidney."

"Rematch," Sidney mumbled through a fat lip. He looked Ainsley in the eye and tried to raise a pointed finger. "Rematch," he said again with more determination.

"Sure thing, kid," Ainsley said.

Jonas left and returned with Ainsley's and Sidney's discarded clothing. With all the grace of a nappy changing, Jonas and Ainsley forced Sidney back into his clothes before Ainsley hastily dressed in his own.

"Damn it, Peter," Jonas said, buttoning Sidney's shirt. "I told you not to fight him."

"You didn't tell me he was related to my boss," Ainsley hissed. "I could have killed him I was so angry with him. He as much as said he was a better surgeon than me."

"That may be but we will never know if you break his arm."

"I should have broken his arm," Ainsley answered

hotly. "That will teach him to be so arrogant."

Jonas broke out in boisterous laughter. "Says the pot to the kettle."

Ainsley just shook his head, his friend fraying his last nerve.

"Come now," Jonas said, hoisting Sidney to his feet, "Let's get him home."

An hour later and Ainsley himself made his way home. He pushed open the front door and was met by no one. Gone were the days when the family butler would meet him at the door and ask about his work at the hospital. Lord Marshall had not hired anyone nor had he promoted any of the lower staff to a higher rank. It seemed to be his opinion, as it was Ainsley's, that no one could replace Billis. A lump found its way into Ainsley's throat, as it did every time he was reminded of what had been. Even though months had passed, the pain remained raw, the only relief found at the bottom of a bottle.

Ainsley hung his coat while listening to the beat of the house. He still lived with his father and sister in Belgravia. With his mother gone and his brother making a home with his new wife in Mayfair, the house seemed starved. Though the house had never been a joyously happy one, Ainsley's father and mother seeing no need for co-habitation, it was far less bleak than it had become since Lady Marshall's passing. There was a time when Ainsley thought things could not get worse and now he would give anything for those days to return.

He climbed the double staircase to the second floor, wincing slightly at the pain in his arm, either from a blow dealt or received. He heard Margaret's voice behind the closed door to her room and was surprised to find her awake. Gently, he pushed open her door to see Margaret and Julia, her maid and newly realized companion, conversing with great merriment. Seated on the end of her bed, Margaret still wore her mourning frock but Julia was dressed in one of Margaret's touring dresses. She giggled happily at her image in the mirror, unaware of Ainsley's presence.

Ainsley could not help but smile at the innocence of it.

Julia's free laughter came to a halt when her eyes raised and met Ainsley's through the looking glass. Margaret turned and gasped. "Peter, what happened to you?" She jumped up and went straight for him, her hand outstretched as if to touch his face. That is when Ainsley realized he must have been a horrid sight.

"It's nothing," he said. He tried to prevent Margaret from touching him but his movement lacked conviction and she was allowed to draw in close, surveying his bruises and running her finger over his brow.

"You're bleeding, sir," Julia said meekly from many paces back.

"My brother has a rather odd idea of sport," Margaret said, her face turning from concern to frustration. She pinched her lips together. "Nothing short of brutal."

Ainsley grabbed her wrist and pulled her hand away from his wounds, wincing at the stings that expanded through his face.

"And your shirt?" Margaret pulled at the collar of his shirt, revealing a smear of blood he had not realized was there. "Off with you," Margaret scolded. "I can't imagine the sight you must have been to any driver," she said as she pushed him down the hall to his room.

Too tired to argue, Ainsley did as he was told and even sat in the chair next to his lamp as his sister bid, practically falling into the chair with exhaustion.

"Getting rather friendly with the help, are we?" Ainsley asked, indicating Julia, who must have stayed back in Margaret's room to change into her regular maid's uniform.

"Do not attempt to change to subject." After lighting the gas lamp, Margaret stood over him, hands on hip, and glowered.

"Why not?" Ainsley teased, "It's as valid a subject as

any other. You both seem rather friendly considering not many months ago you despised the woman." Ainsley poked at the inside of his cheek with his tongue, suddenly aware of a cut on the inside of his mouth.

"This winter has been a rather lonely one," Margaret explained. "She keeps me in rather good company."

"I can't imagine Father supports such a kinship," Ainsley said.

"Father cares little of what I do," Margaret answered, her tone markedly low.

Ainsley raised an eyebrow.

"He leaves for Barbados in the morrow," she said. "Apparently, he will be gone for some time."

Ainsley nodded and then smiled. "So you and I have the house all to ourselves." He stood, and turned to look at his image in the mirror. "Think of all the mischief we could get into."

"I have no desire for mischief," Margaret answered.

"How dull you have become," Ainsley answered. He looked over the cut on his brow, and saw that it had reopened and was bleeding fresh blood onto the already dry bits clinging to his brow hairs. "You and I should—" He turned and found the room empty.

Within a second, Julia walked through his door, a towel over her bent arm and a pitcher of water in her grasp. She had changed into her maid's uniform, but Ainsley had a hard time forgetting the look of merriment on her face when she was wearing Margaret's dress.

"We should see to that cut," she said.

Ainsley nodded, too tired and in too much pain to argue.

Julia filled his washbasin with water from the pitcher and slipped the towel from the same table. She approached him with a wet corner of the towel. She gestured for the chair and Ainsley obeyed.

She held his chin, lifting his face toward her as she dabbed the dried blood. "You may need stitches," she said quietly.

Ainsley chuckled. "I don't mind my scars."

"You have many, I hear," she said before suddenly looking down to his eyes. "You box?"

"Yes," Ainsley answered. "Do you know the sport?"

A slight smile touched her lips. "My brother boxed."

"Oh."

"He's in heaven now," she said quickly.

"Oh."

"Not from injuries in the ring," she explained. Her face fell, though she tried to remain focused on her task. "Other causes."

They were quiet for some time. Julia worked at loosening the blood from his brow while Ainsley tried to ignore the warmth of her hand on his cheek.

"Do you want me to fetch some ice from the cellar?" she said, "Your eye will be black as crows by morning." She stepped back a pace and looked over him, pressing her lips together tightly and trying to avoid his direct gaze while he held the towel to his cut.

He had to admit she was a remarkable woman. Fetching and slim, though not too slim, she possessed a strength that he highly admired in women, and she had proven herself loyal in the last few months that she had worked for the Marshall family. From the first day, when his brother, Daniel, had made disgraceful remarks to her, Ainsley felt a protectiveness toward her that he had only ever felt for his sister and mother before.

When she lowered her hand Ainsley caught her wrist, preventing her from leaving. She did not struggle, though. Instead, she stood over him, returning his gaze with wide eyes and soft features.

"Thank you," he said, using a softer tone than he would have normally.

Julia nodded and he released her slowly. She took her arm back and turned, exiting the room. When she was gone, Ainsley raked his hand through his hair and stood, exhaling deeply. Were she any other woman he would have had her long before then. Never afraid to woo a woman, flirt, and tell her what she wanted to hear, Ainsley found it hard to behave so brazenly with Julia. She deserved more than such vile treatment. She deserved more than the womanizer Ainsley knew himself to be.

Almost as soon as Ainsley dressed in the morning he was summoned to his father's room. A steamer trunk waited in the hall just outside his door and a valise sat on top. Lord Marshall stood at his mirror while Cutter clumsily coaxed his jacket on. Ill-amused, Lord Marshall waved his valet away. "That's enough," he said. "Take my trunk down to the carriage and have Jacob wait for me at the door."

Cutter bowed and left, slipping past Ainsley, who stood just in the doorway.

"You wished to see me," Ainsley asked, bracing himself for contentious discord. He believed his father incapable of reasonable conversations.

"Yes," Lord Marshall answered as he buttoned his jacket. "I will be gone for some time," he began. "I've already spoken with Daniel and Margaret. Daniel will be seeing to my business and affairs of The House while I am gone," he explained, alluding to his work with the House of Lords. "I need you to hire a new butler."

"I haven't the faintest clue how to hire a butler," Ainsley answered honestly. He knew his father to be particular and dreaded putting himself in a position where his father could be disappointed in him. "Perhaps Cutter could fill the position and we can search for a new valet."

Lord Marshall shook his head. "Cutter is an imbecile," he said loudly, obviously not concerned if any of the servants heard him. He walked the breadth of the room and pulled his beaver top hat and gloves from his table. "I need you to do this for me," Lord Marshall explained earnestly. "Can I count on you?"

"Father, I..."

"What is it?" Lord Marshall asked as he put on his hat.

"I had thought it time to look for a home of my own," Ainsley explained. "Soon."

Lord Marshall snorted. "You plan to snub the entirety of your inheritance?"

"No." Ainsley shifted uncomfortably. He despised his family's money. He had never felt at home amongst the wealthy, London elite. He had learned to manoeuver the parties and gatherings well but he could never truly be comfortable in such circles. But he knew he could not remove himself from the family, though he had threatened to do so many times in his youth. Shortly after his mother's death he found out Daniel was not Lord Marshall's son. Despite all of Daniel's interest in the Marshall fortune and business holdings, he was not true Marshall blood.

"You are my son," Lord Marshall said lowering his voice, "and I need you here to look after your sister and our family interests." He placed his hands on Ainsley's shoulders and looked him squarely in the eye. "Can I count on you, at least until I return?"

Ainsley nodded. The timing was not right. He much preferred if Margaret were wed and well cared for than leave her alone with the father neither of them knew well. Their family had experienced too much upset to add more fuel to the fire. He would stay on, and keep an eye on his sister, but hiring a new butler was the task he least looked forward to.

"I'll miss my train," Lord Marshall said, making his way to the door.

"Anything else you need to say before you go, Father?"

Lord Marshall turned, and searched the walls of the room as if they held the answer to Ainsley's question. "No." He turned and walked out into the hall.

Chapter 6

They press and pierce:

Margaret walked down the church aisle on the left, as she had done for a number of Sundays, and took her usual seat to the side of the pulpit. Once settled, pressing down the ruffles in her skirt and crossing her ankles, Margaret stared straight ahead, her worn leather Bible held securely in her gloved hands. She could not cry, so much of her energy spent in the tears shed in the carriage. Instead, she waited patiently, wanting desperately to look around to see if he had come. But she dared not.

Eventually a tall form entered the pew from the same aisle she had traversed, though she dared not look. Jonas shuffled a few steps and carefully took his seat next to her. Still Margaret did not look. Sucking in air, her shoulders relaxed and she closed her eyes.

"Were you afraid I would not come?" he whispered, his lips close enough to her ear she could feel the warmth of his breath on her lobes.

She shook her head. "No," she said. "I knew you would come, like always."

He reached for her hand, which she had placed daintily on her knees, and pulled it toward him. Through her gloves she could feel his radiating warmth and her heart quickened.

This same vignette had played out Sunday after Sunday for many weeks since her mother had passed. Never more and never less. They would take their places side by side in the little obscure church, saying nothing but a promise to meet again the following Sunday.

Once the service ended the congregation thinned. Margaret and Jonas sat for a while, heads bowed toward each other, the air that surrounded them filled with words left unsaid. Margaret could not cypher the meaning of their weekly *rendezvous*. There was no understanding between them. She held hope that one day they would not be forced to meet so secretly, that Jonas would be welcome at her family's home, to dine with them and have a cigar with her father and brothers. She wondered if such mental images were merely self-inflicted torture. No such future existed for them. Ainsley himself had all but forbid their pairing, citing Jonas's penchant for gambling and his spotty reputation. Margaret had little doubt her father would feel the same. Jonas was not high-born. He was a surgeon, a rogue, and not at all worthy of her hand. It was that line of thinking that forced her to meet him in secret because the alternative of not seeing him at all was too much to bear.

"May I walk you as far as the bridge?" Jonas asked.

Margaret glanced around them to find all the pews empty and the rector gone. She nodded at his suggestion, secretly wondering if stepping out together was ill-advised. They had never done so before.

Jonas offered a steady hand as Margaret slipped from the pew. They proceeded down the aisle, Margaret smiling nervously as she matched Jonas's steps. The double doors to the front of the church were propped open, the grey light contrasting heavily with the dark church, which forced Margaret to squint as they approached.

They walked the path to the north of the church, its fringes lined with greenery that hung low over the walkway. Margaret ducked her head and held fast to her hat so the branches would not loosen her hair.

"I plan to speak to your father," Jonas said suddenly, as if unable to hold back another moment.

Shocked, Margaret could not find the strength to look at him.

"It's time we were out in the open," he said. "We shouldn't have to skulk around in neighbourhoods in which no one would recognize us."

She could sense him looking at her, perhaps praying for any sign of encouragement.

"Father has left for Barbados," she said, "We have a tobacco plantation there."

"He's left?"

Margaret nodded, and was surprised to find herself thankful for her father's absence. "I do not think we should be so hasty," she said, finding her throat quickly becoming dry as she spoke.

"Hasty? Margaret it's been many months, and years before that when..." Margaret looked to him but his voice trailed off and he turned his eyes forward. "You believe he will deny my request to court you openly," Jonas said, his words speaking her thoughts aloud. "Has he said anything to you?" Jonas asked.

Margaret kept her gaze forward and her hands locked in front of her. She struggled to find a suitable reply, knowing any explanation she gave would only further degrade him. To any other woman he was an exemplary catch, a surgeon who had won the respect of many in the field. But to her he would always be beneath her in rank and breeding. She was Lord Marshall's only daughter and she knew her father intended to use her marriage to further his political power and expand his business partnerships. She was never meant to choose her own husband and were she ever given such freedom she knew Dr. Jonas Davies would not be one of the permitted choices.

Suddenly, Margaret felt Jonas grab her arm and pull her back to look at him.

"Margaret, say something," he demanded, pain of the conversation evident in the gloss of his eyes.

"There's nothing to say," she said truthfully. "You have met my father. Nothing I say would be of any surprise to you."

Jonas straightened his stance, pulling his shoulders back and effectively distancing himself further from her. "Why do you walk out with me? What is the advantage in meeting me if you have no intentions toward me?"

Margaret could not rightly say. Perhaps she was more like Peter, flaunting her disregard for their father's rules in the same way Peter defied him by practicing medicine. It felt good to have a secret of her own, a time and place with no one in her family controlling her every action. Their disapproval was evident, lacing each encounter with guilt and hints of remorse. But, for the most part, Margaret found a freedom with Jonas she had never felt in any other part of her life.

"Jonas, I..."

Her hesitation only served to anger him more and before she could say another word he waved to a passing hansom and guided her to the kerb.

Chapter 7

Our requiems follow fast on our evangels,—
Voice throbs in verse.

Ainsley hid in his room, looking through his anatomy sketches from school, until midday but no one was about to protest. Cutter, the footman, came in once to retrieve Ainsley's bloodstained clothes but left without a word, most likely supposing Ainsley was deep in thought. In truth, Ainsley was purposely avoiding his duties as man of the house. Ainsley had slept off the pain and alcohol from the night before but a severe headache had crept over him and as the morning wore on he cradled his head in his hand more and more.

He opened the bottom drawer of his desk to retrieve his drawing pencils. The drawer clunked heavily with movement and Ainsley saw the pistol Simms had returned to him earlier. Only ever fired twice it seemed wasteful to have the firearm melted and yet its presence in the house seemed inappropriate. Unsure what to do with it, he pushed the pistol aside and pulled out the wooden box that held his pencils.

"Peter."

A muffled sound came from the hall. Ainsley waited, and eventually lowered the pencil in his hand. He watched the door, supposing any moment it would fly open and his sister would appear, repeating his name.

No one came.

Dropping the pencil on the desktop, Ainsley stood and walked to the hall. He found it empty.

And then he remembered Margaret had already gone to church and would take tea out in the afternoon. Father had already left for Barbados.

Ainsley returned to his room, unnerved. He glanced

around his room, as if expecting one of the servants, but found no one. He had heard his name called, had he not? He listened again, wondering if he had heard something out on the street or in another room that could account for the noise. He heard nothing.

He walked the hall, looking in each room as he passed, and found no one in his vicinity. He spotted Julia in Margaret's room and slipped past the threshold. "Did you call for me, Miss Kemp?" he asked, knowing very well she would have called him Lord Marshall if she had any need to call for him at all.

He looked around the room as if the answers lay somewhere within the wallpaper.

"No, sir," Julia answered. She lowered the hat in her hands, a loose ribbon dangling from the brim, and squared her shoulders toward him as she spoke.

"My sister has left then?" he asked.

"Yes, sir."

Despite the presence of servants, the house felt rather empty. The house was so large a body could occupy its own room and never realize another was about. This must resemble the loneliness Margaret often spoke about.

"Are you fixing one of Margaret's hats?" he asked, stepping further into the room.

Julia smiled and looked down at the velvet-covered headpiece in her grasp. "Yes, it flew from her hand the other day and I chased it down the pavement. I had to step on it to keep it from blowing in the street." She turned the hat over in her hands. "I'm afraid I crushed it."

Ainsley could not help but laugh. "You chased down a hat?"

"It was a very windy day," Julia answered in earnest. Her smile faded and she looked over the mangled bow with consternation.

"Oh, I am not laughing at you," Ainsley said quickly. He raised his hand and touched her arm as he would with Margaret when he wanted her to look at him. "I am entertained at the thought of you running down the road to retrieve a hat when Margaret has an allowance to buy a dozen more in its place."

Julia smiled. "And so said Margaret as well." She fiddled with the bow and bit her lower lip as she smiled.

Ainsley took back his hand. "You should keep it," he said. "If you think you could fix it."

Julia surveyed the hat. "I should be able to, but I could never—"

"I'll talk to Margaret about it," Ainsley said. "It would look pretty on you."

Julia smiled and nodded. She glanced toward him slightly as she passed him and began walking toward the door.

"Miss Kemp." Ainsley turned. "I'm sorry for grabbing your arm yesterday," he said.

"You were in pain, sir," she said dismissively. "We all do things we regret when we are hurting."

Ainsley nodded, glad that, to her at least, their encounter was of no great importance and that he had not embarrassed himself completely.

Julia smiled and bowed her head before leaving the room.

Lady Gemma Brant's house stood unassuming on the outside, a testament to the high-end neighbourhood and well-bred families who resided in similar dwellings up and down the street. But despite being well-bred, Lady Brant stood out as eccentric and rarely entertained visitors. Once past the foyer any visitor to her home was immediately greeted by display case after display case filled with well-preserved body parts, each intricately coloured and showcased for its anatomical properties. Layers of skin were cut back from the bones, revealing veins and arteries, muscles and fat, all of which Lady Brant painstakingly accentuated with dyes, wax and resin, colorant, and stiffeners. Each dissected hand, foot, skull, or heart was displayed as a piece of art to be admired, though many often recoiled.

Ainsley had so often visited Lady Brant's home he did not shy away from inching in for a closer look. Lady Brant's work was a contribution to anatomical study at large. More than once she had referred to her misfortune of being born female. She had never been permitted to attend medical school nor had her womb held a child. In effect, she admitted, she had never entirely been a man or a woman and that suited her all the same.

"Peter!" Half-moon spectacles perched on her nose, Lady Brant greet Ainsley with outstretched arms. "You have not visited me for some time. Come." She ushered him further into the room and led him to a plush, velvet settee. "I will have the girl fetch tea."

Ainsley smiled at Lady Brant's use of the word girl. The turnover for servants in the Brant household was high, far greater than was average, on account of Lady Brant's activities. There was a steady stream of torsos and bloodied body parts making their way through the doors, causing any hired help who hadn't the fortitude to stomach it to find a better position. Frustrated with having to remember the names of her ever-changing staff, Lady Brant began referring to them as girl, boy, man, and woman, sometimes assigning the adjective *young* or *old*, as if it weren't already clear.

Lady Brant rang the little bell on the table beside her chair and removed her spectacles. When the maid arrived, her eyes trained forward with marked determination, Lady Brant asked for tea and the girl left with her eyes to the rug and nothing else. Lady Brant growled slightly at the sight of it. "Girls these days are far too fragile," she said with great annoyance.

Ainsley chuckled. "Margaret would certainly agree."

"How is she holding up?" Lady Brant settled back into her seat. "I worry about her with no other females in the house."

Ainsley watched as Lady Brant took on a pensive look. She may never have borne a child but she was mothering Margaret with a lot more fervor than their real mother ever had. "It's been difficult for everyone," Ainsley said, avoiding singling his sister out.

"Yes, but Margaret"—Lady Brant clicked her tongue—"she needs the guidance of another woman. I don't think your father has given much thought to these matters."

"He's left for the islands."

"Barbados!" Lady Brant's voice rose in disbelief. "The nerve of that man leaving at such a time. He could never be counted on to do the right thing, not when it matters."

Ainsley smiled to himself. Lady Brant never liked the man her best friend ended up marrying and it was never a secret Lady Brant attempted to hide. Ainsley grew up knowing the tensions between Lady Brant and Lord Marshall existed, but the Marshall children were never strangers to tension.

"I believe Margaret has things well in hand," Ainsley said, not wishing to give Lady Brant any room to manoeuver into the family's affairs.

Lady Brant pressed her lips together and shifted in her seat, readjusting her skirt. She looked as if she had more to say, so Ainsley spoke quickly, not caring if he cut her off. "I've come to ask about any new specimens you may have collected." He glanced around her parlour, not noticing anything new or out of the ordinary.

"What do you mean?" Lady Brant stiffened at the mention of her work.

"Raw specimens, I should say." Ainsley stood and walked toward a small glass case at the far end of the room. Inside were bronchioles, the tiny capillary-like stems inside a human lung which looked remarkably like tree branches since they were mounted to the floor of the case. The specimen had been coloured, of course, and injected with a resin-wax mixture meant to extenuate the track. "Is this new?" Ainsley asked, bending over it.

Lady Brant was soon at his side, always eager to explain her art. "Not exactly," she said from behind him. "I've been working on it for a year trying to get the hue just right. I'm still not sure it does the organ justice." Lady Brant walked around the small table slowly. "The human body is such a work of art."

Ainsley envied her sense of wonder after so many years. Clearly, she remained passionate.

Lady Brant plucked a smaller case from the mantel and placed it on the table beside the lung specimens. "I completed this one last week." Inside was a brain, cut into a cross-section, with leathery skin and straggly hair still attached to the bulbous side.

"Has anyone come to you offering organs? Hearts? Livers? Anyone you haven't worked with before? Maybe you have something in your laboratory."

"Peter, your questions injury me. To suggest I would accept such a thing brought to my back door as if I were common rabble." Lady Brant gave him an indignant look. "I only obtain my specimens from the hospital and perhaps, from time to time, the university. But every family is paid a fair price and they are thankful for it, I may add."

"I meant no offence," Ainsley said, quickly turning toward her as she paced the room behind him.

"This is about that *Surgeon*, isn't it?" she asked sharply, her memory suddenly jogged by something. "Oh, please tell me you haven't been pulled into that case with the Yard. You have, haven't you? Oh Peter, what would your mother have to say?"

"I think you may be confused," Ainsley said, "I'm not *The Surgeon*, if that's what you are implying."

"Don't be so crass, of course I wasn't suggesting such a thing." She waved a dismissive hand at him.

"Then why do you speak as if my involvement with the investigation makes me as guilty as the perpetrator?"

"Because I have never known an officer of the law to operate aboveboard, if I may be so bold. You are the company you keep and you have been keeping some questionable company these days."

Ainsley stifled laughter. He never had high scruples for the people he associated with and it was on this tenet that his shaky reputation was built upon. Lady Brant didn't seem to notice. She rounded the back of the settees and leaned in, digging her fingers into the forgiving upholstery.

"I am only helping in the case to find the killer. The police surgeon cannot be counted upon to do his due diligence."

Lady Brant raised an eyebrow at this and began to wring her hands. "And if your name is given to the papers?"

Ainsley shook his head. "No, Simms has assured me."

Lady Brant huffed.

Ainsley decided to keep the conversation on point despite her insistence to meddle. "Has anyone in your circle mentioned a new source for their cadavers, body parts mostly?"

"No." Lady Brant met his gaze squarely.

"Can you enquire—?"

"Peter!"

"It's an investigation. We have to investigate!"

Ainsley had never raised his voice to Lady Brant before. He had taken all her interfering and insinuations in stride, but her impediments to their work was too much. It didn't matter that the subject made her uncomfortable or that people would talk. The only thing that mattered was ensuring the murderer was brought to justice.

After a quiet moment, Lady Brant exhaled and squared her shoulders. "I will ask," she said, "discreetly. But you must promise me to do all you can to keep your names from the papers. I cannot think of what may happen to Margaret should your affair with medicine become public knowledge."

"Is that what this is about? You are afraid my work will make Margaret less desirable?"

Lady Brant avoided his direct gaze and shrugged.

"I see," Ainsley said. "My conduct wields such power?

Above all else? Father and mother's conduct? Lady Evelyn and her brother? All their deeds and scandals can be overlooked but my interest in medicine, my work to bring a villain to task for his deeds, that's a real cause for concern." Ainsley could feel his voice rising with each syllable but he couldn't stop himself. "Lady Brant, if that's your biggest concern then you are demonstrative of everything that is wrong with this world!"

Ainsley stormed from the room, not caring how his outburst was received by his mother's longtime friend. His anger wasn't entirely directed at her. Despite her firm position on the outskirts of proper society, she was the physical representation of it, and her opinions reminded him of society's views and, at the heart of it, that is what angered him the most. He wished he could conduct business in the open without having to care for his family's reputation. He wished he could himself in all areas of his life, not just be half the man he was half the time.

Ainsley had not intended to head to the hospital that day but the oppressive atmosphere of the house and his argument with Lady Brant propelled him to the hospital's door. Absentmindedly, his feet led him along the pavement and soon he found himself standing outside of St. Thomas looking up at the third-story window directly above the front doors. Beyond the pane of glass stood his friend Jonas. Ainsley felt the urge to wave at him but before he could he saw the woman standing next to him, and that's when Ainsley realized she was reaching for his hand.

Transfixed by the peculiarity of the scene, Ainsley found it difficult to look away, even when he saw Jonas lean toward the woman, brushing the hair from her ear.

Someone coming from the hospital doors bumped into Ainsley with marked force.

"My apologies," a porter called over a bundle of laundry. Ainsley tipped his hat in acknowledgement and when he looked back to the window the pair was gone.

The memory of them stayed with him as he made his way down to the hospital mortuary. Margaret had continued to deny any attachment to Jonas but Ainsley had always suspected she was fibbing. She knew nothing could come of it, especially given Jonas's employment. But Ainsley had seen the way they looked at each other. He had caught them a time or two holding hands in the parlour. Once he had even seen Jonas's arm around Margaret's waist as if pulling her in for a kiss.

Ainsley himself had made his position on the matter clear. She was the only female sibling and as much as she toyed with the idea of shirking her responsibility, they both knew she was bound to it by duty. She would marry a man who received their father's blessing, and by doing so she'd restore the family's respectability.

The irony of the situation was not lost on him however. He flaunted his responsibility and threatened the last remaining threads of respectability, all the while anticipating that she would stay the course. The duty that he found stifling was pressed upon her all the more. Perhaps he should have been more supportive of their liaison; doing so might have prevented Jonas from seeking interest from another.

Ainsley wondered if Margaret knew that Jonas had moved on, but then again she may have been the one to end it. The thought did not ease his worry, though. Something inside him told him the woman in the window was another conquest in a rather long line. His only fear was that Margaret had somehow been discarded.

The rooms of the hospital basement were dark and sparsely populated. He saw a colleague in their office, hunched over a book, but Ainsley did not care to announce his presence. Instead, he went down the hall and slipped unannounced into his exam room, where he would be assured quiet amongst the bodies of the dead.

Jonathon's body had been moved to the adjoining room. Ainsley hadn't had the opportunity to examine the others in any great depth. He had skimmed the police surgeon's notes but found them disjointed and vague. The truth of the condition in which they were found was hidden behind neatly stitched torsos and carefully washed bodies. Even so, he must work with them quickly. Within the week, even in the cold basement of the hospital, they would be rendered more of a hindrance than help.

Ainsley went for a cupboard, unlocking the double doors and pulling back at the handles. Inside held his notes, a few of his own sketches he had completed the day before of Jonathon's body, wounds and markings mostly, as well as the sketches completed by the police surgeon. Ainsley had displayed them along the back side of the cupboard the day before. Prominently positioned, yet hidden from the view of others, the arrangement of papers served as a reminder of clues he had already found with the hopes he would eventually see similarities.

Ainsley began flipping through the autopsy reports that had come from the Yard.

Until Jonathon, the victims had been all girls, all under ten years old and all unclaimed. They'd been butchered, their torsos rendered unrecognizable with certain organs missing, though none matched another. Jonathon was the first they could name, and the one who gave his murderer the most trouble. There was a high chance their suspect had visual bruises or cuts to his face or arms, given the damage Ainsley found on Jonathon's hands.

Ainsley pulled up a chair and took a seat in front of the board, his eyes darting from detail to detail as he cross-referenced the cases, jogging his memory and yet confusing it more. Jonathon's stomach was gone, and parts of his intestines, but the girls had their lungs and hearts taken. The blond was missing her eyes. Shuttering slightly, Ainsley turned his gaze away from the sketch of the blond girl.

There was a knock from the opposite side of the room,

and Ainsley turned. The sound was loud enough for him to expect another surgeon or porter had entered the room without his knowledge but when he turned he saw nothing. That part of the room, furthest from the windows, was near black and Ainsley would have shrugged off the noise except one of the off-white sheets draped over Jonathon's body swayed slightly as if touched by a strong breeze.

Ainsley stood, careful not to make a noise, and slowly took steps toward the boy's corpse until finally he was standing over the table. He knew someone was in the room. The air felt different and Ainsley's senses were directing him to beneath the table where Jonathon was laid out. Frustrated at being spied on, Ainsley pounced. He grabbed whoever it was with a forceful fist and dragged a rather small person from under the table.

"Benjamin Catch?" Ainsley's anger morphed into confusion.

Terrified, the boy hit at Ainsley while trying to pull free of the surgeon's strong grasp. "I only wanted to see!" he yelled, pulling at Ainsley's arms to break the surgeon's grip.

"See what?" Ainsley asked. Looking down at him, Ainsley held Benjamin at the shoulders, keeping the boy at arm's length. "Jonathon?"

Benjamin stopped struggling and wiped his nose on his threadbare sleeve. With his jaw clenched, he glared at Ainsley as if the surgeon represented all the misdeeds of the world. And then the resentment slipped away, his eyes growing wide as he took in the sight of Ainsley's face.

"What happened to you?" Benjamin asked, now unable to look away.

Ainsley shook his head and waved off the boy's concerns as he turned away. "You are trespassing, you know this," Ainsley said, slipping his hands into his pockets.

Benjamin nodded. "We don't get funerals," he called out as Ainsley walked from him.

Ainsley turned.

"Us charity cases," Benjamin continued, lowering his voice. "We get put in a hole in the ground with twenty others and no one even knows we were here."

Ainsley knew what the boy said was true. There was no special treatment for the penniless dead; too much philanthropy was given to the homeless and starving that by the time they died no one took notice. Many saw it as a relief, one less guttersnipe to house and feed.

"You were saying good-bye," Ainsley said.

Benjamin nodded, swallowing hard and then wiping his nose on his sleeve again.

Ainsley cocked his head to the side, indicating Jonathon's body. He pulled the sheet back from the boy's face, folding it just at the shoulders. He turned his stool around, placing it at Jonathon's torso and patted the wooden top. "Five minutes."

Benjamin nodded but stayed still. Ainsley eventually turned, leaving the room to give Benjamin some privacy, but he stopped just outside the door, his ear turned to the room, listening.

Ainsley heard the scraping of the chair, as if the boy had moved it closer. Then the room fell silent and remained so for some time until finally Ainsley heard the faint sounds of forcible breathing, then slight whimpers followed by sniffles. For a while, Ainsley thought the boy would not speak, but then Benjamin's voice broke out in a whisper, further muffled by hands clasped in front of him as if in prayer.

"You're not dead," Benjamin sobbed. "You're not."

Sniffle.

"I thought I was going to say good-bye on a dock or something but this will have to do." Benjamin struggled for a breath between cries. "To me you will be in Canada, hunting rabbits, running from bears"—the boy laughed—"eating and drinking with merriment like we said you would. You're not dead. You are just another world away."

Ainsley pressed his palms into his face, wiping his own tears at the boy's words. Jonathon had been scheduled to leave for Canada within the week, and Benjamin eased his pain by pretending his dear friend was across the Atlantic.

A few moments later, Benjamin appeared in the doorframe, shoulders straight and his face stoic. "Thank you, sir."

Ainsley nodded but words failed him.

"I hope you catch 'im that did this to Jonathon and those girls," Benjamin said, while his eyes darted from Ainsley and away again, unable to hold his stare.

Ainsley raised an eyebrow. "Those girls?" It was possible the boy had read newspaper reports, though Ainsley doubted Ben or the orphanage had funds for a two-bit paper.

Benjamin turned slightly and looked back into the room. He pointed to the body placed directly beside Jonathon's. "She was pretty," Benjamin swallowed. "Not now, of course."

"You knew one of them?" Ainsley asked, feeling a slight flicker of hope deep inside him. Even with constables canvassing the streets of Limehouse, knocking on every door and pressing every pedestrian they came across, they had not found out the identity of any of the girls.

Benjamin shrugged. "Not especially," he said, raising his wrist to rub at the remaining tears at his eyes. A slight sniffle escaped him as he stood in front of Ainsley. "A mudlark, she was," Benjamin answered. "Worked just up from the Limehouse Basin."

Ainsley nodded, but waited, not wanting to confirm or deny Benjamin's story. It was still likely the boy was making these facts up, to what end Ainsley did not know.

"It's true!" Benjamin answered forcibly, as if he sensed Ainsley's hesitation to believe him. "Check 'er feet den, if ye don't believe me."

Ainsley glanced to the body, shrouded in a white sheet. Relenting suddenly, Ainsley crossed to her in two steps and pulled the sheet up to her knees. Benjamin appeared opposite him as Ainsley leaned in to look over the girl's feet.

He remembered in the report a sentence that said her feet had been deeply coloured, stained by clay that was common in Limehouse and surrounding parishes. At the time he, as well as the police surgeon, had attributed her tainted skin to her lack of shoes, a luxury few in the neighbourhood could afford, especially for the time when children grew so quickly.

Lifting the girl's foot from the table, Ainsley separated the toes and began counting tiny cuts he found between them. Though she was no more than eight years old, she had numerous cuts on them, healed and reopened on the leathery pads of her feet. However, the condition of her feet was hardly remarkable. Ainsley had processed a number of shoeless children whose feet appeared quite similar.

"I can't say she is a mudlark," Ainsley finally said with a shrug.

Benjamin's expression grew sour. With a growl, he stormed from the room, sidestepping Ainsley's attempt to grab him.

"Hey!" Ainsley went after him, and there was a slight foot chase before Ainsley caught up to him in the hallway, pulling back the sobbing boy, who slapped at Ainsley's grasp. The boy felt slight beneath the threads that made up his clothing. "Stop!" Ainsley yelled. "I did not say I don't believe you, only there is not enough evidence!"

Benjamin scowled but calmed considerably and stopped fighting Ainsley's grasp. The boy shrugged off Ainsley's hands and turned. Ainsley knew better than anyone that despite considerable investment of funds from the gentry, the orphanages and workhouses in the east side only served to keep the children from dying in the streets from starvation, which was enough to allow the upper classes to sleep contently at night believing they had done all they could. Despite his loose clothes and strong attitude, the boy was far from strong. Skin and bones made up the most of him and Ainsley realized why each time it had been easy to overpower him.

"Come then," Ainsley said at last, "Let's get you something to eat."

Ainsley found a pie cart across the street from the hospital and bought two hot pies, one for each of them. Gesturing for a nearby bench, Ainsley turned to Benjamin and saw the pie devoured nearly whole. A trickle of gravy slipped out the side of Benjamin's mouth but the boy paid no heed.

"You will make your stomach ill," Ainsley cautioned but did not expect the boy to slow down.

Once at the bench, Ainsley sat and turned to Benjamin, who was hungrily licking the paper the pie had been served on. Ainsley held out his pie for Benjamin but the boy just looked at him, cautiously.

"It's all right," Ainsley coaxed. "I can't eat much in the morning anyhow," he lied.

As it turned out, not much coaxing was needed. Benjamin took the pie from Ainsley and ate it at a slightly more leisurely pace.

"The orphanage doesn't serve pies often, does it?" Ainsley asked, amused by Benjamin's appetite and glad he played a part in suppressing it.

"No," Benjamin answered with pie filling his cheeks, "never. Mrs. Holliwell is a good cook an' all but I usually give mine to the young' uns."

Ainsley raised an eyebrow at this. "You give your portion away?"

Benjamin nodded, taking his attention from his pie for only the briefest of moments. "I can do better in the streets."

"Pilfering?"

Benjamin's eagerness for the food waned slightly and he paused, thinking over his confession. "Sorry, sir," he said after a time, bowing his head as if in shame.

Anger would serve little purpose, Ainsley conceded. His morals held no value in the streets where every corner held a danger, every day another chance to die. While he and Margaret supped on lavish courses and endless wine at home, countless children slept in archways and under bridges across London with little to keep them warm and even less to keep them fed. To himself, Ainsley vowed to resume his mother's donations to the Society and perhaps pay closer attention to the needs of Mrs. Holliwell and her charges.

When Ainsley looked again he saw Benjamin licking the second paper, intent on extracting every last semblance of flavour from its fibers.

"Would you like another?" Ainsley asked, pre-emptively reaching for his pocket.

"No," Benjamin answered, somewhat out of breath. "I think I have made myself sick." The boy placed his arm over his stomach but the smile on his face never left him. So happy must he have been to experience the bloated pain of too much to eat than the twisting, dry pain of too little.

"Mrs. Holliwell is good to you?" Ainsley ventured to ask.

"Yes," was Benjamin's simple reply. He appeared apprehensive, not much used to being asked his opinion on such things.

"She does not hurt you?" Ainsley pressed. "I only ask because we cannot know what happens when we are not looking."

Benjamin pondered this for some time. "Mrs. Holliwell is a better mistress than others," he explained. "We try to avoid Mr. Holliwell."

Ainsley started. As far as he knew, Mrs. Holliwell was a widow. "Mr. Holliwell?"

"Her son," Benjamin explained. "He can be fierce and the girls shake when he comes to the orphanage." Benjamin's eyes moved to the hospital across the street and his expression became mournful. "Jonathon tried to stand up to him once when Mr. Holliwell was bawling at the girls. Received a black eye for his trouble, he did." His voice became more angered as he spoke and Ainsley caught a glimpse of some threatening tears. Benjamin sniffed, using his shirtsleeve to wipe his nose.

Ainsley vaguely remembered Elliot Holliwell from the time he spent volunteering alongside his mother. Elliot was always sullen whenever Ainsley was around him, distrustful and annoyed, though at what Ainsley did not know.

Clenching his jaw, Ainsley shifted uncomfortably in his seat, wondering how he should best handle this newly discovered information. "How often does Mr. Holliwell visit the orphanage?" Ainsley ventured to ask.

"Not often," Benjamin answered with a shrug. "But I don't have to see him to know he is there. All I have to do is look in the faces of them girls. They don't like him much."

Ainsley's throat became dry. "He bothers them?"

Their eyes met and Benjamin gave a slight nod. Ainsley exhaled, raking his hands through his hair as he leaned back into the bench. It was commonplace enough for children who had known nothing better. Ainsley was more than disturbed by the revelations and it took all the self-control he could muster to remain seated on the bench.

"Tell you what I'll do," Ainsley said, remembering his distrust of the boy earlier. "I will tell Inspector Simms you think you recognized her from the river."

"Her name's Annie," Benjamin answered quickly while licking some the pie's juices from his fingers.

"If you knew her name, why didn't you say so?"

Benjamin shrugged. "You didn't ask."

Chapter 8

We are but orphaned spirits left in Eden

The next morning, Ainsley made his way to Whitehall Place, knowing Simms would likely be there. Inside, the desk sergeant was occupied and Ainsley was able to slip by unnoticed. As he approached Simms's door Ainsley could hear raised voices seeping into the hall.

"You can't do that!" Simms's voice carried down the hall. "How is this supposed to help us?"

"I've only told you as a courtesy," another voice answered.

Ainsley stopped a pace from the threshold once he realized Simms was arguing with Theodore Fenton.

"Get out of my office!" Simms's voice reached a pitch Ainsley had never heard him use before. "Get out!"

Theodore backed out of Simms's office with his hat in his hand. He only noticed Ainsley when he turned to walk down the hall. He smiled slyly as he replaced his hat, tipping the brim toward Ainsley with great emphasis. "Mr. Specialist."

Ainsley sneered as the journalist walked by. He doubted he could hold any more contempt for a single person than he did for Theodore Fenton. Whatever had caused Simms to holler like that Ainsley had little doubt Mr. Fenton deserved it.

Ainsley rapped a knuckle on the doorframe and stepped inside when Simms looked up from his paperwork. His face was red with anger and his breathing heavy.

"I only want good news today, Dr. Ainsley," Simms said gruffly. "I've set my mind upon it."

"I think I may have a name," Ainsley said with an eager smile.

"You have two actually, and I must say it is getting

rather confusing trying to remember how to address you." Simms lowered his gaze to the papers in his hand, propping his head up with his free hand.

"The girl, the last girl, her name is Annie and, according to Ben, she's a mudlark." Without invitation, Ainsley slipped into one of the wooden chairs opposite Simms's desk. "In the Limehouse district, of course."

"Is that so?" Simms answered with little inflection. "I was going to go canvass the area later this morning." Simms slapped one of the sheets of paper down and picked up another. Ainsley had never seen the detective so annoyed with any facet of his position but Ainsley did not visit Simms's office very often.

Ainsley noticed a small pewter picture frame on Simms's desk and pulled it closer to him. Tinted brown, the daguerreotype was a misty portrait of a boy in knee pants and a small cap. He stood ramrod still, a cheeky smile through pressed lips the only pose he could have held for long enough to accomplish the exposure. Ainsley chuckled slightly at the look of the child, who appeared obliging and pleasant.

"Your boy?" Ainsley asked.

Simms eyes flickered up and returned to his paperwork. "Yes."

"Is this a current picture?"

"No."

Simms gave nothing else in response and Ainsley felt he was not welcome to pry. It may have been residual anger felt toward Mr. Fenton, but Ainsley sensed that Simms was in no mood to discuss it and perhaps Ainsley would do better to leave and return later.

Just as Ainsley moved to push himself from the chair, Simms slapped his pen down and stood up. "Confound it!" He reached for his jacket, which he had hung over the back of his chair. "Let us go find the family of that girl," he said, without looking to Ainsley. "I need to be productive."

Limehouse, an east neighbourhood of London, was named for the lime kilns operated by the potteries which used the proximity to the London docks to transport their goods. Still steeped in mariner tradition, the neighbourhood was home to many sailors and dockworkers who earned nothing more than five shillings a day for their backbreaking work. The streets as well were littered with widowed women and orphaned children whose fathers either died in a far off land or abandoned them all together.

On Narrow Street, Ainsley and Simms walked past a shop sign advertising cat meat and sidestepped a knee-high pile of manure that had been raked into the street from one of the backyards. Two pigs tethered to a tree had their ropes twisted together and tightening as they moved to free themselves, their squeals signalling how tight their nooses had become. A lone child stood next to them dumbfounded, only on guard for poachers, not for the sows' well-being.

"Interesting neighbourhood, this," Ainsley said with an amused smile.

The near-constant activity and rush of the crowded street no longer held Inspector Simms's attention as he led the way through the throng. It appeared easy for him to ignore the smell and noise, whereas Ainsley was constantly distracted by the flashes of movement caught in the corner of his sight. So quiet was Belgravia compared to the street they now walked along. So spacious was his house with its rear yard and innumerable rooms. In Limehouse, the doorways were crowded with the grubby faces of half-starved children, many of whom would have loved a small measure of the luxury that Ainsley and Margaret so often took for granted.

The gravity was not lost on Ainsley as he followed Simms. He had been around the poorer classes before, and had visited orphanages and boarding houses, but never had he been affected by the sights and the smell, wafting from the dockyard and the river Thames. Perhaps it was his newfound concern for Benjamin, a child no doubt somewhere in that very throng, looking for cast-offs and scraps in the hopes of bringing them back to the other parentless children.

"Keep up, Dr. Ainsley," Simms yelled over the swelling crowd.

Ainsley pushed through, abandoning the previous care he used to avoid the people around him, and followed Simms between two tall, red brick buildings to the river. The weathered grey wood boards creaked and groaned beneath their footfalls as they stepped forward. Ainsley scanned the muddy banks that flanked the Thames, and saw a dozen or more children knee-deep in the filth. The youngest was no more than five years old and struggled against the pull of the mud.

Ainsley cringed at the sight of it, knowing all the hazards, the broken glass, wire, and rusty metal, that lay unknown beneath the surface. But it was these items and more that the children searched for, reaching their hands beneath the surface for any cast-offs or discarded items that could still be put to use. Any measure of cloth, tin, or iron could be sold for a few dithers and this was how the children sustained themselves and perhaps other members of their family.

They did not know the risk they took. Slaughterhouses further up river routinely tossed discarded pieces of animals into the water, and unscrupulous cesspit workers looking for easy disposal of the waste also used the river. Ainsley's heart quickened at the thought of countless diseases that could be contracted by the slightest exposure to such waste.

"You there!" Simms yelled out while pointing to the eldest boy of the group. "You know a girl called Alice?"

The boy, nearly ten years old, squinted against the oddly bright sun when he looked up to Ainsley and Simms on the overhanging platform. "Yeah," he answered shortly. "What's it to ye?"

"She have a family? An overseer?" Simms asked as

loudly as he could muster.

The boy cocked his head behind him toward Narrow Street. "Lives wit' 'er gran'mudder on Candle."

"Her grandmother, huh?"

The boy nodded. "'Aven't see 'er in a while."

Simms nodded and raised his hand in thanks. Turning to Ainsley, he gave him a quick rap on the stomach as he walked past, a giddy gesture that announced his excitement. Ainsley was slow to move, however. Instead, he stood a few seconds longer, looking at a girl who had just found a muddy cloth, no more than a foot long. She was attempting to wash it in a bit of muddy water but, despite her fruitless task, she smiled slightly at her find, happy to have something for her pouch.

"Ainsley!"

The young doctor turned and saw Simms coaxing him to follow. Ainsley nodded and stepped toward him. "Do you realize how many of those children end up in my morgue?" he asked as he approached the detective. "They die of blood poisoning from wounds to the feet and hands," he continued, without giving Simms a chance to answer. "Painful way to go."

"And you would know from experience?" Simms asked with a hint of challenge in his voice. The detective turned and continued on his way, appearing to not care if Ainsley followed.

"No," Ainsley answered, walking after him. "You are in quite a foul mood today," Ainsley said, with a slight laugh. "Not much yourself, are you?"

Ainsley watched as Simms's jaw became tight and waited for the detective to answer but nothing came.

They walked many blocks, knowing it would be quicker than trying to manoeuver a carriage, finally arriving at a grey wood door. No steps led from the payment and when the door was opened Ainsley and Simms stood on equal ground to a middle-aged woman with her hair in a frayed bun and an apron that barely covered a sliver of her round shape.

"Ma'am, we are looking for the grandmother of Alice, a girl of brown hair and blue eyes," Simms explained while Ainsley remained one step behind him.

From his place on the pavement, Ainsley could see into the room the woman guarded. He could see four babies, swaddled and laying in dresser drawers and baskets placed on the floor. They all slept soundly save one, who Ainsley could see jerking slightly, its eyes wide and vacant as it lay almost forgotten.

The woman at the door moved, marring his view, and Ainsley finally took his gaze from the babes and found her scowling at him. "She ain't got no grandmother."

"Her mother then," Simms said quickly.

The woman shook her head. "Nah. Her mother left the wee Alice with me not seven years ago and I ain't see her since."

"You have quite the collection," Ainsley said, unable to help himself. "All their mothers leave them with you?"

The woman's eyes flickered from Simms to Ainsley, ill-amused and annoyed at their never-ceasing questions. "You want one?" she asked, with a snicker.

"Ma'am, we believe Alice has died," Simms said, bringing the conversation back to the task at hand.

"Well is she or ain't she?" The woman at the door, snorted, as if disbelieving, but then her face fell. "Where is she now then?"

"St. Thomas Hospital," Ainsley answered, taking a step closer and lowering his voice.

"We believe she was a victim of *The Surgeon*," Simms explained, with no care to Ainsley's loathing for that press-given moniker.

The woman was quiet for some time, her eyes trained on the men's feet as they stood in front of her. She did not cry, and this struck Ainsley as odd. But then he remembered she had only a business relationship with the girl and not a loving one.

Finally, she gave a breath of resignation and a nod. "I suppose ye will give her a Christian burial then?"

Ainsley nodded, recalling the parish church he could send her body to, knowing she'd receive better attention than she did in life. "We shall," Ainsley said.

A pair of blond-haired boys appeared beside Simms and Ainsley, slipping past them and into the room. The woman glared at them as they pulled buttons and chains of gold from their pockets. The boys wore the filth of the streets on their feet and hands, as if they'd been left to the elements for months. The woman placed their offerings in a large pocket of her apron and cocked her head toward the inner room. She clicked her tongue sharply and the boys scurried into the house.

"Well, that's it then," she said as soon as they were behind her. The woman moved to close the door but Ainsley stepped forward and braced his arm against the wood.

"I believe the detective has some questions," Ainsley said. He was taller than her, somewhat imposing, and he was glad to have the advantage at such a time. No doubt the woman in front of him was used to sending unwelcome visitors off with either a blade concealed on her person or weapon of some description within arm's length.

She stared at him for a long while, her lips twisted tight with resentment, before she finally released her hold on the door. "Get on with it then," she answered harshly, crossing her arms over her chest.

"How long has she been missing?" Simms asked.

The woman shrugged. "Long enough to be noticed."

"And you did not report it?"

"One less to worry about," she answered plainly. "She wouldn't be the first one to try her luck on the streets."

"She couldn't be more than eight," Ainsley interjected.

"She stayed with me longer than most," the woman answered incredulously.

"Did anyone wish her harm? Did she get in a scrap with anyone?" Simms asked.

"If she did, she didn't trouble me about it," the woman answered. "She knows I got ten wee ones to coax to sleep. As long as she brings me some fodder every day I don't ask no questions."

"What did she bring you?" Ainsley asked, doubting it would provide much for their investigation. Curiosity had gotten the better of him.

"This and that. How is it any concern of yours?" the woman asked, her patience nearly evaporated.

Ainsley shrugged. "I just find it rather repugnant when a woman, such as yourself, sees more profit training pickpockets than finding homes for those babies as you promised their mothers you would."

"Wait a minute now," she said, standing taller. "Who said anything to you about pickpockets?"

"That gold chain," Ainsley said, gesturing to her pocket. "That was not found in the muddy banks or rubbish heaps."

The woman feigned offence, an act as obvious as the haggard look to her hardened features. "I run a legitimate business 'ere and the boys are only contributing to their keep. I ain't got to ask where they come by their ...contributions." Her mouth twisted into a half-smile.

The pickpockets looked no more than five. Their hands were small and their presence overlooked. If raised from a young age, Ainsley had no doubt of their usefulness to a woman such as the one standing before him. So why, Ainsley wondered, did women such as this surrender some of their foundlings to the charities while choosing to keep others for longer spells? Why would a boy like Jonathon be brought to Mrs. Holliwell?

"What about a boy," Ainsley asked, "named Jonathon? Do you remember a boy by that name? You would have brought him to the Limehouse Philanthropic Society Foundling Home twelve years ago."

A snort escaped the woman's mouth. "So long ago, can't remember. The name Jonathon does not sound familiar at all."

"With so many in your charge, how can you be expected to remember their names," Simms offered disparagingly.

The woman before them seemed to take offence to that. Her shoulders straightened and she scrunched her face up in a hardened scowl. "I do my best for them, I do. More than I can say for the likes of some, them what dropped the little things off. Ain't no skin off my back if I cannot find them homes. No one wants a half-pint. Them that wants a child wants a baby and I provide them with one."

"Aye, and ye abandon the ugly and sickly ones, do ya?" Simms asked.

Ainsley guessed there was more to this line of questioning and resolved to ask about it later.

"There's some that do but I am not one of 'em." She nodded and then her smile vanished as she forcibly closed the door, narrowly missing Simms's face.

Ainsley glanced around them, the normal hustle of the street somewhat faded from the norm, and found an audience had gathered around them, eager to take in the interview.

Simms took the discovery in stride. The detective was most likely used to such audiences, and had learned to ignore the jeers and threatening gestures. Ainsley, however, could not help but look at the gaunt faces of the streets of Limehouse. Behind greasy full beards and moth-eaten hats, men glared their disapproval and watched intently as Simms and Ainsley pushed their way through the crowd.

Once a few blocks away, Ainsley spoke, glancing back to see the avenue had returned to normal. "Do you ever feel like they mean to do you harm?" he asked, his nerves still on edge. Never before had he felt at the mercy of a mob.

"All the time," Simms answered plainly.

"That woman must have many friends."

"They are just suspicious of anyone not their own," Simms answered as they walked. "Face it, Ainsley, you and

I don't look like we live 'round the corner."

Chapter 9

A time ago:
God gave us golden cups,
and we were bidden
To feed you so.

Hands on her hips, Margaret stood in her mother's sitting room, the furniture and trinkets arranged as they had been while her mother lived. Lady Charlotte's bedchamber and sitting room remained a museum of sorts for the months that had slipped by since her passing.

Standing in the room the first time since, Margaret hardly knew where to start. She turned in place, twisting her little mouth as she took it all in. Julia waited amongst crates, straw, and newsprint she had absconded from the kitchens.

"I haven't the faintest clue where to begin," Margaret said at last, looking at the concerned face of her lady's maid.

"'Tis a difficult chore," Julia said.

Margaret laughed slightly and raised her hand to her chin, propping her elbow with her other arm. "I'm afraid I haven't the stomach. I wish it were possible to leave it as it is."

Julia knelt down, her skirt billowing slightly as she took her place amongst the boxes. "Perhaps we should start at the beginning." She chose a small bud vase, hand-painted with gold details, and held it gently in both her hands. "Shall we return this to the Ainsleys?"

Margaret slipped heavily into an armchair near her. "I haven't the faintest clue," she said with honesty. "Mother's family hasn't bothered with us for many years. I couldn't say what is an heirloom and what is bumpf."

Julia eyed the delicate vase, a hint of a smile tickling

the corners of her lips. "Where I grew up bumpf had a different look entirely." Julia set the vase aside. "Perhaps you'd like to take it when you marry."

Margaret gave a short chuckle. "I doubt I shall ever marry. All the men who come to call are silly boys, superficial in thought and deed. I could no more see myself spending the rest of my life with them any more than I could see myself marrying the king of Spain." Margaret and Julia smiled at Margaret's jest.

"And your gentleman friend?"

Margaret's face fell as soon as the words were said. "Father would never allow it," she confessed. "Perhaps if my mother were here I could borrow some strength from her." Margaret played with a loose strand of the armchair's seam. "Jonas and I both know nothing will ever come of it. Besides, he's not much of the marrying kind. A rogue by all accounts...he cannot be tamed."

Julia smiled. "Then why do you meet with him?" she asked.

"Because it feels good," Margaret confessed, "to know someone cares when it feels as if no one else does. I suppose it's a bit self-serving really. I don't expect him to wait, not for me."

Margaret could feel the eyes of her maid on her but she did not look up. Instead, she bit her lower lip in an attempt to hold off threatening tears. What she said was true. There was no hope. Jonas would never have permission to ask for her hand, just as she would never be permitted to accept it. They enjoyed each other's company but nothing else could come of it.

"And you, Miss Julia, have you any plans?" Margaret asked teasingly in an effort to change the subject.

"No," her maid answered plainly. "I try not to plan. I learned long ago that plans are made of clay, easily shaped and contorted, or simply washed away."

Margaret flinched at Julia's eloquent words. There had always been hints of higher education during their talks, something Margaret had never before experienced with her father's staff. While Margaret had learned pieces of Julia's life before Marshall House, she was well aware that the true story of Julia's background lay buried beneath the surface. Despite a close kinship developed from tragedy and proven loyalty, Margaret wondered if the maid would ever feel comfortable telling her about her past and the childhood she left behind.

"Julia—"

"These books, would you like to keep them?" Julia said with a marked directness. It was clear she had an interest in changing the subject and smiled while she held the volumes up for Margaret to see. Margaret nodded, conceding the change in topic and accepting the books as Julia handed them to her.

A moment later, Cutter arrived, stepping inside the threshold from the hallway. "A Lady Gemma Brant to see you, Lady Margaret."

Margaret furrowed her eyebrows, surprised that Lady Brant would come to the house. She had not visited Marshall House for as long as Margaret could remember.

"Show her in, Cutter," Margaret said. "I doubt Lady Brant would mind if we continued with our work." Cutter bowed at the waist and left to escort the guest up to the room.

Margaret sighed. Lady Brant often visited Margaret's mother while they stayed at The Briar, but at the time Margaret and Ainsley were still young enough that they were not required to entertain her. As soon as they would see her carriage making its way down the long lane from the main road, Margaret and Ainsley would take off into the trees, climbing as high as they could, and then spy on her and their mother. They'd make an afternoon of criticizing Lady Brant's dress or hat, her facial expressions, and the way she ate with her fingers. It all seemed rather harmless at the time, though now the memories sat heavily on Margaret's heart.

While the days she spent in the treetops with her brother solidified their attachment for all time, she now felt she should have spent more of her days learning the ways of sophisticated women rather than making sport of them. She had taken it for granted that her mother would always be there to flank her or, in the very least, guide her in social settings. Now, it seemed, Margaret was on her own.

Margaret rose from her chair just before Lady Brant entered from the hallway. She saw the look of displeasure on Lady Brant's face by the way she scrunched up her nose and looked about the room.

"I have not darkened these doors in many moons, Margaret. I heard your father has left town and took it upon myself to pay a call," she said.

Julia stood to leave the women to their visit.

"Oh, don't bother yourself," Lady Brant said, waving a dismissive hand toward Julia. "Stick to your task. I won't stay but a minute."

Margaret approached and received a soft embrace and brief kiss on her cheek.

"How are you, my dear?" Lady Brant asked.

"We are well," Margaret answered as if by rote, not caring to take a moment to ponder her true well-being.

"Are you truly?" Lady Brant pressed. "I worry for you, Margaret dear, all alone in this big house with your mother gone."

"I am not alone," Margaret answered. "Between Father and Peter—"

Lady Brant huffed. "Your father prefers the bottle and your brother is far too busy with hospital business."

"We have innumerable servants," Margaret offered, glancing to Julia, who had returned to her work amongst the crates. She did not wish to concern Lady Brant with the true extent of her loneliness.

"Servants are not companions," Lady Brant answered, walking further into the room. She turned about, lingering for a moment as she took in the late Lady Marshall's mantel and returned her attention to Margaret. "I wonder if it would be best for you to come live with me."

Margaret's gaze shot to Julia, who had looked up suddenly from her task.

"'Tis not an unusual thing," Lady Brant pressed, no doubt seeing the look of concern on Margaret's face. "Your mother has passed and your father cannot be bothered with you. I would see that you receive all manner of invitations. I shall have you married off before the summer is out."

"Lady Brant—"

"I know what you are about to say," Lady Brant said, raising a hand as if to halt any protest from Margaret. "You do not wish to marry at present, but you are nearing twenty-five."

Margaret winced at this. She was a couple years from twenty-five but the date loomed as if a prison sentence to spinsterhood. For a moment, Margaret felt resigned, accepting even, to the proposal before her. Lady Brant had been married off in a very similar fashion many years ago despite her secret yearnings to defy convention and study medicine. Lady Brant had been lucky though, of a sort. Her husband had died within the first year of their union, leaving her with a large sum of money, enough to allow her all manner of unconventional indulgence. She had always spoken out about the way she was sold to the highest bidder, and now it angered Margaret that Lady Brant thought she could do the same to her.

Unaware of Margaret's internal struggle, Lady Brant continued. "I have no doubt your father expects these things to happen in the committee room but us women know it happens in the ballroom. Now—"

"Lady Brant, my answer is no."

The woman blinked at Margaret as if not fully comprehending what Margaret had just said. "What did you say, dear?"

"I thank you for your interest but my answer is a decided no."

"You need to think about this," Lady Brant pressed.

"I have thought of it all I need to. I am more than happy to stay here and to live the life as providence has decreed. I will not lower myself so much as to chase eligible bachelors about town." Margaret stole a quick glance at Julia, who smiled as she packed the crates.

"You'd not be the first to do so," Lady Brant answered with a slight laugh.

"Is this the entire reason for your visit?" Margaret pressed, only somewhat regretting her solid stance.

"Well, no," Lady Brant admitted. She hesitated for a moment, no doubt put off by the brash manner in which her offer had been rejected. "Your mother's charity, the Limehouse Philanthropic Society, has requested my assistance later this week. I am to perform routine health checks for some of the children, smallpox, you know. I'd like you to come assist me."

There was no doubt why Lady Brant had been asked. Trained in anatomy and sufficiently wealthy, Lady Brant could provide the service without any expectation of being paid.

"Actually," Lady Brant continued more sternly, "I *expect* you to assist me."

Margaret swallowed hard and fought back the urge to protest. She had already created division between them and was loathe to create another subject on which they would disagree. It was not the charity work that Margaret disapproved of, but rather the commanding way in which Lady Brant ordered Margaret about. Conceding to help would only serve to reinforce a behaviour that Margaret could not abide.

Margaret nodded. "My mother would wish for me to assist."

Lady Brant placed the palm of her hand on Margaret's cheek, and smiled "That she would, dear."

Chapter 10

But now our right hand hath no cup remaining,

Medical bag in hand, Ainsley walked through the front door to the Marshall home and nearly tripped over a crate which had been left to the side. Startled, Ainsley looked around to see a number of crates and furnishings lined up in the foyer. He recognized a side table that had been in his mother's room and a large oil painting, a still life, that once hung over her mantel.

"Margaret?" he called up the stairs, expecting her to be on the second floor.

"Goodness, Peter, no need to shout," Margaret answered, revealing herself. She had been crouched behind the painting, and held a brass candelabra in her hands.

"Why are Mother's things strewn about the foyer?" he asked, placing his bag on the floor at the foot of the stairs. He noticed an open crate in front of him and pulled a decorative bell jar from it. Inside held dried wild flowers, hardened and painted with a rare blue butterfly fastened to one of the flowers.

"Father wishes the room repurposed," Margaret answered with an exhale of breath. "He's placed me at the helm for this project." She gestured toward the display jar in his hands. "If you see something you like, you may keep it."

"Where will the rest of it go?" he asked, looking about at the variety of items between them.

Using the back of her hand to pull tendrils of brown hair from her brow, Margaret glanced around. "Well, much of it belongs to the Ainsleys. I suspect they will want it returned; the valuables, in any case."

"Haven't you any interest in keeping some for yourself?" Ainsley pressed. He began to move about, surveying the towers of crates as well as the odd piece of furniture scattered throughout. Movement caught his eye, and he looked to the stairs just as Julia began her descent, a small crate in her arms. Ainsley fought back an urge to relieve her of the burden, knowing the maid would refuse his help.

"I've claimed what I'd like to keep," Margaret answered, not noticing his distraction. "I don't care to keep much. Most of the things I associate with Mother's memory are at The Briar." She placed the candelabra in a nearby crate, its match visible above the top. "At first, I was reluctant to touch anything, but I found a sudden urge to get to work once Lady Brant left."

Ainsley raised an eyebrow. "Lady Brant paid a call?"

Margaret smiled out one side of her mouth. "I was just as surprised as you. She has a way of instilling guilt in me. Must have spurred me into action. I swear I haven't much tolerance for her."

"After Lady Brant took her leave Lady Margaret blew through the room like a strong wind, Mr. Marshall," Julia said as she walked by Ainsley. "Suddenly able to make decisions without much thought." She placed the crate on top of another and knelt down near the one Margaret had placed the candelabra in.

Ainsley watched as the maid began to wrap the brass in straw. She looked up, and Ainsley quickly turned away.

"Well, yes." Margaret placed her hands on her hips. "I fear I may have gone too far."

Ainsley shook his head. "Certainly not. It needed to be done. Though I cringe to think of what Father has planned for those rooms."

Margaret shrugged. "I haven't the faintest clue."

"Are you about done?" Ainsley asked. "Will you join me for a late tea?"

Margaret gave a quick nod. "Yes. I shall wash up, though. I am nothing but dust and straw at present."

Ainsley nodded and made his way to the parlour while

Julia disappeared along the hall to the stairs that would take her down to the kitchens.

Ainsley made himself comfortable on the settee near the window, leaning back into the pillow and drawing his feet up onto the couch. He raised his hands to his face, rubbing eyes that hurt from the smoke of the streets. A few moments later, Margaret came into the parlour and took a chair near him. She looked just as weary as he.

"Have you found him yet, Peter?" Margaret asked without further need to explain.

Ainsley shook his head. "These children live their lives unnoticed and their deaths even more so. It's like he planned it this way, banking on their irrelevance to society."

"That's rather harsh," Margaret said. "They are children."

"They are not children as you and I know them," Ainsley answered, leaning farther back into his chair. "These are abandoned children, left to fend for themselves in the streets. Some as young as three years old. These are not children in hoop skirts and hair ribbons walking with their governesses in Hyde Park. They sleep in alleys and rubbish heaps, often in groups of children in similar circumstances. If they are lucky, and I use that term loosely, to have an adult looking out for them it's usually because the child is of use picking pockets, or garnering sympathy for beggars. Half of the bodies brought to my morgue are that of children, dead from starvation, exposure, or wounds inflected on them in life."

Margaret shifted uncomfortably in her chair.

"My apologies, but it is the truth," Ainsley answered.

"I am only uncomfortable with myself," she explained, "Lady Brant asked me to assist her at the orphanage later this week. What a spoiled brat I am for behaving as if I'd rather not."

Ainsley smiled. "Lady Brant does not make good company. I am not surprised you would wish to stay at home."

Julia walked in then, her arms laden with a tray of tea. She placed the tray on a table to the side and began to pour a cup for Margaret and a cup for Ainsley.

"I shall try to be more obliging," Margaret said, "in this case, at the very least. I should like to do more for the orphans than just administer medicine."

Ainsley looked up to Julia as she handed him his cup of tea.

The maid started when their eyes met and Ainsley's playful grin vanished.

"My apologies, Mr. Marshall." She raised her hand to her chest. "Your wounds look as if they are healing well."

"With thanks to my nurse who dressed them," Ainsley answered with a pleasant smile.

Julia swallowed nervously.

"Thank you, Julia, for the tea."

Julia bobbed a curtsey, retreated to gather her tray, and left the room.

"Look at you," Margaret said as soon as the maid had left. Ainsley looked to her, expecting some teasing, but instead he found a cold, immovable stare. The lightness of his smile faded.

"Is something the matter?" he asked, knowing very well she meant to chide him for becoming familiar with the staff.

"Was it not you who warned me about becoming attached?" Margaret asked, raising her cup of tea to her lips. "Although I must admit you are rather entertaining when you flirt."

"I don't recall any flirting," Ainsley answered.

"Perhaps I shall ask Julia if she felt you were flirting," Margaret offered.

"Margaret!"

A gentle laugh escaped Margaret's lips. "Very well then," she said, still amused. "I will allow you to have your fun. But please do not make yourself into another Daniel."

Ainsley shuttered and turned his gaze away. "Of that I have no interest."

Since the wedding, their eldest brother, Daniel, had little reason to visit Marshall House and so Julia had been spared further unwelcome attention from him. For a while, Ainsley was very protective of the newest housemaid and worried that he and his brother would have yet another topic on which to disagree. It seemed that Daniel had forgotten all about Julia and it pleased Ainsley to not have to worry about her, though he held little doubt regarding her ability to protect herself if it came to that. She had a strong right hook, if Ainsley recalled. His jaw stung at the memory of it.

"You were saying you'd like to do more for the children," Ainsley offered, hoping to change the topic.

Margaret shrugged and placed her teacup on the small wooden table beside her. "Yes, now that I feel like a total miscreant."

Ainsley laughed. "Your words, not mine."

"Perhaps we should hold a fundraiser, like the ones Mother used to plan. We could have it here at the house, if Father should agree."

"If you schedule it soon there would be no need to ask Father," Ainsley offered.

"Yes," Margaret's voice trailed off, as she twisted her fingers in front of her. "We shall have an auction in Mother's memory with all the proceeds benefiting the Limehouse orphanage."

"You'd like to auction off Mother's things?" Ainsley asked.

"Why not? Father told me to get rid of it. We would be selling it off or giving it away anyway and it's not like any of us need the money more than the children."

Ainsley watched as Margaret's eyes began to glisten and she turned her head to the side with the hopes he would not see.

"I could not bear it if you did not support me, brother,"

Margaret said. "I cannot tell you how much enjoyment this would give me."

Ainsley stood, placing his empty teacup beside Margaret's on the table. He knelt before her, taking her hands into his and looked her directly in the eyes. "I wholeheartedly support you in everything you wish to do and I know Mother would too."

Margaret smiled, and a tear rolled down her cheek. She laughed as she wiped it away.

Standing from his crouched position, Ainsley planted a kiss on her forehead. "I must to bed or I shall fall asleep in my teacup."

In truth, he was not interested in bed at all. He knew he could not sleep one wink for all the information that swam in his head. As soon as he was in his room, he locked the door and headed for his desk, pulling his sketchbook out from his medical bag. He sat in the limited glow of his desk lamp, flipping pages and outlining images with his fingers as if they held clues he had not seen before. For many hours he sifted through pages, replaying the scene as he had seen it when he first arrived.

When he looked at Alice, the girl Benjamin had recognized, he wondered why he had not detected she was a mudlark. The police surgeon had not noticed it either. Other children like her had been brought to him, nearly caked in mud with bits of rubbish from the Thames in their hair and ears, and yet Alice had none of this. Nothing was noted in the report Simms brought him. She had worn less of the muck of the streets than the other victims and Ainsley had thought she was freshly bathed, though now that he saw where she slept he felt such care would have been inconceivable.

Almost resigned to his dead end, Ainsley laid down his sketch of her, smearing his penciled notes with his thumb as he did so, and realized the rationality that had alluded him.

Alice had been bathed by *The Surgeon* himself.

Chapter 11

No work to do,

The next morning Ainsley woke to the sound of his bedroom door opening. He jumped, sitting up abruptly, and found that he had fallen asleep at his desk, copious notes scattered over the desktop.

"Pardon me, Mr. Marshall," Cutter said feebly. "His lordship has left instructions for you. I was supposed to give them to you yesterday but..." The footman stood slightly straighter as his voice trailed off. "Sorry, sir. I had expected you would be up by now."

Ainsley rubbed his face and twisted his shoulders as if to stretch. "What could the old goat need of me now?" Ainsley asked with a smile. Cutter betrayed nothing as he handed Ainsley the note.

"Shall I have Cook save you a plate of breakfast?" Cutter asked when back at the door.

Ainsley shook his head. "No, Cutter, I'll venture down after a time and get something of my own."

Cutter looked only slightly surprised at this. No doubt the London staff was getting used to Ainsley's odd, self-sufficient behaviour. Where most, if not all, of the aristocracy enjoyed the luxuries their wealth could afford them, Ainsley avoided them and often preferred to do things on his own.

"As you wish." With a slight bow, Cutter left and Ainsley ripped into his father's note.

Peter,
The placement agency is sending over a few candidates for butler. Please interview them in turn and prepare to give me a report on each, as well as your reasons for who

you decide to hire. I shall not return to London for many months and so I expect he will be well-versed in the running of the House by the time I arrive. I have left notes from the agency in my desk drawer should you need to peruse them prior to your interviews.
—Father

Ainsley exhaled and ran his hand through his hair as he laid his father's letter on the desktop. In some respects he loathed the task before him. Never in his life had he been involved with the hiring and firing of household staff and yet if Ainsley expected to take a household of his own, perhaps he'd better learn. Though he doubted who he thought was a stellar candidate would please his father. Hiring staff for himself would be one thing, hiring someone whom his father would like was an entirely different matter, especially since their previous butler had been with the family for nearly three decades.

After dressing in fresh attire, Ainsley ventured downstairs to the long, narrow corridor at the back of the house that led down to the kitchens and scullery. As he approached the stairs, he saw Julia coming up. When their eyes met her gaze dropped to the floor and she slipped to the railing as far as humanly possible so he could pass.

"Good morning, Miss Kemp," Ainsley said with a smile.

"And to you, Mr. Marshall."

Ainsley paused at the doorway and gestured with his arm that he was making way for her to pass. She pressed her lips together but kept her gaze down as she slipped by. Keeping an eye on her form, Ainsley turned as she went and intended to speak but the words did not strike him. He paused in place, watching her scurry down the corridor and turn into the main part of the house.

She hadn't seen his awkward attempt to converse nor did she hear his heart quicken when he first saw her. And thank God for that.

At the bottom of the basement stairs he could hear the undermaids' and Cook's hushed voices from the kitchen. The open archway was three more steps forward but he remained at the bottom of the stairs listening in as they spoke disparagingly.

"And to think she puts on such airs!" he heard Cook say.

"Who is she anyway?" one of the younger scullery girls asked. "The way she acts you'd think she was Queen Victoria herself."

"She's an orphan, that's what," Cook replied matter-of-factly. "Them that brought her into this world took one look at her and didn't want her, and that's the truth of it. No need for her to go on ordering us about like her slaves."

"I heard her tell His Lordship about a brother of some sort," a girl said. "She can't be an orphan if she's got a brother."

"Yes she can, you doff," a maid snapped. "No parents what makes you an orphan."

"It's a lie, the whole bit of it," Cook said. "She ain't got no one that cares for her but Miss Margaret, and knowing how fickle that girl is, she'll tire of her new pet soon enough."

The group erupted with laughter.

Having heard enough, Ainsley stepped forward and rounded the archway. Instantly, they sprung up from their various chairs and stools scattered around the kitchen to stand at attention. One girl hopped up so fast she knocked her stool over behind her. She did not move to replace it to its feet and instead lifted her chin an inch or so higher.

"Lord Marshall, we don't often see you down in the kitchens anymore," Cook said, attempting to avoid a dark silence. "Did Cutter not bring you a plate in the dining hall?"

She, above anyone, would know the valet had not, though he mustn't have mentioned Ainsley's wish to fetch his own food from the kitchen.

Ainsley stepped past one of the younger girls and snagged some biscuits from a cooling rack behind her. The four women watched as he rounded the kitchen, scooping up tidbits of food as he found them along the way. "Don't let me interrupt, ladies," he said, taking a bite of one of the biscuits.

The scullery maid bit her lip and turned suddenly, pulling a clean pot from the counter behind her and disappearing into the scullery. The other young girl followed her empty-handed, which left Cook and her undercook at the stove.

"Will you or Miss Margaret be home for luncheon?" Cook asked cautiously.

"I can't rightly say," Ainsley answered. "Perhaps Margaret has given up eating all together. You know how fickle she is." Ainsley popped the rest of the biscuit in his mouth and left the room assured that he had made his point.

Ainsley brought his foraged food to his father's study and took a seat at the large mahogany desk. He laid the morsels in front of him, and surveyed his position as interim head of the house. The piece of furniture had been so imposing when Ainsley sat on the other side, often chided for one misstep or another. The view from the opposite side was far more to Ainsley's liking. He chuckled at the thought of his father seated in a chair opposite him and how insignificant the great Lord Marshall would look. From his current angle, it was just a desk but from the opposite side it was as good as any throne.

As he ate he contemplated the conversation he had overheard. He had not realized Julia was an orphan and the revelation surprised him all the more when he remembered his father's resistance to hiring people without legitimate parentage. Lord Marshall hadn't the rigid views many of the elite touted. But where his staff were concerned he was quite scrupulous. Knowing this, Ainsley quickly became incensed, wondering what the women in the kitchen were playing at. Why would they perpetuate such a myth? What gain would it provide Cook to alienate Julia from the rest of the staff?

Ainsley opened the top drawer of his father's desk and found nothing. He proceeded down the drawers until he discovered a dossier marked "staff." Slapping it on the desktop, Ainsley pulled his chair closer. He opened the file and found employment records and documents from Colbert's Staffing Agency, which included a list of nine potential candidates for butler and the times when each prospective employee would arrive. Each interview was granted thirty minutes and the first one was expected to arrive in little under an hour. It looked to be the beginning of a very long day.

Ainsley rang the servant's bell. When Cutter arrived, dishevelled and out of breath, he rocked as if he could fall over at the door.

"Are you well?" Ainsley asked, wondering why he had not noticed his valet's behaviour before.

"Very well, sir," Cutter answered with a slight gasp. "I was in the yard, was all. The coal cart has arrived."

Ainsley nodded. "Ah," he said, "Well, can someone in the house be spared? I need two letters delivered." Ainsley stood, scooping up the hasty messages he had scrolled out as he waited for Cutter. "One is for Dr. Crawford at St. Thomas."

Cutter nodded as he accepted the first envelope.

"The other is for Inspector Simms at the Yard." Ainsley presented him with the second envelope. The letter inside described Ainsley's suspicion that Alice had been bathed either before or after she was murdered. It upset him that he could not tell the detective himself but he was glad for the change of pace the day of interviews brought him.

"The Yard?" Cutter's young voice rose in alarm, his eyes wide at the thought of the detectives back at the house.

"It's a private enquiry. Nothing to concern yourself about, I assure you," Ainsley said in an even tone.

Cutter nodded but his expression remained dubious.

"Please, just deliver the letters," Ainsley said, forgoing any more reassurance.

Cutter nodded and left hurriedly to find an underservant with quick feet and a discreet tongue.

Once settled back in his seat, Ainsley opened the file again and took out the sheets of references that pertained to each candidate, and started when he saw Julia's name on the paper under them. Without hesitation, he set the necessary papers aside, took up Julia's employment record, and began skimming the page.

He knew so little of the woman and it was the mystery of her that intrigued him. She had come to them at a time of complete turmoil and Margaret had been hell-bent on disliking her. After a time, Julia confessed to him that she had been hired to find out all she could about Lady Charlotte Marshall, Ainsley's mother, while she lived. She proved her loyalty and Ainsley told his father she should be kept on, if only for Margaret's sake. At least that is what he told his father. Never would he admit to being drawn to the woman and her unmistakable fortitude.

He skimmed her references, recognizing some familiar names of families in the neighbourhood. She hadn't stayed with any of them long, he noted. Given such short tenures she had most likely been hired to assist in the houses for Christmastime or a wedding. He saw that she had come to the Marshall family through the same agency which was sending the candidates for that day and then he found a letter of introduction from the agency which had most likely come along with Julia when she arrived.

Without shame, Ainsley skimmed the letter. "... *strength of character... discreet and modest...difficult childhood which has made her less desirable to other houses though for your purposes she is the ideal candidate.*"

Ainsley placed a hand over his mouth, rubbing his

unshaven chin as he read. Had Julia been aware of what the agency had written about her? Could she have known of the task that would be asked of her, to spy on the lady of the house?

Ainsley turned to the paper beneath the letter and saw the words Limehouse Philanthropic Society scrolled under *"education."* Ainsley placed the letter of introduction down and checked and rechecked the words he was reading. If it were true, Julia had been raised in the neighbourhood where all *The Surgeon's* victims had been found. She was raised in the same orphanage where Jonathon had also lived.

Ainsley slapped the paper down, angered that the employment records raised more questions than it answered. He cursed his curiosity and wondered why he had looked at the papers at all.

Just then the door opened and Cutter slipped in. "Mr. Bellfort has arrived."

Ainsley nodded, recognizing the name of the first candidate he was to interview. "Thank you, Cutter," he said with marked resignation. "Show him in."

The hours slipped by unnoticed and by the time Ainsley bid farewell to the last candidate he craved a strong drink.

"Thank you, Maxwell," he said, with an overwhelming sense of relief. He stood, offering the prospective butler his hand as he rounded his father's desk.

"Do you think I have a chance, my lord?" Maxwell asked. He was the youngest candidate, only slightly older than Ainsley himself, though he had much experience in lesser houses. First as a footman, then a valet, and briefly as butler to a widow who had passed away suddenly. The man himself was rather unremarkable. He might just be the type of personality to compliment Lord Marshall, especially during their time of bereavement.

"As good a chance as anyone," Ainsley answered

noncommittally as he walked toward the door that would lead them to the foyer. He opened it wide and stepped back, allowing Maxwell to walk through first.

On the other side of the threshold Julia struggled with a large crate in her hands, tall enough to nearly cover her face, her skirts shifting slightly as she walked, inching closer to an unseen rug that had been rolled up and placed amongst Lady Marshall's belongings. Ainsley moved to assist her, save her from a guaranteed fall, but Maxwell rushed to her aid, taking the crate from her grasp.

"Allow me," he said, giving Julia a smile.

Not noticing Ainsley standing near the door to his father's study, Julia returned Maxwell's smile and smoothed out her skirt as she looked at him. Ainsley watched as she directed Maxwell to the spot where she had intended the box to go. Margaret smiled from her spot amongst the cast-offs.

Irritated, Ainsley's patience was at an end. He had been moving to assist Julia and yet this man, a stranger in this house, had superseded him.

"Thank you, sir," Julia said demurely.

"Maxwell," he answered quickly, with a slight bow. "And you, Miss?"

Ainsley stepped forward, his face stern and gaze hardened. "Her name is Julia," he answered crossly. He slipped his hands in his pockets and stood with an air of challenge.

As if caught in an indecent act, the two servants tore their gazes from each other.

"Thank you," Julia said again, though she dared not look his way. She retreated to where Margaret stood and knelt down to a box at her side.

"You will hear from the agency should we feel you'd suit us," Ainsley said, slightly less optimistically.

Maxwell must have noticed Ainsley's change of mood and made a step forward as if to protest and then thought better of it. "Thank you for your time, sir," he said. He gave a nod and made for the front door.

Once the man was gone, Margaret spoke up. "He seemed to be a nice fellow," she said, only glancing to Ainsley briefly before looking back to the papers she held in her hand.

Ainsley snorted, his interest in the man completely erased.

"What's the matter with him then?" Margaret asked, placing her pages down and walking toward Ainsley. "He looks much more energetic than any of the others I have seen walk through here."

"By energetic, you mean young?" Ainsley asked, glancing to Julia, who remained on the floor taking stock of the items in front of her.

Margaret shrugged. "Strong, polite, and enthusiastic. Is that not what one would look for in a butler? Has he no experience?"

"He has been a butler for two years," Ainsley answered. "He comes highly recommended."

"Then what can be the problem?" Margaret asked with a slight laugh. "Father shall not care. Billis could not have been any older when he was first hired on."

Ainsley gave a scowl and raked his hands through his hair. "Margaret, please," he said, unwilling to give further reasons for his distrust of the man.

Margaret gave him a disparaged look. "Peter."

Ainsley shook his head and turned his eyes from her. He found himself looking to Julia again and Margaret must have seen. She smiled crookedly. "Come then," Margaret said, turning into him and sliding her hand into the crook of his arm. She began to lead him away from the pile of auction items in the foyer. "Let us ask Violetta for some tea and you and I can have a chat."

Lacking energy to protest, Ainsley allowed himself to be pulled along.

"Lady Margaret, allow me," Julia spoke up from her place on the floor.

"No thank you, Julia," Margaret said over her shoulder. "You are busy. I shan't be long."

Margaret led Ainsley down the hall and into the library. Pulling the cord behind the door, Ainsley watched as Margaret crossed the room to the cushioned window seat that lined the library window which looked out over the rear yard. A sly look of amusement passed over her face as she sat, crossing her ankles beneath her skirt and folding her hands in her lap. Ainsley was standing at the door when Violetta appeared.

"We'd like some tea, Violetta," Margaret said once the maid appeared.

The seasoned maid looked from both Margaret and Ainsley. "Julia is—"

"Thank you, Violetta," Margaret answered forcibly.

The maid bobbed a slight curtsey and left with her lips pressed together tightly.

"She has become quite idle since Mother died," Margaret explained. "Julia has been run ragged for some time. I imagine it's time for us to expect things from her again."

Ainsley rounded the couch and took a seat amongst the cushions. He sat for a moment before reaching behind his back to pull out a pillow that had become lodged between him and the cushion.

"I think it's charming that you have taken to Julia so well," Margaret said.

"Do you?" Ainsley asked as he looked over the accent pillow. Giving Margaret a twisted smile, he tossed the pillow in her direction. "That is for your meddling," he said with a broad smile.

She raised her hands, protecting her face and, more importantly, her hair from the pillow. She was able to grab it before it hit her. "Meddling?" Margaret's mouth dropped at the suggestion. "Why should I meddle when you bear your interest on your face so plainly?"

"Is it so plain?"

"You cannot deny the man his position because you fancy Julia and wish to cocoon her."

"I have no interest in cocooning her," Ainsley answered, stumbling over the word *"cocooning"* and the image it implied.

"What are your intentions then?" Margaret asked. "Only good, I hope."

"I have no intentions," Ainsley answered as solidly as he could muster.

"She is a very lovely woman," Margaret pointed out. "Intelligent. Beautiful. Not at all inclined to dramatics or gossip. I am not surprised you are drawn to her."

Ainsley shrugged. "She is not the first woman I have found attractive and I daren't say she won't be the last." Ainsley leaned into the arm of his chair, propping his elbow up and playing with the piping of the fabric with the tips of his fingers. He was ashamed of the attraction he felt, not because Julia was a maid and deemed unworthy of his affection but rather because as a servant in his family's house she fell under their protection, fed and housed from a world that otherwise would cast her off. "I heard the kitchen staff say she was an orphan," he said suddenly.

Margaret's mouth opened and closed quickly. "I do not believe it."

Ainsley shrugged. "It's true. Her file in Father's desk confirmed it."

"You looked in Father's files!"

"I had to for my interviews," Ainsley answered quickly in his defence.

Margaret pressed her lips together as her gaze drifted to the floor. "It shall not change the way I feel about her," she declared, raising her eyes. "She is more than a maid now. I feel for her like a sister, in a way. And should your interest in her interfere with that I shall never forgive you."

Ainsley chuckled at her sincerity. "Have no fear, sister. I am not interested enough to see it through to its natural conclusion."

Margaret gave a sly smile and eyed him from across the room. "Enlighten me, brother," Margaret said teasingly. "What *is* a natural conclusion when a man is attracted to a woman?"

Ainsley laughed, knowing very well she was not as innocent to the ways of the world as she proclaimed. "Perhaps someone will tell you once you cease to be a child."

With the greatest force she could muster, Margaret tossed the pillow back at him. Her aim was off and the cushion flew toward the door, narrowly missing Violetta as she walked into the library with the tray for tea.

Chapter 12

The mystic hydromel is spilt, and staining

Margaret's day started as the ones before. She and Julia had allowed the auction to consume their every thought and deed. As word of their endeavour reached the staff, Lady Gemma Brant, and her brother Daniel, the mountain of goods for the auction grew and the need for organization grew with it.

"If Father came home to see this..." Margaret let her words trail off as she looked over the furniture, boxes, and miscellaneous trinkets from the second-floor landing. From overhead she could see how expansive their project had become, congesting the foyer and impeding on access to the stairs.

"We need to hand out the invitations soon, Julia," Margaret said as she made her way back to her room. Crossing the threshold, she found her maid at the tiny writing desk near the window, leaning over the tabletop with a fountain pen in her hand.

"Forgive me, Miss," Julia said, turning slightly in the chair at the desk. "I had meant to finish the invitations last night but Miss Violetta asked for my assistance."

"Doing what, may I ask?"

Julia smiled. "Mending mostly. I was so tired when I finished I could not think of another thing."

Margaret scowled. It was more than a little unnerving to hear her Mother's lady's maid was giving orders to the others, as if Violetta herself hadn't enough desire to do them herself.

"I apologize," Julia said.

"No, I am not cross," Margaret answered suddenly, realizing she must have misinterpreted the look on her face, "not with you, at least."

Julia nodded but a look of concern remained on her face. Margaret smiled reassuringly and patted Julia on the shoulder as she walked past to the window seat.

"Who shall we address the invitations to?" Julia asked, as if hoping to change the subject.

Margaret reached for her address book, a tan, leatherbound book that remained more empty and out of date than she'd like to admit. She exhaled as she flipped through the pages. "I have the addresses for a few of mother's friends, the Pennyfeathers, Talbots, and Careys, but aside from that I haven't the faintest clue," she said. "Mother used to handle the society side of things. I just did what I was told." Margaret released a slight laugh at her words. To think she was firmly in her twenties and not well acquainted with anyone featured on the society pages. She had more friends back at The Briar than she did in the city and this contributed greatly to her incessant boredom.

"Perhaps Lady Brant would help," Julia suggested.

"Certainly not," Margaret answered quickly. "I cannot deny a need of her one day and crawl back the next."

Having witnessed Lady Brant's offer of guardianship and Margaret's vehement refusal, Julia nodded.

"I would ask Evelyn but I don't care to bother her," Margaret said. "Daniel said she is still not well."

"We can head for a walk in the park," Julia suggested. "Seeing someone might jog your memory and in the very least we shall get some exercise from it."

Margaret smiled. "Maybe we could place invitations in the hands of random people in the hopes they will spread the word."

The two of them laughed uproariously at the suggestion, knowing very well that was not the manner in which a society hostess supplies invites. A walk seemed a good idea to Margaret, even if their task remained to plague them another day.

"This is a grand endeavour, Miss Margaret," Julia said with a smile as she gathered the envelopes. "The orphanage will be grateful for your efforts."

Margaret watched as her maid generated a tiny pile of invitations, positioning them on the flat corner of the writing desk.

It broke Margaret's heart to think of Julia growing up in a place like the orphanage. As good as Mrs. Holliwell was at providing a stable home for the children it was the stigma of the address that plagued their little hearts the most. The humiliation of being an orphan would haunt Julia for all her days, following her wherever she could find a position of employment. It did not matter how dependable or discreet she was, society would never be able to see past her unfortunate circumstances.

"I'm so sorry you had to live there," Margaret said, willing away tears that stung at her eyes.

The maid's gaze shot up quickly, her eyes wide and expression startled.

"Peter told me," Margaret said by way of explanation. "Perhaps he shouldn't have."

Julia regarded Margaret in stunned silence.

"I'm sorry," Margaret said quickly, seeing how uncomfortable her maid had become at the mention of the orphanage. "I should not have said anything."

"I understand, Miss," Julia answered, though somewhat awkwardly.

"I won't speak of it ever again," Margaret availed. "I can't have you uncomfortable on that account."

Julia gave a slight smile but said nothing, which made Margaret deeply regret her slip of words. She cursed Peter for being so nosey and, worse, sharing his findings with her.

Margaret slipped her address book on the window seat beside her before standing suddenly. "Let us go for that walk then, shall we?" she asked cheerily, forcibly changing the subject.

Julia nodded and hurriedly snatched the envelopes.

Margaret and Julia walked down Bond Street, a bundle of invitations clutched in Julia's gloved hands. They had asked Jacob, the family's groom, to convey them to Hyde Park, knowing from there they could walk the streets of Mayfair. There he would wait until they were finished with their promenade. It was too early to be making calls but Margaret could not wait. She'd have to pounce on anyone remotely recognizable, make dreaded small talk, and somehow slip the auction into conversation. It was not a task she was looking forward to but the success of her event depended upon it.

Margaret had hoped she would happen upon a few of her friends on the pavement, which would save her visits to individual houses and perhaps from a few awkward exchanges of dialogue. She chose Bond Street, where she knew many of London's socialites would be perusing the shops and spending their generous allowances. The streets, though, were surprisingly empty and with each determined step Margaret's conviction suffered.

"Perhaps it's too early in the day, Julia," Margaret said with a forced smile. "Perhaps too many of them are still abed."

Walking slightly behind her ladyship, Julia looked as if she was suppressing a laugh.

"Well, it's true," Margaret said, seeing the amusement on her maid's face as she glanced back. "You may be out of bed hours before the sun but the women in my circles haven't a care to leave the covers until hours afterward." Stopping and turning, Margaret let out a disparaged sigh. "Is it any wonder I cannot stand any of them?"

"Margaret!"

Margaret turned to the sound of her name but at first she could not see the source. Then across the street she saw Miss Bethany Brundell, an obnoxious soul, waving her hand. She scanned the street for an opening between carriages before crossing.

"Bethany! What a pleasure!" Margaret played along as

Bethany kissed the air on both sides of her face. The Brundell family had spent much time in France and, despite being back for many years, they still observed many of the French customs, a situation that often left Margaret befuddled and unsure, to say nothing of the great deal of annoyance the greetings were to her.

"Mama was just speaking of you the other day. We are so sorry to hear of your tragedies." Bethany clicked her tongue in sympathy, which only vexed Margaret further, though she was able to hide it from view. "I had no idea your family had been so troubled." Bethany placed a gloved hand on her chest to feign disbelief. "I can't imagine a mother killing herself and leaving a daughter unwed."

"Who told you such a thing?" Margaret charged.

"Oh, Margaret dear, please don't think I have any interest in such goings-on. I love you as a sister and I shall never believe a word of it." Bethany rounded, heading in the same direction as Margaret and Julia had been, and slipped a hand under Margaret's arm, leading her down the street. Margaret glanced over her shoulder to ensure Julia followed.

"How is Peter?" Bethany asked. "Not intended yet, is he? Please be kind, Margaret. I haven't the stomach to hear he has been matched as Daniel has."

"No," Margaret answered. "He assures me he has no interest at present."

"Oh excellent," Bethany said with a wide smile. "We've been touring the continent for the last few months, Grandmama and I, and we only just returned last week. I must admit my heart jumped into my throat when I had heard Daniel had been wed."

"Oh yes," Margaret said, remembering the somber yet sweet ceremony she had attended for Daniel and his new wife Evelyn just a few weeks prior. It had been a private affair, with only a handful of guests. Neither the Marshall nor Weatherall families wanted a fuss after what led up to the original wedding date. "They are very happy."

"Oh, lovely," Bethany said, her voice a little too high for Margaret's liking.

Margaret licked her lips, regretting the words that threatened to leave her lips. "I'm auctioning some of Mother's things for her charity," she blurted, against her better judgement. "Perhaps you and your mother would like to come?"

"An auction!"

"It's for the orphaned children—"

"Oh, the darlings," Bethany said.

Margaret stopped and turned to Julia, who had already pulled out an enveloped invitation from the pile. "Thank you, Julia." She turned and handed the envelope to Bethany, who held it to her breast as if it were a cherished possession.

"I will not dream of missing it," she said with a broad smile. She glanced over Margaret's shoulder to Julia. "Are those for others?" she asked with a pointed finger.

"...Yes," Margaret answered hesitantly.

"I am headed to tea this afternoon with Mama and the Pennyfeathers. Shall I give them an invitation?" Bethany reached for another invite without waiting for a reply.

"Well, of course," Margaret said with a slight laugh. "I was not sure who would be in town and hadn't really planned a guest list. Truth is, I am not sure many will attend."

"Fear not," Bethany said, snagging nearly three-quarters of the pile of invitations. "I shall hand them out to the most generous socialites. Do not worry on that account." Smirking mischievously, Bethany gave Margaret a wink. She stuffed the envelopes in her reticule and patted Margaret on the hand.

"Bethany!"

Both women turned to the street at the sound of someone calling. A man stood on the step of an open carriage door, waving to Bethany. The carriage had been pulled over to the side and the driver commanded the team to wait, trotting their displeasure into the cobblestones.

"You remember my brother Joseph, do you not?"

The man tipped his hat at Margaret but his position amongst the traffic did not permit him to alight from the carriage.

"My morning shop is spoiled," Bethany grumbled. She gave Margaret a sympathetic smile. "Give my regards to Peter. Take care, my dear." Gingerly, Bethany slipped between two parked carriages and used her brother's offered hand to step into her family's carriage. She waved as they rolled away and then gave her brother a playful smack when he winked at Margaret.

With Bethany gone Margaret and Julie stood stymied. Margaret looked from the empty space where the over-animated Bethany had stood and then back at Julia.

"I do believe you had planned that, Miss Margaret," Julia teased.

"I doubt anyone could have planned better," Margaret answered with a laugh.

Chapter 13

The whole earth through.

Using the back of his hand, Ainsley wiped perspiration from his forehead as he leaned over the torso of a man who had been found dead in a lodging house a few blocks from the hospital. Although Ainsley suspected an undiagnosed disease, a cause that would have fascinated him immensely at any other time, he found it hard to concentrate. His mind wandered unrelentingly to the children in the adjoining room who begged him to find their killer.

The deaths of pauper children were hardly a priority for the hospital and, as far as Dr. Crawford was concerned, Ainsley had done his duty by performing the autopsy. The supervising surgeon had stopped asking when Ainsley could be expected to release the bodies. So many times Ainsley had denied the request, citing further tests, but in truth Ainsley had no desire to let any of the children go. To where? Ainsley would ask himself. Some hole in the ground left unmarked and unvisited? The thought had sent so many chills up Ainsley's spine he began willing himself to think of it no more. The least he could do would be find the murderer and prevent the fiend from striking again. Perhaps then the cold graves of the children would haunt him a little less.

Ainsley hadn't realized he was frozen mid-movement over the body, moving neither scalpel nor hand, until he heard someone clear their throat.

"Do you plan on completing the dissection sometime in the near future, Dr. Ainsley?"

Ainsley looked up and saw Dr. Crawford on the opposite side of his examination table, a clipboard held tightly to his chest. Behind him, Ainsley saw Sidney, his one eye still somewhat puffy from the boxing match the other night. He did not approach Ainsley's table as Dr. Crawford had. Jaw clenched, Sidney gave a hardened stare at Ainsley.

Failing to suppress a self-pleased smile, Ainsley stood tall and jerked his chin toward Sidney's face. "You've looked better," he said without any concern for how cruel he may sound.

Sidney snorted and turned away.

Dr. Crawford scoffed, shaking his head. He gave a quick glance to his nephew before turning back to Ainsley. "Runaway carriage, apparently," he said. "Though I have my doubts," he added through the side of his mouth.

Ainsley felt a sudden chill and looked beyond his visitors to the door, expecting Frisker or another porter to appear. At first he saw nothing and when he looked back to Dr. Crawford he found the head surgeon giving him a dubious look. "My apologies, sir," Ainsley said. He laid down his scalpel and wiped his hands on a nearby towel. As he turned to toss the towel aside a movement in the shadows caught his eye.

It was brief, there as a solid mass, watching the trio intently. When Ainsley looked back the form was gone.

"What is it, Ainsley?" Sidney asked, a deep frown setting upon his face.

Not wishing Sidney to see him unsettled, Ainsley shook it off. "Nothing." As soon as he said it however, he felt a light touch on his hand at his side. The touch, faint but cold, began at his smallest finger, expanding to the rest of his hand before Ainsley snatched it away quickly. He turned and stepped away, shocked to find nothing there. He looked to his hand, feeling the chill in his flesh with the other.

Sidney laughed. "The dead unnerve him," he said, crossing his hands over his chest.

Ainsley sneered, angered at himself for behaving so foolishly. And in front of those two, no less.

Crawford cleared his throat and turned to Sidney

unapologetically. "Wait outside, boy," he said in an authoritative voice.

Sidney looked up suddenly from a body he was studying, his eyes wide as if he were caught doing something he shouldn't have been. "Sir?"

"Go wait outside." Dr. Crawford punctuated each syllable separately.

Begrudgingly, Sidney turned and left. Only once the door latched did Crawford begin to speak. "He is an embarrassment to me," he explained, speaking to Ainsley as if they were old chums. "I cannot tell if that boy has any grey matter in that big head of his."

Ainsley pressed his lips together tightly to suppress a laugh.

"He's scored so low on his last two examinations the school is threatening to expel him. I just don't know what to do," he continued with a shake of his head. "I promised my sister I'd see he got along in London. I haven't the heart to write and tell her he's a lost cause." The pained look on Crawford's face was enough to garner some sympathy from Ainsley, though not much. He cared little for the overly confident scoundrel. The fact that Crawford was not aware of the origins of Sidney's injuries meant that the boy knew he should never have challenged Ainsley in the first place and it was that choice that saved him. Somewhat.

"I haven't the patience to tutor him," Crawford confessed. "You're my best man—"

Ainsley flinched at this. Never had he heard a word of praise from the head surgeon. Each conversation began and ended with a glare, words of admonishment, or disappointment. Only once had Ainsley heard hints of Crawford's unwilling praise. This was the first time the man had ever said anything to Ainsley directly. It had been a conversation Ainsley was only partly interested in, and Crawford's comments brought Ainsley quickly to full attention.

"I'd like you to allow him to shadow you," Crawford

said quickly, as if to bury his compliment amongst his true motive. "Perhaps you can penetrate that thick skull of his." Crawford scoffed a measure of disgust evident on his face.

Ainsley shook his head. "Absolutely not," he said, raising his hands as if to create distance. "I have too much—" Ainsley glanced to the room to the side where the bodies of Jonathon and the others remained. He could just see the table where Jonathon's body lay. He knew if he had a shadow he'd not have as much time to work with Simms on the case as he would like.

"It would just be a few days or so. Until he passes his final exam," Crawford explained. "I'd be indebted to you."

Ainsley stopped his protest, his eyes on the spot where Benjamin had stood, weeping as he said good-bye to his friend.

"Are you willing to do something for me?" Ainsley asked, suddenly inclined to entertain the idea.

Crawford hesitated. "As your superior I could include it as part of your duties," he threatened.

Ainsley snorted. "That would not be allowed. I'd hate to have to inform the Board of Governors." Ainsley gave a half-smile, knowing Crawford would not be able to refuse his request, not if he wanted him to help his nephew.

Crawford's shoulders sank as he stared at Ainsley.

"I will allow Sidney to shadow me if you hire Benjamin Catch, one of the boys from the orphanage."

"To do what?" Crawford's voice bellowed with protest. "Has he been a practising surgeon long?" Crawford asked, mocking Ainsley's suggestion.

"We could train him as a porter," Ainsley answered, immune to Crawford's objection. "It's either that or the boy goes to Canada as a farmhand. A fate worse than death, so I hear."

Arms crossed over his chest, Crawford regarded Ainsley suspiciously. "What does it matter to you where this guttersnipe ends up?"

Ainsley took offence to Crawford's use of the word

"guttersnipe." Almost all the children who ended up in their morgue could be classified as such. It was clear Crawford held little regard for the populace they were meant to serve.

Ainsley shrugged. "Those are my terms." He turned to his tools, ensuring they were replaced in their proper spots. "Perhaps you should ask Sidney to pen the letter to your sister. It might give the boy a sense of responsibility for his own predicament." Ainsley turned, satisfied everything was in order.

"So you've resorted to blackmail then?" Crawford asked.

"Extortion, actually."

Crawford's eyes narrowed. "Fine. Tell the boy he's to be here no later than five a.m. I have no use for tardiness."

"Tell your boy to keep his arrogance at home. I have no use for his ego."

Crawford nodded, effectively agreeing to Ainsley's terms. As if to seal the deal, Crawford offered his hand, which Ainsley shook forcibly. There was no telling if the head surgeon would renege on their deal. Ainsley would simply have to trust the man's word and handshake.

When Crawford left, Ainsley leaned in on the examination table in front of him. Ainsley had been so concerned with getting a better deal for Benjamin he almost forgot he had agreed to spend time tutoring his least favoured person. He pounded his knuckles into the table.

"Damn it!"

It was late by the time Ainsley left the hospital. The darkened streets were made even darker by the mist that clung to the pavement and buildings. Ainsley felt the rain, like pinpricks, on his face as he walked into the wind. He knew he should head home but he wanted to let Benjamin know of his new position at the hospital and hoped the boy could start soon.

The rain turned to ice pellets and Ainsley arrived at

the orphanage door, hunched against the cold, one gloved hand clutching his collar closed while the other knocked on the orphanage door. He knocked a second time, louder than the first, and finally someone opened the large door. A man stood on the other side, his face deep in a frown, his eyes squinting against the barrage of ice that flew at him from the street.

"Can I help you?" he asked, holding up a hand to shield his face.

Even in the dim light Ainsley recognized him as Mrs. Holliwell's grown son, Elliot, the man Benjamin said bothered the girls at the orphanage and made all the children scared. Ainsley had no doubt Elliot would recognize him as Lady Charlotte Marshall's son, as Mrs. Holliwell had, and so Ainsley knew he must introduce himself accordingly, though he had not yet figured out how he would describe his connection with the hospital where Benjamin had been hired to work.

"Mr. Peter Marshall," Ainsley said, offering his free hand. "Lady Marshall's second son."

Elliot squinted against the barrage of ice and rain. "Peter?" A look of recognition came over his face and he ushered Ainsley in. "Quick, quick," he said, his voice denoting some concern. "You must be frozen stiff."

Once inside, Ainsley released his collar and removed his hat.

"Let me put these by the fire," Elliot said, taking Ainsley's coat, gloves, and hat. "We are not used to late-night visitors. We lock the doors before the supper hour. I was trying to recall if any of the older boys had not returned from their positions." Elliot motioned with his arm for Ainsley to follow him down the dark hallway.

The building was quiet and near black. Ainsley realized Elliot must have been walking the hall from memory and Ainsley tried to keep up but his steps were less assured. "Mother told me you had stopped by the other day," Elliot said from the darkness.

"Yes, I happened by a scene involving one of your charges."

"And a detective," Elliot interjected. "We've spoken with the lad. No further need to worry on that account."

Finally, the man opened the door to a sitting room where light from a small fire illuminated the room. With the door opened, the light and warmth radiated into the hallway.

"Mother," Elliot said. "Mr. Peter Marshall has come to pay a visit."

Ainsley stepped into the room and saw Mrs. Holliwell seated in a high back chair near the fire, a small girl, perhaps no more than four years old, curled up in her arms. The orphanage matron stroked the girl's hair as the child slept. "Mr. Marshall!" she explained in an animated whisper. She reached out her hand in greeting but dared not move. "My apologies, Mr. Marshall. I'd rise to shake your hand but I just managed to get her to sleep."

Ainsley shook his head, dismissing her need to apologize. "Let her sleep."

"She hasn't been herself today," Mrs. Holliwell said, glancing down to the child and pulling a strand of hair from her face.

"Is she severely ill?" Ainsley asked, his professional curiosity getting the better of him.

"No, no," Mrs. Holliwell answered, smiling at his concern. "Nothing I have not nursed before."

"Mother was supposed to come home this evening. It was her night off," Elliot explained while standing beside Ainsley. "I found her here coaxing Louisa to sleep."

Mrs. Holliwell pressed her lips together and gave her son a look of apology. "I simply cannot leave them," she said. "There are others who help, Mr. Marshall, but I have taken these children on as my own."

Elliot cleared his throat and gestured for an empty chair opposite his mother. When Ainsley took it, Elliot pulled a wooden chair that had been placed against the wall closer to the circle of light emitting from the fire.

"For what do we owe the pleasure of your visit?" Mrs. Holliwell asked, maintaining her quiet tone.

"I have come about Benjamin Catch," Ainsley said, adjusting in his seat.

An audible sigh escaped Elliot. "What has the boy done now?" he asked, clearly annoyed.

"Why must you always be so disparaging?" Mrs. Holliwell asked her son. She turned to Ainsley. "Benjamin is a good boy, a bit troubled, but good."

Ainsley saw Elliot's jaw tighten, most likely embarrassed by his mother's admonishment.

"So I have observed. The boy is clearly wanting more responsibility," Ainsley said. "It's why I spoke of him to a friend of mine at St. Thomas Hospital."

"The hospital?" Mrs. Holliwell looked to her son.

"Ben has been selected to take Jonathon's place as a farmhand to a Canadian family—"

"But I would hate to see him shipped off," Ainsley stammered. "There are no advocates for them there."

"Elliot assures me he is going to a good family," Mrs. Holliwell said, her face betraying her worry for the child.

Elliot leaned back in his chair, his body language hard against any correction Ainsley might offer.

"I have no doubt," Ainsley lied. "I only thought he should be given the option of work here in London, should he so choose."

"What kind of work?" Elliot asked.

Ainsley turned to Elliot. "As a porter in the morgue."

Mrs. Holliwell's gasp caused the girl on her lap to stir before settling into sleep again.

Ainsley reached out a hand of reassurance. "Believe me, it is not as morbid as it sounds. Benjamin can stay here, where surroundings are familiar and he will learn a trade that will see him comfortable for the duration of his life."

"And who shall pay for his board?" Elliot asked

doubtfully. "Are we to carry his expense until he is old and grey?"

"Elliot, hush!"

"It is true, Mother. All these children cost money and you bring home more charity cases every day, faster than we can find homes for them." Elliot's voice grew animated with frustration. He turned to Ainsley and toned down his worry. "Benjamin's assignment to the Dominion was to relieve some of the burden."

"He would receive a wage and be able to assist the orphanage until he is able to acquire a room of his own," Ainsley explained. He could tell Mrs. Holliwell was pleased with his plan. A light smile touched her lips but when her gaze drifted to her son it quickly vanished. Ainsley looked over and saw Elliot had become agitated.

"I cannot see how this differs all that much from our standard procedures," he said sharply, bouncing his knee. "Why such a sudden interest in the foundlings, Mr. Marshall?"

Feeling the tension in the room rise, Ainsley leaned back in his chair in the hopes it would make him less intimidating. He had not anticipated such a reaction. Elliot was a naturally suspicious man, Ainsley could see as much, and not nearly as charitable as his mother was. The man was a bookkeeper, a person centered in facts and numbers but he also harboured supressed resentment and anger, which now he directed toward the children. It was clear Ainsley's offer to help had made Elliot look miserly in front of his own mother, and that was something that bothered Elliot greatly.

"Elliot, please. Mr. Marshall is doing it in memory of his mother." Mrs. Holliwell gave a gentle smile. "She spoke fondly of the physicians at St. Thomas. I do not doubt your motives, Mr. Marshall." She shifted in her chair, scooping the child up in her arms somewhat awkwardly but the child made no indication that she was aware her bed was on the move.

Ainsley stood, offering with outstretched arms to take the heavy child from her.

"Oh, yes, thank you."

Together, Ainsley and Mrs. Holliwell shifted the child's weight until she was secured in his arms. Mrs. Holliwell straightened the ripples in her skirt and turned. "Follow me. I shall show you to the girl's room."

Again, Ainsley followed through the dark corridors, and then up a wide set of wooden stairs. The girl was so light, and almost curled into him as he walked. He need not have worried that she would slip from his grasp. Ahead of him, Mrs. Holliwell opened a door and a small aura of light escaped the room. She walked in ahead of him inciting whispers of joy from the other girls as she did so.

"Hush now," Ainsley heard her command gently.

When Ainsley slipped passed the threshold, there was an audible gasp and then quiet murmurs. Mrs. Holliwell again begged the girls to quiet themselves and showed Ainsley to one of the beds. Bent over the metal-framed bed, Ainsley slipped the girl under the cold covers and then helped Mrs. Holliwell pull one of the blankets over the child. Gently, Ainsley placed a hand to the girl's forehead, checking for fever. Satisfied she was in no danger, he turned and followed Mrs. Holliwell from the room.

"Good night, girls," she said as she pulled the door closed. "No more stories." A sheepish groan rose from the girls just as the door latched. "The older girls take turns telling the younger ones tales."

"You have taught them to read?"

Mrs. Holliwell tilted her head to the side slightly and bit her lower lip. "When I can. It's rudimentary at its best but it will do well enough once they enter service or other work."

Service? Ainsley was reminded of his discovery about Julia. She had been raised here at this very orphanage, if the employment records were to be believed, and he did not doubt his father would have ensured precise accuracy in that regard.

They walked the hall, approaching the stairs, though their pace was slow.

"Mrs. Holliwell, do you recall a girl named Julia living here years ago?"

"Julia?" Mrs. Holliwell knitted her brow in an attempt to recollect the name.

"Julia Kemp. She'd be around my age, lovely girl with cinnamon-coloured hair. Gentle enough but somewhat of a fighter as well."

Mrs. Holliwell smiled as they reached the stairwell. She grasped the railing and stopped, turning to Ainsley. He could just make out her features in the dim light that filtered in from the gas lamp outside the window.

"Lovely girl. She entered service at fourteen, I believe."

"Do you know if she reunited with her mother at some point? Either while she lived here or afterward?"

"Mother? No, certainly not. Her mother passed many years ago when she was a child. That's how she came to us." Mrs. Holliwell shook her head and placed her free hand over her stomach. "Such a mournful child..." The headmistress's voice trailed off and she began to tackle the stairs.

"Mournful in what way?" Ainsley pressed.

Mrs. Holliwell heaved a sigh and paused on the landing. "Mr. Marshall, I doubt she would want me to say. If you know her in some capacity might you not ask her yourself?"

Ainsley walked through the door of Marshall House, a much-needed refuge from the wet streets he had been traversing on his way home. Removing his coat, Ainsley caught a glimpse of Julia and when he turned he saw her asleep on the floor, her body slouched over a low table, a pen poised in mid-task, her page blotted with ink escaping the pen's tip. He draped his coat over the bannister at the foot of the stairs, and quietly walked toward her. His intention was to wake her, save her a chill or stiffness that would surely plague her the next day were she left to sleep in such an awkward way, but as he crouched down beside her he hesitated.

He glanced to the paper held to the table by her hand and saw that she had been making notes of some of the auction items. Her handwriting was beautiful and her spelling flawless, a testament to Mrs. Holliwell's tutelage. Ainsley would never have guessed Julia's upbringing was so tumultuous had he not seen her employment record for himself. She was so cheerful and agreeable, it hardly seemed fair for Mrs. Holliwell to describe her as mournful. During her time with the Marshalls, Julia had only ever been loyal, accommodating, and fair. She worked hard, often taking up extra tasks that should have rightly been Violetta's and yet she never complained, not that Ainsley was aware of. She even endured snide remarks and jeering from the other staff but never said a peep about that struggle to him or Margaret.

Julia was quickly taking her place in the Marshall household, and Ainsley could not deny the way he was drawn to her. It was not simply her beauty, he decided. There was something else entirely that bade him to protect her, to want her as his own.

He watched her sleep for a few moments, running thoughts through his mind, searching for meaning in these forbidden feelings. She was household staff, off limits in every way. In any other world, there'd be no such internal debate. He smiled to himself as he pulled the spilling pen from her loose grasp.

She stirred, startling somewhat when she saw him. "Mr. Marshall, I did not hear you come in," she said, trying hard not to appear groggy.

Ainsley stood up and offered her his hand to help her to her feet.

Pressing her lips together, Julia avoided his stare as she climbed to her feet.

"Shall I fetch you some tea?" she asked.

"No," he said, turning from her quickly to put the pen away. "I couldn't leave you there. I'd not have caught a wink had I known you were sleeping on the cold floor."

Julia bowed her head and pressed the creases from her skirt. "That is very kind." She noticed his coat hung over the bannister. "I shall hang up your coat at least." She moved to slip passed him, the only access to the bannister through a thin aisle between the auction items.

Ainsley should have stepped back and given her more room but he did not. A near magnetic force propelled him to stay in place as she brushed by, head low and gaze unsure. He could smell a hint of cinnamon in her hair and resisted the urge to draw closer.

Awkwardly, she stepped back, his damp coat draped over the crook of her arm. She turned as if to leave but hesitated. Ainsley watched as she opened her mouth, preparing to say something but stopping herself.

"What?" he asked, "What is it?"

Julia swallowed. "Only that you..."

Ainsley's throat grew dry at the myriad of possibilities of what she would say next. If it was anything remotely like what he had been thinking he was sure he'd be the happiest of men for the rest of his days.

"You told Miss Margaret about the orphanage." Her eyes glistened in the dim light as if readying to cry. However, she did not. Instead, she stood returning his stare, a quiet yet unmistakable challenge to a long-held belief that servants were merely chattel, nothing more. It was clear she had wanted him to respect her privacy as she had done for every member of the Marshall family during her brief but tumultuous employment.

"I... I—" Ainsley struggled for something to say.

"It is a time in my life that I do not wish to dwell on," Julia explained. "Mrs. Holliwell is like a mother to me and I will always love her for that but those years were not my happiest."

"I understand."

"I doubt you do," Julia charged, the tears spilling over onto the crest of her cheeks. "I applaud Miss Margaret for her work with the auction but you must know how hard it is for me to hear her friends speak of orphans as..." Her voice stopped, as if unwilling to say the words aloud. "I have been trying to keep these feelings to myself. I never wished to burden her with my woes." Her free hand went to her face to wipe the tears and it took all of Ainsley's strength not to step forward to help her. "I know you are my employer and my personal information is yours to do as you wish but I cannot help but feel betrayed by you."

"Betrayed?" Ainsley could hardly believe the words he was hearing. "It wasn't a secret. Everyone knew, everyone accept Margaret and myself. I had to hear it from the kitchen staff before I ever thought to look at Father's files."

Julia opened her mouth to protest, her lips tightened in anger, but she stopped herself.

"I only wanted to know if what they said was true," Ainsley said.

"What business is it of theirs whether or not I came from an orphanage?" Julia's voice became loud, a stark contrast to the sheer quiet of the house.

Ainsley looked to the second-floor landing above them, half-expecting Margaret to come to see what the fuss was about. When he looked back to Julia she was gone. He could hear the sounds of her shoes on the floor as she made her way down the hall to the back of the house.

"Wait!" Ainsley went after her, quickening his pace when he saw how determined she was to get away. He couldn't let her leave crying. He wasn't sure what to say to her but he could not have her crying on his account.

He caught up to her in the tight hallway that would lead to the kitchens. He grabbed her arm to force her to look at him. "Julia, I'm sorry." She tried to push him away, the tears coming forcefully, but he held on to her, unwilling to be scared off. His coat fell into a heap on the floor amidst the ruckus.

"Let go of me," she said. "I will pack my things and leave in the morning," she said sternly, as she gave one last heave to pull herself away. Ainsley stepped back, his hands held aloft, signalling his concession.

Julia hung her head, pushing back one last tear. She gathered up his coat and turned to walk down the stairs.

"Please don't leave," Ainsley begged. "Margaret would never forgive me."

Julia stopped just before the stairs. The irony had not been lost on him. Not six months before she had slapped him across the face in that very hall and now he was begging her not to go.

"She loves you," he said, stepping toward her. "I—" He reached for her hand and pulled her back toward him. For a long while they stared at each other, an evident passion between them held at bay by their opposing duties.

Leaning in, he pressed his lips to hers. She lingered for the briefest of moments, returning his kiss, before he felt her hand on his upper arm, bidding him to stop. Begrudgingly, he released her but did not back away. He nudged her cheek with his and relished the feeling of her eyelashes fluttering over his skin.

The hand that had pushed him away slightly now clung to him as if forcing him to stay.

"Don't go," he whispered, pushing a loose strand of hair away from her face.

Julia nodded and looked up, her eyes searching his face in the failing light. She kissed him then, holding him tightly before wrapping her arms around his neck. Ainsley placed his hand on her hips as she straightened her body and then he wrapped his arms around her waist. She leaned into him, allowing herself to become lost in his embrace. Eventually, his mouth left her lips and began trailing over her chin to her neck. Slipping even further into his control, Julia's breathing became heavy and her grasp grew tight as his kiss moved down her neck to her shoulders. Gently, he tugged at her lace collar, testing her willingness to go further.

She exhaled slowly, her warm breath exciting his skin. She made no protest as his arms enveloped her and soon they were both lost in each other, forgetting their argument, the uncomfortable truth of their roles in the family, and the sinister world that lay beyond Marshall House.

Chapter 14

Most ineradicable stains, for showing
(Not interfused!)

"Mr. Marshall, your sister asks if you would join her for breakfast."

Ainsley sat up in bed, startled by the sound of Cutter's voice in his room. Panicked, he turned to the other side of his bed, sure that the footman would spot Julia.

The bed was empty and Ainsley was alone.

Ainsley ran a hand through his hair, exhaling slowly in an attempt to settle his rapidly beating heart.

"Are you all right, Mr. Marshall?" Cutter asked as he walked around Ainsley's bed, gathering discarded clothing from the night before, saying nothing of their odd placement.

Julia's absence was typical. Not once had Ainsley awoken with a woman still beside him. They often left, either satisfied or ashamed, but either case having no further need of him. Each arrangement was precisely as Ainsley wished it and yet waking up without Julia at his side stirred up regret in his heart.

Shielding his eyes from the morning sun that slipped in through a break in the drapes, Ainsley nodded. "I'm quite all right," he answered without thought. "Tell my sister I shall be down momentarily."

Cutter bowed slightly and left. Ainsley never allowed anyone to help him dress and his father's valet was so accustomed to Ainsley's constant refusal he scarcely ever asked anymore.

Ainsley dressed quickly, hoping to find Julia before she started the bulk of her daily duties. But before he could button the length of his shirt he heard footsteps at his door.

He turned quickly, hoping it was Julia.

No one was there.

Adjusting his collar, he walked to the door and found it partly open. Ainsley peered into the hall, looking the full width of the house from one corridor to the next, and saw no one. Puzzled, Ainsley looked again and that's when he saw movement heading down the stairs. It was Julia who had come to speak to him, he knew it, only now she retreated.

Tie in hand, Ainsley darted out into the hall and to the top of the stairs. "Juli—"

There was no one there.

He saw something, he knew he had. Waiting for the sound of a door or footsteps on the floor, Ainsley heard the dead quiet of the house and suddenly the air felt heavy. At the railing on the second- storey landing looking over the foyer, Ainsley put on his tie and adjusted his cuffs.

The floor creaked markedly behind him and he turned with fright. No one had been in the hallway a moment ago and the space was empty. Once again, he looked down both corridors and saw nothing. He had sensed something, though. A presence, as if someone were staring at him at that very moment.

He laughed at how suggestible he had become. How easily he was startled by the slightest noise. How easily he jumped to conclusions. Ainsley returned to his room to finish dressing and even as he walked down the stairs to breakfast he smiled thinking over his folly. He knew such things were possible. He had seen the ghost of a child many times over many days during the previous year. He still hadn't been able to piece together what he had seen and he reasoned it was better than way, the not knowing. The chances of such an event happening again were scarce, so scarce; in fact, it seemed ludicrous to give credence to the thoughts running through his mind.

Ainsley made his way down the hall and was about to turn into the dining room when the billowing of a skirt caught his eye near the library door. It was unmistakable, as if a woman had been standing in the hall and turned into the library. It was a full skirt, certainly not a type any of the maids would wear.

Unsure of what he had seen, Ainsley approached but found the library empty. He retreated to the hall slowly without taking his eyes from the doorway.

"Peter, why are you standing there staring down the hall?" Margaret asked from her usual seat in the dining room.

Ainsley shook his head, willing himself to forget what he had just seen. He spied Cutter at attention in front of the buffet, and nodded in greeting. It was perhaps a good thing only Margaret and he remained at the house with such a skeleton staff. Without a butler or head housekeeper, the staff would be run off their feet catering to the needs of everyone.

As it was, breakfast was light but Ainsley cared not. Margaret seemed chipper and worked steadily at her plate of food. "Who were you looking for?" she asked as Ainsley took his seat opposite her.

Ainsley shook his head. "No one. I thought I saw something. That is all."

"Was it Mother?" Margaret's voice rose gleefully, unaffected by the idea that her brother may confess to having seen their departed mother.

"No," Ainsley answered with slight hesitation.

Margaret shrugged and continued to spoon out her hardboiled egg. "I only ask because of your propensity to attract spectres."

Ainsley's jaw tightened at the mention of it. "One dead child hardly befits a *propensity*," he answered.

"Well, if you do see her, ask if she believes I am doing the right thing," she said, her voice somewhat downturned. "I am beginning to second-guess this whole auction thing. Perhaps it is not the right thing to do."

"Mother would want you to continue," Ainsley

explained. "If only for the children."

Margaret nodded, her gaze fixated on an upper corner of the room. "Father certainly would not approve." She turned her focus to her food, snatching another egg from the plate between them.

"Then we are fortunate that Father is not here, at present."

Margaret smiled. "The invitations have been issued. It's not as if I can run the span of London retracting them all."

Ainsley raised his cup of tea to his mouth. "My, Margaret, you are efficient."

Margaret shrugged. "I had some help. I ran into Bethany Brundell yesterday."

Ainsley nearly spat out his tea back into his cup. "Bethany?"

Margaret nodded. "She suggested I leave the invites with her since she would be seeing many of the socialites that afternoon at tea. I did not see the harm in it."

"I suppose you are to tell me Bethany is coming as well," Ainsley said, letting out a controlled breath.

"Of course." Margaret pursed her lips, eyeing her brother with a bit of contempt. "I know you two had an issue a while back—"

"An issue?" Ainsley slipped to the edge if his seat. "That woman convinced Mother that we had been promised to each other. She said I wanted to keep it a secret and that's why I had not told her or Father. Mother nearly had me go through with the blasted thing as well. She did not believe me when I told her we had no such understanding."

Margaret shook her head. "Could you blame Mother, truly? You had made such a name for yourself as a rake, Mother and I thought Bethany had finally tripped you up and snagged your heart."

Ainsley almost choked and leaned back in his chair, refusing to touch another morsel of food. "Not that woman, I assure you."

Violetta entered the room, a carafe of coffee in her hands. Margaret looked over. "Violetta, how is Julia?"

"She's fine now, ma'am," Violetta explained, placing the carafe on the buffet table on the far side of the room. "Resting is all."

"What's the matter with Julia?" Ainsley asked, unable to hide his anxiety at the thought of her being unwell or, worse, feeling as if his actions had been the cause of it.

"She's not feeling well, or so I hear," Margaret explained while surveying the remaining food between them.

Ainsley moved to stand. "Perhaps I should go see if she needs—"

"Oh, Peter, sit. She's perfectly fine. Just overtired with all my demands with this auction." Margaret pressed her lips together and looked from Ainsley and then back to the food. She had a look of regret about her, as if ashamed. "I'm told she fell asleep in the foyer last night working on something I assigned to her. I attempted to apologize this morning but she wouldn't let me in the room." Margaret squared her shoulders and reached for some fruit. "She said she would just like some time to rest."

Ainsley felt sorry for his sister and sorrier still that he could not alleviate the sense of responsibility she felt. He could not tell her of Julia's true whereabouts without jeopardizing the maid's reputation and position within the staff, not to mention the tarnish it would bring to him were it found out he had been fraternizing with one of the maids. Margaret in particular would never forgive him.

"What do you have planned for today?" Margaret asked, forcibly changing the subject.

Ainsley hesitated to give an answer, his mind still processing feelings of guilt.

"Your case involving the children," Margaret pressed, "have you and Simms any leads?"

Ainsley shook his head slightly. "Nothing has been pinned down," he answered.

"Well, you must have your suspicions," Margaret pressed with a slight laugh. "I've never known you to be so quiet on the subject."

Ainsley could feel a rising tension in his shoulders. It wasn't the sort of topic he had meant to bring up at the breakfast table. He had little interest in sharing the intricate details of the grisly case. Not that he felt Margaret couldn't handle it. He knew she had a stronger stomach than most men. The case, however, was unrelenting, creeping alongside him wherever he went and colouring every facet of his life. Each hour that passed he felt his noose of obligation tightening. He and Simms had been working tirelessly on their own portion of the investigation. The sleep he had just awoken from had been his first real night of slumber since Simms first brought him on to the case. Ainsley couldn't be blamed for wanting a few moments of the morning without incessant reminders of what reality awaited him beyond the house walls.

Ainsley pushed his plate away.

Margaret mustn't have seen his discomfort. "What are the common threads between them?"

"There are none, only the manner with which they were killed." His voice became strained and already he felt defeated before the day had begun. He raised his hands to his temples.

"Are they not from the same neighbourhood at least?" she insisted.

"No," Ainsley snapped. "There is nothing. Not age, nor gender, nor address. They were butchered carelessly and cast aside like rubbish. I have only the answers the bodies themselves provide, nothing more. Perhaps you should apply at the Metropolitan Police. An occupation there may satisfy your meddling." Ainsley reached for his tea but before he grasped it the remorse hit him.

Too much of his heart had become involved in this case. He worried for Ben and the others in Mrs. Holliwell's care and feared the Yard would find another before Ainsley and

Simms had a chance to hunt the bastard down. All these fears and worries made him impatient and unkind.

Ainsley raised his gaze to apologize but found Margaret had left, his chance evaporated.

Ainsley had never felt more dread than when he left the house that morning. After breakfast he had gone to Margaret's room and found her not there. He lingered amongst her auction items for a time, hoping to happen upon her or Julia but neither of them came and eventually he was forced to move on. During his half-hour walk to the hospital Ainsley vacillated between being angry with himself for the words he had spoken and chiding Margaret for her insensitive questioning. He knew he was entirely in the wrong, and wished he'd had the opportunity to express as much to her before he left.

The fact that Julia did not wish to see him affected him more than he ever thought possible. Her avoidance of him hurt far more than his quarrel with Margaret. His behaviour toward his sister's lady's maid was inexcusable and would no doubt cause awkwardness between the two of them in a relationship that had otherwise been rather cordial. Never before had his philandering extended to the staff, at least not his own family's staff. It was not that long ago he was chastising his brother Daniel for making eyes toward Julia. That was different, though, he told himself. Daniel's advances were unwanted and Julia responded to his own with equal desire, hadn't she? Had he forced himself upon her and made her couple with him? Perhaps she thought he demanded it by virtue of his position of authority. What should have been a sweet encounter between the pair quickly turned sour at the thought of his insatiable lust overriding his duty.

At the time, Ainsley thought it was a mutual desire between the two of them and had not cared what any long-term recourse would be. Now that Julia had taken to her room, feigning illness, Ainsley feared he had overstepped his bounds, making a budding kinship into something cheap and tawdry. It pained him greatly to think he had hurt her in any way. This was so unlike him. Never before had he felt an ounce of regret and now he was riddled with it.

Walking away from the house, knowing two women inside were vexed with him, made each step all the more difficult. And what awaited him at the hospital promised to be less than elevating.

Deep in thought, Ainsley did not notice the police carriage pull up beside him until Simms called out his name.

"Dr. Ainsley. Ainsley!" Simms leaned out of the carriage, holding his hand out to help Ainsley in. "They found another one."

Chapter 15

That brighter colours were the world's foregoing,
Than shall be used.

In a dockyard not far from the Tower of London, Ainsley stood over victim number five with his hands shoved deep in his pockets and jaw clenched, a feeble attempt to suppress the bile that slowly crept up his oesophagus. The sight was typical for *The Surgeon*, another girl slit from pelvis to sternum, her organs rearranged, some spilling from the opening. Her body lay next to a red brick building, slightly hidden behind a heap of broken wood crates and barrels. Ainsley closed his eyes to the sight, his mind slow to comprehend any possible reasoning for the attack.

A gawking crowd of dockworkers and sailors had gathered before he and Simms arrived. Two uniformed constables had stood on guard for a time, keeping the growing throng at bay until reinforcements arrived. Ainsley wondered how the pair of them had managed to keep everyone back from the scene and when he looked to the crowd he saw the curiosity on their faces. They had no intentions of intervening. They just watched and waited as if to see what the Yard would do.

Simms pulled a handkerchief from an inside pocket and, in an act of generosity Ainsley would thank him for later, laid it on the girl's face.

"What do you think, Dr. Ainsley?" Simms asked from the opposite side of the body.

"I think we are just players in their Greek tragedy," Ainsley answered, cocking his head toward the crowd.

Simms surveyed the group. "You get used to it," he answered with resignation. He turned to the uniformed officers and pointed to the crowd. "Go ask if anyone saw anything. Who lives in the area? Who does this child belong to?"

A senior constable nodded and they dispersed toward the crowd.

Ainsley inched toward the child's body, carefully watching his footsteps in the gravel so as not to disturb any possible evidence. He doubted there would be anything, but Ainsley was nothing short of meticulous. The location seemed odd to the young surgeon. All of the other bodies had been found in urban dwelling areas, and this location seemed quite remote in comparison.

The dockyard was a maze of warehouse buildings with only enough leeway for one slender cart and no more between them. Empty crates and barrels were stacked along the outsides of the six-storey, red brick buildings. Planks and catwalks crisscrossed above the alleys between the warehouses, offering an advantageous view to the murder scene.

When Ainsley looked up he saw no lamp or source of light. "Was it a full moon last night?" Ainsley asked, shifting his gaze to look at Simms.

The detective shook his head. "We'd have noticed too. All manner of discord happens on nights of the full moon."

Ainsley nodded, knowing Simms spoke the truth. "He'd have needed light then," Ainsley reasoned, "A lamp of some kind to perform his work."

"You think he cared much about precision?" Simms rebutted.

Ainsley looked toward the detective. "In a way, yes." It was clear that accuracy was not the ultimate goal, however. It did not seem to matter how the act was carried out as long as suffering was the end result.

"Anything missing?" A familiar voice rose up from the crowd and when Ainsley looked he saw Theodore Fenton standing nearby, his notebook poised and pencil at the ready.

Ainsley stood and inched toward Fenton, using his broad shoulders to shield the girl from the reporter's view.

"Trying to get the details for the evening edition then?" Ainsley asked, working hard to keep his anger in check.

The crowd began stepping back from the two men, as if expecting the duel to come to blows. Fenton too expected some physical altercation and flinched when Ainsley raised his hand to scratch the tip of his nose.

The doctor plucked the pencil from Fenton's grasp and, reaching over the body, he ran the sharpened graphite over the bricks of the wall, ruining the writing utensil. When Ainsley presented Fenton with his pencil he raised an eyebrow and smiled slightly at the expression on the reporter's face.

Ainsley turned to the constables. "Get him out of here," Ainsley commanded, gesturing to Fenton. "Take him twenty blocks from here, I don't care. Just don't let him come back to my crime scene."

The constables nodded, and walked over. They flanked Fenton on both sides, each taking an arm, and led the reporter off through the crowd.

Simms smiled when Ainsley turned back to him. "Better you than me," Simms said.

Back at their task, they knelt side by side, looking over the body and speaking in hushed tones so the crowd could not hear.

"The organs," Simms said, pointing to the mess of her midsection. "As mangled as the rest?"

"Cannot tell," Ainsley answered after a time. "I'd need to take a look at the hospital. At first glance, I'd say everything is here." Ainsley looked up, knowing the revelation would bring about more questions.

"He did not take anything?"

"Like I said, I need to look closer to be sure but"— Ainsley glanced over his shoulders—"I'd hate to do more here."

Simms nodded and bid someone toward them. "Come

forward then."

Ainsley turned to where Simms gestured and saw a man in a bowler hat and loose clothing coming forward, a box on stilts in his fumbling grasp. The box had a brass cylinder on the front and a folded mass of black fabric attached to the back. Ainsley stood, backing away slightly, anticipating a debacle. The man placed the three stilts on the ground, displacing the gravel, and carefully placed a wooden box at his side. The man lost his grip on the stilted apparatus and it would have fallen had Ainsley not reached out for it. The man nodded in thanks and smiled slightly as he readjusted his hat.

"What is this?" Ainsley asked Simms, knitting his brow.

"Paris has been using cameras for over a year now, documenting crime scenes," Simms said. "Inspector Wright commissioned this man specifically for this case."

As if on cue, the man lost grip of his stilted camera again, forcing Ainsley to lunge to catch it. Instead of handing the camera back to the man, Ainsley positioned the legs into a tripod, negating the need for someone to hold it.

"Much obliged," the cameraman said, with another dithering nod.

Ainsley watched as the man squinted toward the overcast sky and then back toward the body in front of him. "Right then," he heard the man say before repositioning the stilted camera further back from the scene. "Everyone out of the frame then," the photographer said as he folded the black fabric up over the top of the camera.

Simms cocked his head to the side and Ainsley followed him as they backed up and out of the scene. The crowd looked on in rapt interest, most likely never having seen something so technologically advanced. Once at a safe distance back, Ainsley crossed his arms over his chest and looked on as the photographer adjusted the brass tube on the front of the camera, checking and rechecking through the back of the camera box. The repetitive scene played out for what seemed like a lifetime before the photographer pulled the black fabric down the back of the camera. Unclasping his wooden box, he pulled a black square from a cache of similar objects and brought it beneath the black fabric with him. A moment later, the photographer placed the black square on top of his wooden box on the ground.

Intrigued, Ainsley watched, piecing together what little he knew about the science of photography. He knew the photographer had taken out the nickel plate from the black case and slid it somewhere in the back of the camera. The fabric was to prevent exposure to light, which would reach to the nickel prematurely.

Ainsley smiled despite himself. The entire process was enchanting.

After a short time, the photographer came out from under the fabric, careful not to lift the fabric too high and reached for the cap protecting the glass lens in the front cylinder. "Ready then?" the photographer said, positioning himself just behind the lens and out of view of the camera. "One, two, three."

Ainsley narrowed his gaze, wondering why the man insisted on behaving as if he were doing a portrait for some wealthy family. The crowd fell into a nervous silence, afraid even the slightest noise would somehow disrupt the photograph and undo all the man's careful work. Ainsley too found himself holding his breath as he waited to see what the man would do next.

After a long moment, the man replaced the cap on the lens and disappeared behind the black fabric. "That should about do it," he said after stowing the protected nickel plate back into his square box. The man smiled at Ainsley and Simms. "Perhaps you gentlemen would like a picture at some point. I could give a good rate for men in uniform."

Ainsley gave a glance to Simms, who waved the man off. "Just make sure you get the prints to us in a reasonable time, alright?"

The man tipped his hat and stepped back, kicking one of the legs of the tripod and then stumbling to catch the camera. Ainsley bowed his head to hide his smile. It was a miracle the man had survived so long in life without suffering a calamity of his own making.

"I will send the body to St. Thomas," Simms said, turning from Ainsley to an approaching constable.

"Sir, this man says he saw the girl yesterday 'round the corner from 'ere," the uniformed constable said as he approached. He gestured to a rotund man in tattered clothes who followed sheepishly behind the officer.

"Is this true?" Simms asked, taking on a commanding tone.

The sheepish man nodded. "Yes 'em. She was standing for a while near west building, and when I came back 'round near midday she'd taken a seat on an overturned crate."

"You are sure it was this girl?" Simms asked. He knelt down by the girl's head and lifted the handkerchief so the man could see.

The man nodded, glancing to the body for a brief moment before turning away. A bead of sweat slipped down over his brow. "Yes 'em. She's the very one."

Simms nodded.

"Sir! Sir!" Another constable pushed through the crowd, a paper held in his hands. Finally bursting through, he looked to his notes. "I have a name, sir. One of the witnesses recognized her as Maryanne Blight, of the Limehouse orphanage."

Ainsley's heart stopped. The thought of another victim from Mrs. Holliwell's orphanage made his stomach churn. "Are you sure?" Ainsley pressed, reaching for the paper in the man's hand.

"Yes sir," the constable answered, somewhat shaken by Ainsley's directness. "The witness was quite convincing."

Ainsley could not believe the words he saw on the paper. It was exactly as the constable had said, and seeing it in writing made it no less horrific.

"Who will tell Mrs. Holliwell?" Ainsley asked.

Simms let out a quick breath of air, his shoulders slumping suddenly at the thought. "Come with me then," he said. "Your presence will help to soften the blow."

Ainsley doubted the detective's words. He was certainly a familiar face but he was no better acquainted with Mrs. Holliwell than any other on the force. In fact, it was his mother's history with the charity that made Ainsley the worst person to perform such somber duties. An attack on his mother's charity was like an attack on his family. The killings had become personal.

Chapter 16

Hearken, oh hearken! ye shall hearken surely

Margaret winced slightly as Lady Brant edged closer, a gleaming grey needle poised at the ready. It was silly, really. Margaret was not squeamish in the slightest and yet the sight of that needle drew the blood down to her toes. The young girl in Margaret's lap, no more than two years of age, squirmed as well and nearly slipped away had Lady Brant not held her to Margaret.

"Goodness, Margaret, you must hold the child," Lady Brant admonished as she kept a firm grasp of the child's arm.

"Yes, Lady Brant, my apologies." Margaret held the girl in place, unsure if her grip was too tight, but leery of another reprimand.

Lady Brant said nothing as she slipped the needle into the child's skin, focusing instead on the process of vaccination. Not a mother herself, Lady Brant had not the time nor the patience for children, a reality Margaret was reminded of again and again throughout that morning at the orphanage. Lady Brant was a woman of anatomy and medicine, lending her expertise to the administration of mandatory vaccines. She had invited Margaret along to stand in as mother, holding the children still and wiping runaway tears. The young girl was their first patient and Margaret could already tell it was going to be a long day.

Clutching the site where the needle pierced her skin, the girl slipped from her perch on Margaret and fled, sniffling back tears as she went.

"Make sure you mark their paperwork," Lady Brant called as she readied another dose of smallpox vaccine. "Don't want the government accusing us of not doing our due diligence."

Margaret nodded and shifted her focus to the form beside her. "I thought the House was still debating whether the vaccine should be mandatory?" Margaret asked.

Lady Brant chuckled slightly and then looked over her half-moon spectacles at Margaret. "And why should the Lords doubt what they have already made law?" Margaret saw her mother's friend shake her head in disagreement. "There is no better way to ensure healthy poorer classes than through mandatory vaccines. All this debate about vaccinations being harmful is hogwash. It's saved many lives, Margaret dear, and the only ones wondering at its necessity are the ones who don't know the first thing about science." Lady Brant turned, the needle poised and ready. "Now, next child."

Little one after little one, Margaret held them steady and forced herself to watch as Lady Brant pinched some skin on the upper arm before inserting the needle. After a time, Mrs. Holliwell approached, patting their most recent patient on the shoulder as they passed each other.

"This is not their favourite day," she remarked as she looked over the sullen faces of the children who had already been treated and those who waited with apprehension. "I have prepared a special custard for them as a reward."

Margaret smiled at this but her pleasure vanished when she saw the look of disapproval on Lady Brant's face.

"Mrs. Holliwell, these children have no need of sweets any more than I have need of my womb." Lady Brant clicked her tongue as she shook her head. Her face was stern and cold.

"I think it's a wonderful idea," Margaret said, seeing the joy slip from Mrs. Holliwell's face. It was hardly Lady Brant's place to be advising the administration of the orphanage, and despite many meddling comments made to Margaret in the past, she could not see how Lady Brant had any vested interest in what the children were served for lunch. "Something to look forward to after a morning of discomfort." Margaret smiled toward the children who still waited in line.

Lady Brant shook her head, obviously disagreeing, but she said nothing.

Disheartened, Margaret turned away. There could be no pleasing this woman and she had noticed Lady Brant's admonishments were becoming more and more demeaning since Margaret's mother died. Margaret could not remember a time when Lady Brant had ever been overly kind, but she hadn't been quite so harsh either.

Margaret's eyes scanned the room, secretly hoping there where not so many children yet to be treated, but instead her gaze found Ainsley slipping into the dining hall, followed closely by Inspector Simms.

"Peter?" Margaret stood.

"Margaret!" Lady Brant must have looked over as well, suddenly seeing the somber pair at the doorway, because no other words followed.

They watched as Ainsley and Inspector Simms weaved through the line of children, stopping at Mrs. Holliwell.

"Have you come to see Margaret?" Mrs. Holliwell asked, "She is doing remarkably well..." Suddenly her voice trailed off as her gaze found Inspector Simms. A wave of recognition came over her features and Margaret saw her hands begin to shake.

"Not in front of the children," she said quietly.

Simms looked around them and nodded. "Is there another room?"

Inhaling forcibly, Mrs. Holliwell nodded and turned, ushering the two men away. Margaret followed, without care to Lady Brant and the task they had come to perform. Margaret knew of the last child found dead, the adolescent boy Ainsley had said resided at the orphanage. She hoped their visit brought news of the culprit's apprehension.

Mrs. Holliwell led the group through the kitchen to a small office on the other side. She held the door as the three filed in and then closed it. Margaret watched as Mrs.

Holliwell lifted a trembling hand to her mouth, as if to steady a quivering chin.

"Mrs. Holliwell," Simms began. He glanced to the floor, as if searching for the words.

Ainsley licked his lips. "There's been another," he said gently. "Maryanne Bl—" But before Ainsley could finish Mrs. Holliwell let out a deep throaty growl and stumbled to the chair behind her. One hand went to her mouth, the other grasped feebly to Margaret's skirt. Margaret sank beside her, eager to hold the sobbing woman in her arms.

"Peter, this cannot be," Margaret pleaded in disbelief.

Ainsley's gaze went from Mrs. Holliwell to Margaret but no words came. An uneasy quiet came over the room. The only sounds were that of Mrs. Holliwell's gasps for air.

After a time, Ainsley knelt before them, holding Mrs. Holliwell's hand before the woman calmed down enough to speak.

"How?" she asked. "Where?"

Ainsley glanced to Simms and then turned back to Mrs. Holliwell, pulling a clean handkerchief from his inside pocket. "They haven't determined how," he explained. "They found her in the dockyards."

"Mrs. Holliwell, how is it you did not notice a child in your charge was missing?" Simms pressed, appearing less sympathetic than Ainsley or Margaret.

"How can he ask that?" Margaret asked Ainsley incredulously. "He hasn't the right—"

Ainsley put a hand out in front of him, bidding Margaret to calm down.

A sniffle escaped Mrs. Holliwell. "Maryanne was visiting her father. He had been at sea for nearly a year." Mrs. Holliwell turned to Margaret, perhaps searching for a friendlier face. "He gave us money to help with her upkeep. If she was not housed here she'd have nowhere else to go. Two days ago we received word that his ship was expected to dock yesterday." Mrs. Holliwell turned back to the detective. "She begged me to let her go surprise him as he disembarked. I hadn't the heart to say no. I did not think her missing as much as I thought she was with her father." Her last few words gave way to sobs and finally she sank into Margaret's accepting arms.

The room became uncomfortable as the woman grieved, her tears marking the death of two children in her care. Simms shifted and Ainsley stood. When Mrs. Holliwell finally looked up to Margaret she spoke in near desperation. "The children are not safe in my care," she wailed. "I cannot keep them safe!"

"No, no, don't say that. That's not true." Margaret tried her best to soothe Mrs. Holliwell and after a time her loud sobs became slight whimpers.

"Perhaps we should come back another time," Simms suggested. "Once you have had a chance to get over the shock."

Mrs. Holliwell said nothing but Margaret nodded. Before Simms and Ainsley could take their leave, Elliot Holliwell pushed through the door. "What is it?" he commanded. "What have you told her?"

"Maryanne," Margaret said, peering over Mrs. Holliwell's shoulder. "They have found Maryanne."

Elliot raked his hand through his hair and clutched the doorknob behind him as a brace.

"She was like my own child!" Mrs. Holliwell yelled in Margaret's shoulder.

"Mother," Elliot demanded, "this is why you cannot work here. Look what it's done to you."

Mrs. Holliwell looked away, as if trying to avoid the subject.

"We have had reporters coming to the door asking questions for days," Elliot said to Ainsley as if looking for an ally to agree with him.

"Who asks questions?" Ainsley asked.

Elliot shrugged. "I don't know his name."

Ainsley and Simms exchanged glances.

"But Elliot, the children," Mrs. Holliwell sobbed.

"Let the Society hire someone else," Elliot said, as he began to pace the room. "Look what this work has done to you. Remember what it has done to us!"

Mrs. Holliwell's cries continued, and Margaret tried in vain to give some support.

Simms nodded toward Ainsley and they turned to Elliot. "We shall return at a later time with further questions," Simms explained at the door. He glanced to Mrs. Holliwell before placing his hat back on his head and leaving.

Margaret's eyes drifted from Elliot, who displayed grief through anger, to the floor, all the while rocking Mrs. Holliwell ever so slightly. After a time, Mrs. Holliwell quieted and pulled herself from Margaret's arms.

"My apologies, Lady Margaret," Mrs. Holliwell said, sniffling into the handkerchief Ainsley had given her. "The tragedies have been great as of late."

Margaret watched as Mrs. Holliwell gathered herself and stood, pressing out the creases in her apron and skirt. Margaret stood as well, and watched to ensure Mrs. Holliwell would not collapse again. Mrs. Holliwell turned to her son, who leaned back into the desk with his arms folded over his chest. "Elliot, I understand why you ask but you know and I know it is something I cannot do."

Elliot shook his head, a look of disgust on his features.

"Please excuse me, Lady Margaret," Mrs. Holliwell said, grasping at a few last ounces of dignity she still possessed. "I must freshen up before I come before the children. You and Lady Brant must carry on. I will inform the children later."

Margaret nodded but said nothing. She watched as Mrs. Holliwell left the room with Elliot close at her heels.

Chapter 17

For years and years,

Ainsley stepped out into the dining hall, the solemn faces of the pauper children looking up at him as he followed closely at Simms's heels. A line of girls waited nervously near Lady Brant, who seemed altogether out of her element amongst the hoard of orphans. "Stand back," she pronounced authoritatively, though Ainsley could see how awkward the situation was. Lady Brant held out an outstretched palm as if keeping a curious predator at bay. "I will not have you all dismantling my workstation."

Ainsley glanced over the tools, recognizing their purpose and remembering the vaccination training he had participated in during his schooling, held in an orphanage in Germany much the same as this. He remembered his mother assisting Lady Brant during other such charitable visits and thought it fitting that Margaret should take up the duty in her memory. Ainsley could not help but smile.

"What is it, Peter? The boy?"

Ainsley was pulled from his thoughts and found Lady Brant staring up at him expectantly.

"No, 'tis another," he answered quietly. "A girl." Ainsley glanced to the throng of eavesdropping faces around them. "Margaret will tell you more." Ainsley gestured to Simms, who turned at the door, waiting for Ainsley to follow him. "I must keep with the detective now."

Lady Brant pressed her lips together. "Yes, well, need I remind you to be careful of the company you keep?" Her eyes shifted to look beyond Ainsley, to where he imagined Simms stood, and then back to Ainsley.

"I fear you may be needlessly suspicious," Ainsley answered, trying hard to temper his annoyance. "Simms has given me no reason to question his character."

"His profession is enough to cause me to question his character. What sort of man wishes to consort with thieves and murderers on such a regular basis?"

Ainsley shook his head in disagreement. "A similar question could be asked of me." A smile began to spread over Ainsley's lips. "You, as well, for that matter."

He left her, speechless thanks to his rebuttal, and walked toward Simms, who waited for him out in the hall. Before he quitted the room, Benjamin caught his eye. Seated near the window, the young man looked utterly despondent against the chattering of the other children. One of the little girls ran up to him and placed a paper heart in his hand. She said something Ainsley could not hear and Benjamin smiled before thanking her.

When the little girl skipped off, Ainsley approached with his hands in his pocket. The boy could have easily barked at the girl, driven her away, and demanded to be alone, but he did not. He accepted her small gift and brightened her day, perhaps even viewing the tiny offering as the bright spot of his day.

"You have an admirer," Ainsley teased as he drew near.

Benjamin shifted in place, glancing to the group of girls nearest him and then back to Ainsley. "Nah," he said, "They'ze always doing stuff like that." Benjamin placed the paper heart on the wood of the windowsill and watched as it soaked up the moisture from the chipping paint.

"Has Mrs. Holliwell spoken to you about the hospital's offer of apprenticeship?" Ainsley asked.

Ben gave Ainsley a quizzical look.

"Dr. Crawford has offered you a place as porter," Ainsley said, taking a seat beside Ben. "You can remain living here until your apprenticeship is done and then find a place of your own when the time is right."

"Will I have to work with the bodies?" Ben asked cautiously.

"You aren't bothered by them, are you?"

Benjamin shook his head but Ainsley could tell he

lacked conviction.

"You get used to it," Ainsley answered.

Ben looked across the room to the line of children getting their vaccines. "Mrs. Holliwell doesn't know you work there, does she?"

"No," Ainsley said. "My father does not want me to be a surgeon, so I hide it. I'm Dr. Ainsley at the hospital and Mr. Marshall when I'm with my family."

"Mrs. Holliwell isn't your family," Ben offered.

"No, she knew my mother rather well and..." Ainsley hesitated, "I just haven't worked up the courage to tell her."

"Being a doctor is better than anything else I've seen," Ben said. "I don't think you should be ashamed of it."

"I'm not," Ainsley answered.

"You are if you do not tell people," Benjamin said stoically.

Ainsley gave a half-smile. "Can I count on you to keep the secret a little while longer?" Ainsley asked.

"I'll do anything if it means I can have a proper job," Ben said.

Ainsley nodded. While he hated the fact that he asked the boy to lie for him, he knew, for the time being, it was the best thing to do.

"Tomorrow morning, six sharp," Ainsley said as he stood up. Ben nodded and Ainsley left to meet Simms in the hallway.

"What do you think then?" Simms asked as Ainsley approached.

"Elliot clearly disapproves of his mother's profession," Ainsley answered, glancing back into the room. The murmur of the children began to rise as they grew restless. "Perhaps he takes his anger out on the children."

"You thought that as well?" Simms asked.

"Benjamin told me Elliot is a formidable presence here at the orphanage. I suspect he's been inappropriate with the girls."

Simms turned away, clearly angry. Ainsley saw his free

hand curl into a fist at his side.

"Trust me when I tell you it has been hard to keep myself from bashing his skull since I found out," Ainsley said quietly.

Simms looked over Ainsley's shoulders and then cocked his head toward the door. "Let us take this out to the street," he said. "Our continued presence is making Mr. Holliwell uneasy."

Ainsley turned slightly and saw Elliot in the dining hall, leaning on an opposite wall with his arms crossed over his chest, his eyes staring right at him and the detective. Ainsley thought to retrieve Margaret, preferring that she follow him home, but then thought better of it. She was in Lady Brant's company and was a pillar of strength in her own right.

"Come, Ainsley," Simms called, while he held the door open. Ainsley nodded and followed the detective out into the hazy light.

The street was shrouded by fog, giving everything soft edges and a dreamy appearance. Immediately, Ainsley felt his face become damp as he and Simms descended the front steps and approached the police carriage.

The stout driver, hidden beneath weather-beaten black cloak and tall hat, appeared to have fallen asleep, reins in hand. Simms used a spoke of the carriage wheel to provide a step and tapped the driver's leg. "St. Thomas," he commanded with a shove.

Ainsley saw the driver nod, as he gathered the reins more tightly, and Simms stepped down. They slipped into the carriage one after the other.

"I have an idea but you are not going to like it," Simms said as they settled into their seats. The carriage jerked into motion and soon what little of the street they could see through the fog became a meaningless blur as they rolled along.

"What's that?" Ainsley asked, admittedly intrigued.

"We create a trap," Simms said, "We catch our killer in

the act, as it were."

"How do you suppose we lure him?" Ainsley asked, doubtful.

"Benjamin."

"No," Ainsley answered sharply. "Absolutely not."

"He's more than capable. Strong. Observant. We could use him in many capacities."

Ainsley shifted in his seat, made uncomfortable at the idea of the boy becoming bait in the sadistic game of "cat and mouse" the Yard was playing with the child killer.

"You are not his father, you cannot stop him should he agree," Simms pointed out.

"No, but I'd strongly advise him against it."

"Which do you think is stronger—his newfound respect for you or a decade-long love for his friend?"

Ainsley adjusted his coat and looked out the window.

Simms exhaled and softened his tone. "I understand the affection you have for this boy, the care you have taken for this case demonstrates that but unless you are—"

"I do it for all the children, not just Ben."

"Then you agree with me, we cannot just sit back and wait for this child killer to slip up. If I were working this case alone I wouldn't need to ask your permission," Simms reminded him.

"So why are you?" Ainsley asked.

Until then their relationship had been fairly easy. Both required something of the other and their goals were so similarly aligned. But the stress of discovering another body was evident on Simms's features, especially with the list of likely suspects so short. Ainsley knew the detective was not blaming him for their inability to track down the culprit but Ainsley felt the pressure nonetheless.

"Just give me more time," Ainsley pleaded. "Let me have a look at wounds, compare them to the others. There must be something I'm not seeing." Ainsley relaxed somewhat when Simms began to nod, if somewhat begrudgingly.

"I won't do it yet," the detective said, "but it doesn't mean I am not considering it as an option."

Ainsley nodded, aware that their agreement would be temporary but relieved all the same. It was clear the murderer held a total disregard for the lives of London's poorer children. Capable or not, Ainsley was not willing to put Benjamin up as some sort of decoy.

Simms let Ainsley get off at the front doors to the hospital and shouted instructions at him even as the carriage rolled away. "Send a messenger as soon as you find anything. I'll be back later to go over your report."

Ainsley nodded and waved him off teasingly. "Anything else?" the young doctor shouted against the clip-clopping of the horses' shoes on the pavement.

"Lay off the drink for a while, eh?"

A snort escaped Ainsley's lips as he stood there, the carriage too far along the road for any further words between them. *Lay off the drink*? The detective's words resonated as if an echo trapped inside Ainsley's head. How much drink had he assumed Ainsley would have? Certainly not enough to interfere with his duties. Ainsley groped his coat pockets, searching for his flask, which felt surprisingly light. Funnily, he had not remembered taking many sips from it that day but now that his mind was on the topic, that is exactly what he wished to do next.

In the morgue, Ainsley found Sidney hunched over the body of the girl, Maryanne, already laid out on Ainsley's examination table, and he was suddenly reminded of the promise he had made to Dr. Crawford to assist the budding surgeon.

Sidney stiffened as Ainsley drew near and his eyes followed him as he rounded the examination table.

"Do you drink, Sidney?" Ainsley asked sharply and he opened a high cupboard door near his work area.

"No, sir."

Ainsley snorted as he pulled a bottle of Scotch from the

shadows, and then two tumblers. "You will before long." With a heavy clunk, Ainsley planted the two tumblers on the wooden surface next to his tools. He pulled the cork from the Scotch with a determined yank and poured them each a glass. Sidney made no move to retrieve the one intended for him and yet Ainsley raised his glass slightly, a toast to Maryanne, before downing the entire contents without stopping for air.

"Is this part of my tutoring?" Sidney asked, somewhat mockingly.

Ainsley shrugged. "Why not?" He thrust the glass into Sidney's unsure hands and then poured himself another. Again, he emptied the tumbler's contents without stopping for breath and then placed the empty glass near his neat array of tools. Moving toward Maryanne, he surveyed the rest of the room, where even more corpses awaited his attention. They had been there the day before.

"You might want to consider taking up smoking, as well," Ainsley teased as he looked over the examination table. The platform was a bit higher than he was used to and he started to fiddle with the table legs. "It's either that," he said with a grunt, "or you grow accustomed to the smell, which is worse on certain days more than others."

Finally, the table gave way and the one side, the head side, dropped half a foot, which caused Maryanne's arm to slide from the table, a sudden movement that caused Sidney to jump back a few feet from fright.

"Do you expect her to come back and whop you on the nose?" Ainsley asked with a laugh.

"No, sir."

"Oh, sir, is it now?" Ainsley raised his eyebrows as he positioned himself to drop the other side of the table. "Far from the boxing ring now, aren't we?" Ainsley teased.

With the table lowered, Ainsley grabbed his leather apron from the hook and threw a similar one, though one used with little frequency, to Sidney. "Make yourself useful and check to make sure I have everything," Ainsley said with a nod to his cache of instruments on the workbench that lined the wall.

His apprentice now occupied, Ainsley found his clipboard and snagged a pencil. He pulled back the thin sheet used to cover the body before slipping into his high podium desk, which overlooked the table. He began a rudimentary sketch, indicating the wound to her abdomen, and then quickly wrote a list of the organs he could identify.

"How did she die?"

The sound of Sidney's voice interrupted Ainsley's concentration. He furrowed his eyebrows and stared at his apprentice, hoping to draw attention to the absurdity of his question.

"I mean, what did he do? Just tear her stomach open?"

Ainsley did not answer straight away. He hadn't thought of how the victims were approached, only that the murderer must have been a man to be able to overtake them so easily. For the first time he thought of the girl, seated most likely, and waiting for her father. She probably would have been looking around her, eager to recognize her only kin amongst the rush of dockworkers. She would have looked at the culprit, seen him as he approached.

Ainsley closed his eyes, a feeble effort to banish the thought. Who could approach a child with an intention to kill them so heinously? The young surgeon shifted around the table to move toward Maryanne's face, lifting the lids of her eyes.

"If only there were a way to know what she saw last," Ainsley said. "Her lips are dry," he said suddenly. He saw that they were cracked on the surface, though not deep enough to bleed. "And her skin all around too." Ainsley pointed while Sidney came over to have a look.

The young apprentice shrugged. "It must be the winter winds."

Ainsley shook his head, doubtful at such an explanation. "The temperature has warmed considerably.

Besides, it doesn't look the same." Ainsley studied the marks close, pondering possible causes. Gingerly, he touched them with his finger.

"Do you smell something?" Ainsley asked suddenly.

He stood up straight and found the smell suddenly gone. When he lowered his nose to the girl's lips he could smell it again, something sweet though not very strong. He opened her mouth, her jaw rather tight against his pressure. There was nothing inside her mouth, nothing sweet the murderer could have used to gain the girl's trust. Ainsley swept her discoloured molars with his finger and found no sugary residue.

His body straightened, Ainsley leaned in on the table and surveyed her body once more. The last time he smelled a dead body so closely was during a case of arsenic, but arsenic leaves the smell of garlic, not a sweet smell. This smell reminded Ainsley of something, though it was so faint he could not put his finger on it.

"I know this smell," he said. "Take a sniff. Tell me what you think."

Ainsley watched as Sidney came in closer to Maryanne's face.

"Do you know it?" Ainsley asked.

With a look of apology Sidney shook his head. "Perhaps we should just continue?" he suggested.

"Just give me a second," Ainsley answered as he leaned in one more time. "Chloroform."

"What?"

"It's chloroform." Ainsley slapped his hand down on the examination table and let out a whoop of excitement. "I knew I'd recognize it. It's used in surgeries all the time. In school we were trained in its uses, not to give too much. A small amount can incapacitate a person for fifteen minutes. A good surgeon can do his duty before the dose wears off. Any more than that and the patient may die." Ainsley was giddy, running his hands through his hair as he explained the surgical aid. "He subdued her with chloroform."

Suddenly, Ainsley's elation at his discovery gave way to the realization she had been unconscious and hopefully had not felt a thing.

Ainsley closed his eyes at the thought and wondered if the other children had been treated the same. He rushed into the adjoining room, and one by one went to each of the victims. Sure enough, they all showed signs of a severely dry mouth, though none had the same distinct smell.

"They have all been washed," Ainsley said as he walked back to Sidney at the examination table. "But I am certain they all were subdued the same." Ainsley's discovery made sense. How else could Jonathon, as strong as he was, be overtaken?

"So what now?" Sidney asked.

"You are going to have one of the most thorough anatomy lessons of your career," Ainsley answered in complete seriousness. With one major discovery under his belt he wasn't about to let anything by him.

Chapter 18

The noise beside you, dripping coldly, purely,

Ainsley walked slowly down the second-floor hall at Marshall House, weary from another long day. He began to unbutton his shirt and then slipped off his waistcoat, draping it over the crook of his arm. He required sleep most of all but he knew he would not find it that night. His mind was held hostage by the images he saw that day, another child snuffed of life and butchered like an animal. Ainsley had not slept well in the past weeks and he held little hope of finding any rest in the coming hours.

He turned the corner to his room and found Julia next to his desk, leaning in while surveying some sketches he had drawn.

"Julia."

Startled, she looked up and quickly backed away from the desk, clutching the feather duster in her hand, closer to her chest. "My apologies, my lord," she said avoiding his gaze. "They only caught my eye for a minute."

Ainsley stepped closer, interested in seeing which ones she had seen. His often gruesome, anatomical sketches he left at his office, always fearful one of the maids or even his father might see them. At home, he made sure his subjects were more neutral, and not related to his work. He could see she had found his sketches of his mother, visions he had held in his memories for years, images he was eager to get down on paper after her passing lest he forget them entirely. He pulled the pages off his desk, aligning them so that the corners and edges matched. One remained unfinished, abandoned once he had started work on the surgeon case.

"They are quite good," Julia said, as she eased away from the desk, heading for the door.

"Margaret told me you were unwell," Ainsley called after her. He placed the pages down, hiding them beneath a leather portfolio.

"Not unwell," Julia answered turning, "just overtired."

Ainsley nodded. There was a quiet tension between them, filling the room like a mist from the Thames. Ainsley wanted so much to go to her, pull her into his arms, but she looked guarded against him. He had wondered if she regretted their coupling, more so if she was angered with him for it.

"I wanted to offer an apology. I never meant to take advantage of you in that way." The words almost choked him. He wanted her and presumed she wanted him too. She was a stunning woman, but there was more to it than that. There was an unspoken passion between them, there always had been, and he wished there could have been an easy solution to their mutual desire. "It was wrong for me to abuse my position and I shall never do anything like that again." He turned slightly to hide his discomfort at the words. He could not tell her he cared nothing, for it simply was not true.

"I'm not angry," she answered, almost panicked, "if that's what you think."

Ainsley turned toward her. "You aren't angered with me?"

"No," Julia answered, before she glanced toward the door. "I thought perhaps you would be angered with me," she said, "or already grown tired of me."

Ainsley let out a quick breath and shook his head. "Absolutely not. I will never tire of you!" He stepped toward her, pulling her behind his open door, where no one walking down the hall could see, and kissed her freely.

Later that night, with the entire house dark save for the lamp at Ainsley's bedside, the young doctor looked over the sleeping woman in his bed and quietly watched the gentle rise and fall of her breathing. Resting on her side,

Julia's cinnamon hair lay loose on the pillow as she cradled her cheek in the crook of her arm. Ainsley reached over, brushing her hair back from her face, and touched her cheek with his finger. Never had he been with anyone so pure. It seemed almost a dream that she could consider him worthy of her attention. Maid or not, she bore a confidence, an air of royalty that placed her well above the station of her birth. Ainsley smiled, remembering how he had seen that in her the moment he first laid eyes on her.

It seemed unfair, he realized, for her to be born into such circumstances. For her to grow up in an orphanage, to be trained for service from such an early age, her first and lasting misfortune to be born to a poor, sickly mother while he, Margaret, and Daniel bore no such burden.

Ainsley's hand trembled at the thought, the cruelty of fate. Julia stirred and opened her eyes, a smile touching the corners of her lips. "You do not sleep," she said softly.

"I cannot," he answered, disheartened.

She looked him over, pensive and concerned. "Your work haunts you," she said. "I can see it in your eyes."

Ainsley nodded. "I will not tell you the horrors that I see." He stroked her hair gently, letting it trail over the curves of her back.

"You could," she answered earnestly. "It will help ease the burden you carry."

Ainsley smiled at her offer but shook his head. "No, it is my burden alone."

She slipped closer, wrapping her arm over his bare chest and snuggling into him. He grabbed her hand and pressed it to his lips. Before long he heard the slow, rhythmic sounds of sleep come over her and he turned to snuff the light of the lamp.

When Ainsley came down for breakfast he found Maxwell standing at attention in the foyer and immediately Ainsley's mood was soured. The man was not his first choice for butler but, out of the list of candidates, he had been the most qualified. He'd have to answer to his father, at any rate, who would wonder why Ainsley had passed up the chance to hire such a candidate when there were so few to choose from.

"Good morning, Lord Marshall." Maxwell gave an exaggerated bow as Ainsley reached the bottom of the stairs.

"Has Cutter shown you the butler's office?" Ainsley enquired, forcibly hiding his contempt for the new staff member.

"He has, Lord Marshall, and a fine office it is, sir." Maxwell began to follow Ainsley as he passed. Eager to get back to his morgue, Ainsley went straight for the cloak closet, opened its double doors, and began riffling inside.

"Is there any way I can be of service to you, Mr. Marshall? I'm afraid our interview ended abruptly and, well, the fact is, I was surprised when the agency called me. I thought for certain I had displeased you in some way."

Finding his coat, Ainsley turned and refused help while putting it on. "Do not mistake my hiring you as an acceptance of your character," he said as he adjusted the collar. "In this house we frown upon our maids fraternizing with the male staff and I suspect we are not the only house in the city that operates so."

Maxwell nodded, keeping a sharp eye on Ainsley as he spoke.

"We expect discretion in all things and will not tolerate deception." Ainsley saw the hypocrisy in his words. His real intent was to scare Maxwell away from even looking at Julia. He couldn't have cared less whether Maxwell entertained anyone at the end of his shift, but he wasn't going to let this man make eyes with Julia ever again.

"Am I clear?"

Maxwell nodded obediently. "Yes, sir. I would never dream of it, sir."

"Very well." Ainsley turned to the clutter that made the foyer look more like a warehouse than a Belgravia entranceway. "Margaret's auction is this evening and I am sure she will be instructing the staff most of today with auction business. Please indulge her. One more day and we shall be back to normal." Ainsley began pulling at the cuffs of his shirt beneath the sleeves of his coat and shrugged his shoulders to entice the coat to sit properly on them.

Maxwell nodded. "Is Lady Margaret expected back soon?"

"What do you mean? Has she left the house?" Ainsley stopped his fidgeting and looked to the new butler with confusion. "It is not yet nine o'clock."

"Yes, sir, I thought it strange as well but nor did I see it my place to question the young woman's coming and goings." The smile that crept over the butler's features fell abruptly when his eyes met Ainsley's. "Forgive me, sir."

"You must understand, Mr. Maxwell, she is my sister and the only remaining member of my family with whom I am close. It is my wish to protect her from all things and I shall need you to be my accomplice."

Maxwell nodded, eager to please. "Yes, sir."

"I will speak with her when I return." Ainsley reached into the closet and pulled down his hat from one of the shelves. "Cutter will be in charge this day but in the morrow I should like to see you at the helm. I hired you for a particular purpose and I may not like you, but I believe you will do well." Ainsley cocked his head toward the back stairway that led down to the kitchens. "Go to Cook and familiarize yourself with our family's requirements. My father will not return for some weeks and it is my intent that you should be thoroughly educated regarding the intimate details of this house."

"Yes, sir." Maxwell slipped past Ainsley and headed for the stairs.

The exchange left Ainsley depleted. The family had been spoiled for years with Billis's quiet presence. He knew everything with regard to the family, the staff, and the needs of the house. Aside from the odd request, Billis knew what the family would need long before they did. Those days were over, Ainsley realized as he watched the new butler make his way down to the kitchens. The next few months would be fraught with mistakes, forgotten chores, and flaring tempers, and it certainly was not something Ainsley was looking forward to.

Chapter 19

Of spirits' tears.

Margaret pulled at her gloves as she walked the halls of the hospital, cautiously peering through each doorway as she passed in the hopes Jonas could be found. Each room held horrors more gruesome than the last. The cries of agony, some muffled, some shrill, were easy enough to ignore but the expressions on the faces of the patients, those seeking relief from their pain as well as those wishing a quicker and more humane end to their suffering was almost too much for her to bear. It was this that made her doubt her early conviction to be a surgeon. Her brother had taught her how to detach herself from the dead, but it was the suffering of the barely living that crumpled her resolve. Since her mother's death she hadn't had much time to think about it, which was all the better, she told herself. She doubted she had the fortitude to challenge the establishment's view regarding female doctors, to say nothing of the views society had for a high-ranked person going into trade.

She envied Jonas and Peter, though. They had such freedom to do as they pleased, though Peter would argue it was nothing of the kind. Margaret never wished she had been born a man—she was well-suited to her female form—but it was the lack of understanding that she could do without. She wished there could be more people advocating for the issues of women and less advocacy for control over them.

Margaret's intent was to arrive early and find Jonas before he started with his surgeries. Her plan seemed so well-formulated in her mind that she had not considered tracking him down would be so involved. There was one final door on that floor to try and when Margaret peered around the corner she found a great beast of a woman scowling back at her, her face so sour Margaret was sure she had been raised on a strict diet of lemons.

"What ye want?" she asked hoarsely.

Margaret stammered, put off by this woman who had to be three times her size.

"Ye can't go 'round spyin' on all and sundry because yer ladyship wants ta. We 'ave rules, you see."

Margaret nodded. "Yes, sir, er, ma'am. I beg your pardon. I was only looking for Dr. Davies. He's a surgeon—"

Margaret was cut off by the woman's cackle. "Ye and everyone else, I s'pose." Margaret waited as the woman turned in place, rocking her excess weight back and forth from one leg to the other as she tried to pivot in place. Retreating to a desk Margaret had not even realized was there, the woman used it to hold herself up as she spoke.

"If 'er was up ta me, I'd 'ave never 'ired him. Too distracting for my girls, you see. I'ze needs workin' girls, not swoon and giggle girls."

Margaret nodded, for a moment feeling she could have easily been talking to a calculated madam in a den of ill-repute, instead of a head nurse at a respected hospital.

"Dr. Davies is usually on the second floor, visiting patients. Best if ye start there." The madam gave Margaret a black-toothed grin, which did little to soften the manner of her delivery.

Margaret nodded, expressed a quick thank you and retreated with haste.

Grateful for the relative quiet on the second floor, Margaret noticed most of the doors were closed and felt less inclined to brazenly snoop for Jonas. Instead, she approached a handful for girls, nurses in training or so Margaret guessed, huddled a few yards away. Judging by their size, they could have been no more than fourteen and their matching giggles only served to reinforce that belief.

"Excuse me," Margaret said as she approached.

The girls, all childish and ill-mannered, turned quickly

at the sound of Margaret's voice. "Shh!" one of them hissed. "It's a right proper lady."

"Can I help you, Miss?" a second one asked, forcing down a mischievous smile. She swatted her hand at one of them that pulled at her skirt.

Margaret smiled. Their youthful mischief made her nostalgic. "I am searching for Dr. Jonas Davies."

One of the girls gasped and was quick to place a hand over her gaping mouth. Margaret's smile faded as her impatience grew.

"Dr. Davies, ma'am?" the second one asked.

"Yes." Margaret decided to use her authoritative voice in this instance. The girls seemed to respond better to it. "Where is he?"

The girls looked to each other and finally the second girl pointed to the door they had been pressing their ears against. Confused, Margaret approached, but the girls did not dissipate. They allowed her to pass between them but waited on bated breath as Margaret opened the door.

Inside, Margaret found Jonas, half-seated on the edge of a desk and a young woman, older than the girls in the hall, thank goodness, pressed against his legs teasingly. They moved quickly at the sound of the door but not quickly enough. Margaret had seen Jonas's hand at the back of the woman's neck as if kissing.

Margaret straightened her spine, pulling her shoulders back and inching her chin slightly higher. She raised an eyebrow coolly, unwilling to allow either of them to see how much she was actually trembling.

"Good morning, Jonas," she said. She offered a calculated smile as she looked from Jonas to the woman and back again. "I came to ask you to breakfast," she lied. "I see you have already had some."

Turning on her heels, Margaret left, not caring in the slightest if he ever spoke a word to her again. She imagined he'd follow, running after her, begging the opportunity to explain, but he didn't. She pushed through the group of girls at the doorway, who feigned scandal and made for the stairs, but Jonas still did not come. By the time she reached the front doors, she realized how much she had expected his rebuttal and even thought to slow down some, and give him the chance to catch up. Once outside the front doors she looked up to the second-floor windows, wondering if she could catch a glimpse of him begging her to wait. Instead, she saw nothing and it was his silence, more than anything, which hurt her the most.

Jacob had dutifully kept the family carriage at the front doors, though off to the side. He gave a look of relief when he saw her approaching and quickly opened the door and offered a hand for her to climb in. "Where to now, Miss?" he asked.

"Home, please."

Jacob nodded and snapped the door closed quick enough to latch. Margaret slid to the opposite side of the carriage bench, the extra half a foot giving extra distance between her and the cause of her pain. The carriage rocked into motion, easing into the traffic of the other carriages while Margaret stewed.

Her brother had been right. Jonas Davies was a rogue, a scoundrel, a womanizer, and she deserved better than that. The reality of these statements, however, did not ease the pain nor halt the cascade of tears.

Chapter 20

The yearning to a beautiful denied you,

The hospital looked like a fortress that day, and though Ainsley once looked upon it with awe and admiration he now saw it as a prison for the dead and dying. No longer did he look forward to his work; instead, he dreaded it and further regarded his tasks with little hope of gaining further information. He wondered whether the honeymoon was over and this was the drudgery others spoke of, when work, once enjoyed, became nothing more than repetitive actions toward a repetitive reward.

As Ainsley walked the hall, and down the back stairs toward the morgue he could feel a sense of despair begin to creep into his consciousness. He had identified chloroform as the murderer's first contact with the victim. Alice, the mudlark, had been bathed, but from what he could tell, the others had not. Maryanne and Jonathon specifically looked as if he had butchered them where they lay. Ainsley could not say so for any of the others since he did not see where they were found. And his original thought that the murderer was known to the children was not entirely true. Though it could be, Ainsley interjected, and so completing the circle that kept funnelling in his head.

Ainsley pushed the door to the morgue with a bit more force than usual and was startled when it hit a closely placed bed. The cadaver on the slab shook from the impact and its arm slid from the side peeking out from under the sheet. Ainsley exhaled and placed the arm gingerly back in place. As he did so he noticed the room was at capacity. Body after body was laid out in front of him in neat rows, a single rather slender aisle the only way from the examination table to the door. It was undeniable. His work was piling up. Ainsley had been so engrossed in the workings of the case that he had not noticed before.

A second after Ainsley turned from the door it reopened, again hitting the table with a thud. Ainsley turned and saw Benjamin and Frisker coming in with yet another body on a stretcher between them.

"Over there," Frisker said, indicating with a nod of his head where the boy should go.

Ainsley did his best to slide out of the way as they passed.

"Excuse us, sir," Frisker said with a nod as he passed.

Ainsley watched as they choose an occupied slab and hoisted the body between them on top of one already there.

"You can't do that," Ainsley protested, drawing near with a hand held out in front of him. "These are people."

"Sorry, sir, Dr. Crawford's orders," Frisker said, as he looked about them. Ainsley followed his gaze and saw a handful of other stretchers laid out the same.

It was no secret Ainsley had been neglecting his duties. Too often did he leave with Simms to a crime scene or, more recently, to search out witnesses. He could hardly say he was earning the wages the hospital paid him, and the evidence was piling up in the morgue.

Ainsley pulled back the sheet from one and surveyed the boy's face. It was obvious he had been pulled from the Thames; the filth from the water clung to his flesh while the stench created an aura around him.

"All right then," Ainsley said, replacing the sheet. "Let's get started then and get these people their rest."

Between Ainsley, Frisker, and Benjamin, the work was quick. Ainsley had to discipline himself not to get carried away with the details. He had to remind himself of the intent of his work, to examine the bodies, superficially if need be, and give the families a small measure of reasoning for their pain. It was not the time to dally and it was this internal dialogue that made quick work of half the room.

"Hold the bucket," Ainsley commanded sternly to

Benjamin. "Hold it." A second later, Ainsley tilted the body on the table enough so that a gush of blood, bile, and Thames water slid out, most missing the bucket and hitting the floor.

"Sorry, sir," Benjamin said, still shocked by what he had just witnessed.

Ainsley shook his head, but he wasn't angered. Frisker appeared a moment later with a mop and together the two porters worked around Ainsley to clean up the mess while the doctor turned back to his patient.

So focused was Ainsley that he did not notice when Simms entered the room. Pulling up beside the examination table, the detective watched as Ainsley did his work.

"He's working out then?" Simms asked, indicating Ben with a slight tilt of his head.

Ainsley huffed. Perhaps Crawford wasn't the only one who expected Benjamin to fail. "I've had worse, if that's what you mean." Ainsley quickly sorted through the organs in the abdomen. "Did you get my message?" he asked while still bent over the body.

"Yes, chloroform you say?"

"Both Sidney and I could smell it. It's quite clear."

"I understood chloroform to be odorless."

"It is, for the most part. That's why we didn't smell it on the others. Our murderer splashed some on Maryanne's clothes and that's where the smell is coming from," Ainsley explained.

Simms nodded, thinking over Ainsley's words. "Did it kill them straight away?"

"We can hope," Ainsley said. "I want to show you something." Ainsley turned to his sink and began to wash his hands. "Why don't you two go have lunch then?"

Frisker and Ben nodded and turned to leave. While he watched them go, Ben following behind Frisker, he could not help but feel a twinge of pride for having given the boy such a chance. He was holding up remarkably well.

"The cuts are interesting," Ainsley said, turning to Simms. Together they walked into the adjoining room, where Maryanne waited. Her exam had been completed and her torso sewn up but what Ainsley intended to show the detective did not require her to be unstitched. Pulling the sheet back, Ainsley leaned in and pointed to the top of the scar in her torso.

"He cut her here, in what I thought was a circular pattern, a bit haphazard."

Simms shrugged. "He was in a rush."

"Yes, but then I found this." Ainsley pointed to a part of her wound just above the others. It was an inch long and formed a nearly perfect line. "Seems odd to try to be so precise just to hack away at her insides."

"Did you find this on any of the others?"

Ainsley shook his head. "No, they were too mutilated to see much of anything. The only consistency I found was he used a dull blade, no more than three inches long. All of their wounds were jagged."

Simms nodded absentmindedly. "So he drugs them, lies them down, and then attempts to cut them open quickly with a blade that could barely give a decent shave?"

"That's right."

"For what purpose?"

"Well, he wanted some organs. He took her stomach and one of her kidneys. And he reached up and cut out a lung but he only cut off half of it."

"Half?" Simms gave Ainsley a look of puzzlement.

"His blade was not big enough or sharp enough to cut through the sternum." Ainsley turned and went back to his cache of tools arranged along the far wall of the other room. When he returned he held up one of his sharpest knives; though thin it could open a chest cavity in less than two minutes. "He'd have to have this to cut through the ribs with any kind of speed. He knew he wouldn't be able to do it. He had tried on Jonathon." Ainsley pointed to the body of the boy behind Simms.

The two men turned and Ainsley pulled down the sheet, which revealed a half-dozen shallow cuts into the boy's chest. "He tried here and here," Ainsley pointed, "but his knife was too dull. So he must have not bothered with the girl."

Simms listened intently while Ainsley explained. "If he wanted a lung, why doesn't he just get a better blade?"

Ainsley shrugged. "Perhaps he can't afford one."

"He could steal it," Simms put forth.

Ainsley nodded. He doubted any man who thought nothing of murdering children would have scruples against theft.

"A constable from Surrey Constabulary stopped by my office this morning," Simms said. "That's why I was so late coming in to speak with you."

"Surrey?"

"He said he read about our surgeon in the papers and thought he might have something of interest to us. About a year ago, a body was found in Guildford, a young girl, not much older than Maryanne here, killed in the same manner."

"Did they catch him?"

"No. The clues at the time were limited and the perpetrator never struck again."

"So you think these cases could be related," Ainsley said, anticipating where the detective was headed.

"The medical examiner still works in the area, if you care to speak to him," Simms said.

Ainsley looked about the room, the remaining corpses waiting for his attention. If he left to pursue the case with Simms there was no doubt Crawford would be cross. But in his own way Ainsley felt he owed it to the children who lay dead in the other room.

Ainsley smiled. "I have a sudden hankering for a train ride, don't you?"

The Royal Surrey County Hospital was housed in a

newer red brick building with arched windows and a stout white bell tower centred on the roof. Ainsley and Simms walked the few steps to the front door before turning to a nurse stationed at a desk near the front door.

"Pardon us, ma'am, where may we find Dr. Ferris?" Simms asked, reading the name off his notepad.

"He'd be in the south wing, you'll have to follow this corridor all the way down," she said as she pointed to the hallway behind them. "Turn left and it is the last door to your right, I believe. But he might not be in. He's so rarely at the hospital."

"Has he a general practice in the area? A dentistry?"

"Well, no," the nurse answered thoughtfully. "I'm not sure what he does when he's not here."

Ainsley and Simms nodded their thanks and headed in the way she directed. It was a much smaller facility than St. Thomas, and Ainsley marvelled at the brightness to the rooms and overall uplifting atmosphere.

"You seem chipper," Simms remarked as he followed Ainsley's gaze. "Far cry from London-town."

"Everything is so new," he said, peering into each doorway as they passed.

"The hospital itself is only a few years old," Simms said with a smile. "Thinking of transferring?"

Ainsley shook his head, frowning at the thought. "No," he said, without missing a beat. "I think I'd be bored."

They walked the entire length of the hospital, each step taking them farther and farther from the regular hum of the nurses and visiting families. Another corridor, this one short and dark, led them to a door marked "Mortuary" in hand-painted, white lettering.

Simms looked to Ainsley. "Should we knock?" he asked.

Ainsley shrugged and turned the knob. The room on the other side was nearly empty. The only light was from a small window on the farthest wall and the light it filtered just gave the objects shapes and little shading. Arranged neatly, the shelves and tables made the place look as if it were never used. Only two bodies were hidden inside, both under sheets and situated against the wall.

"Hello?" Ainsley called out as he stepped inside. "Dr. Ferris?"

"We must have just missed him," Simms suggested.

Ainsley saw something out of the corner of his eye, and studied the bodies to the left closely.

"Scotland Yard," Ainsley said. "We rode the Brighton train for half an hour just to get here."

One of the corpses moved, first rolling to the side and then sitting up. Simms jumped, preparing to make for the door, but Ainsley grabbed his arm. He cocked his head toward the moving sheet. "I think we found our doctor."

Dr. Brindle slipped from under his sheet, the look of an afternoon nap betraying his secret.

"If I didn't know you were there I'd have left thinking the place empty. How often does that trick work?" Ainsley asked.

"More often than you'd think," Dr. Ferris answered, adjusting his glasses and dusting off his shirt and trousers. "How did you know I was there?" he asked, pointing to his hiding spot.

Ainsley smiled. "I am a morgue surgeon at St. Thomas. I know what a dead room feels like."

Dr. Brindle eyed him, titling his head back slightly to look at Ainsley through his spectacles. "Usually, the other bodies scare people away. Nurses tend to not stick around for long with that smell in the room." Dr. Ferris gestured toward the second body and laughed slightly. "I guess I have gotten used to it." The doctor stepped forward, rubbing his hands quickly on his shirt and offering it to Ainsley first, then Simms. "Morgue surgeon, you say," he said as he greeted them. "I thought you said Scotland Yard."

"He's Scotland Yard, I'm Dr. Peter Ainsley."

"Detective Inspector Simms, sir," Simms said.

"Dr. Ferris." He crossed his arms over his chest. "What

can I do for you? I can't say I know anything about the goings-on of London."

"You may, actually," Ainsley explained. "We are looking into the case of *The Surgeon*, you may have read the papers."

Dr. Ferris dropped his arms to his side, obviously startled at the change in conversation. "Oh, yes."

"We understand from a detective with the Surrey Constabulary that there was a similar instance here about a year ago. If it's true, there may be a connection." Ainsley turned to Simms, suddenly aware that it was usually he who explained their case. However, given that they were meeting one of Ainsley's counterparts, it only seemed fitting that he should be the one to do the questioning.

"The boy found on"—Simms opened his notebook—"Tunsgate. Do you remember?"

Dr. Ferris looked confused, as if silently searching his memory. He began to shake his head.

"He would have had missing organs, a wound from here to here," Ainsley indicated where on himself. "We'd like to see the file."

Dr. Ferris looked from Ainsley to Simms, a look of doubt coming over him. He adjusted his spectacles and let out a deep breath. "I'm sorry, gentlemen—"

"It must be in your files. Can we sort through your reports from last August?" Ainsley pressed.

The doctor gave them a look as if he didn't want to, as if he didn't trust them.

"We won't be but a minute," Simms pressed.

Finally, Dr. Ferris nodded, and motioned for them to follow him. He led them around a corner to a set of tall wooden filing cabinets and pulled on one of the doors. He fumbled with some files, looking at them and placing them back. Opening another drawer, he gave the pair of investigators an apologetic look. "I'm not as organized as I used to be," Dr. Ferris explained.

Ainsley began to doubt Dr. Ferris was looking in

earnest and stepped forward to look for himself. He'd be damned if he came all that way, with hope of finding a new lead, only to go home empty-handed because of some two-bit country doctor. Standing beside Dr. Ferris, Ainsley searched, trying to make sense of the filing system. Eventually, Ainsley moved to the second cabinet and Dr. Ferris took a step back.

"Here are a few we can search in," Ainsley said, pulling out a handful of files. He handed them to Simms, since Dr. Ferris's help had been proven unreliable.

"Is there a table, Doctor?" Simms asked.

Dr. Ferris started, as if surprised someone was speaking to him. "What? Oh, yes. Table."

Ainsley grabbed a second handful and followed Simms and Ferris back to the examination room. With two stools pulled up to the exam table, Ainsley and Simms sat opposite each other while Ferris slipped back onto his original bed and bit his nails while he watched.

Ainsley saw Simms eye him from across the table as they flipped through the pages. If he wasn't already fuming, Ainsley would be laughing at the ludicrousness of it all.

After some minutes searching Ainsley found it, a brief report and a grouping of rudimentary sketches. "Here," Ainsley said, laying the papers flat between himself and Simms. Ainsley read the notes while Simms looked over the images.

"Do you remember the case?" Ainsley asked.

Ferris slipped off his seat and drew near, leaning in to look over the file. He grabbed one and read his notes quickly before grabbing another. "There were hardly any clues, if I recall. The boy was six years or so and worked as a sweep." Ferris placed the pages down. "His stomach was missing and his liver. It looked as if the kidneys had been scratched by the blade but that's it. It was truly a nightmare," the doctor said, shaking his head, "I couldn't get the body sewn up properly."

"What about chloroform?" Ainsley asked sharply.

"What?"

"Did you smell it on his body, his hair, clothes?"

Ferris laughed. "Good God, I don't smell them. It's bad enough I have to operate on the street urchins as if I cared for them. No one was pressing for answers, not even his employer, who I suspect had already procured another to take his place easily. Vagabonds are a dime a dozen." The doctor laughed softly at his own joke.

Ainsley felt his body stiffen at his colleague's words. Secretly, he dared the doctor to continue so Ainsley would have an excuse to give him one to the nose. He saw Simms watching him, shaking his head slightly as if he could read Ainsley's thoughts. In the end, Ainsley decided to ignore the doctor and instead concentrated on the papers in front of him.

"So this is related to that *Surgeon* case?" Ferris asked, unaware of the anger he was inciting. "Golly, those murders are getting quite a bit of attention." He whistled. "I bet all the papers are begging for interviews and the like. I bet everyone wants to see what you'll do. You're like a West Side play, you are."

Ainsley jumped to his feet. "These are children!" he yelled, stepping within an inch of Dr. Ferris's face. "Any man who seeks fame at the expense of dead children is a blackguard!"

Dr. Ferris raised his hands as if to push Ainsley from him. Simms pulled Ainsley back.

"Come on, Peter," he said, grabbing at Ainsley's shoulder.

Ainsley turned to the file and gathered the papers. "I'm taking these," he said. "They're liable to get lost for all time in your care," he sneered. Ainsley righted the stool and replaced the other files they had been sorting through but was careful to keep the one they needed in his grasp. He left without waiting for Simms to follow and marched down the hall, flipping through the pages in an effort to refocus his energies.

"Dr. Ainsley!"

Ainsley did not stop at the sound of Simms's voice behind him but he did slow down a bit.

"I fear you gave that man a heart attack," Simms said once he was at Ainsley's side.

"And he'd deserve it. Who would hire such an imbecile?" Ainsley asked, not expecting an answer.

Ainsley set the pace, eager to get out of the hospital, assured that he had all he needed in his left hand. "He didn't want us to find these," he said, holding up the pages he held tightly in his grasp. "I have never seen such ill-organized notes."

"How are you so sure he won't come after you for them?"

"He won't. The hospital board would pull him from the payroll if they knew such workmanship took place." Ainsley shook his head, still disbelieving he had met such a character.

"I'd suspect he's behind these murders if he weren't so damned incompetent," Ainsley said once they were far enough away from the hospital's front doors. The suggestion was almost laughable until Ainsley really thought it through.

"Think of it this way, he kills one, almost gets caught," Ainsley raised the file in the air slightly, "so he decided to head to London where things are more ubiquitous."

"Ainsley," Simms spoke as if doubted him.

"It's less than half an hour by train, many workers take the train daily to London for work. You heard the nurse yourself, he's hardly there. Why, I'm surprised there's enough dead people to keep an undertaker in business here."

"I suppose it's possible," Simms said.

"He has no connection to the children," Simms interjected.

"That would be better, don't you think? Considering

what he did to them?" Ainsley exhaled and slipped his hands deep in his pocked. "Perhaps I only wish it were Dr. Ferris behind it all. Think how much closer we would be to apprehending this monster."

Simms grew quiet. It was no secret he had little experience with such criminals, and Ainsley's training never touched upon the reasons behind death as much as it did with the methods. Together they made an unlikely pair, less adept than others to the task before them but never once had they tried to shirk their duty. Each step brought them closer but never quite close enough, always leaving their quarry one step ahead.

"We will get him," Simms said, breaking a steady silence. "He can't hide from us forever."

Ainsley shook his head, giving the detective a sideways glance. "I can't let anyone else die," Ainsley said, his voice hinting at defeat, "not because of my inability to decipher the clues."

Chapter 21

Shall strain your powers.

By the time Margaret reached Marshall House her tears had dried. She donned a stoic expression, determined to betray nothing, and instead would deal with the emotional pain later. Within a few hours' time she'd be host to a house full of society elite and could not risk greeting attendees with puffy eyes and a red nose. With a clenched jaw, Margaret pulled the hatpin to remove her hat and allowed Maxwell to take it from her.

"Good afternoon, my lady," he said with an overly obediently bow.

Margaret smiled, nodded, and walked past him, her silence merely a means to keep her emotions from pouring out freely.

"Everyone is on task for the auction this evening," he explained as she approached the stairs. "Miss Julia has everything well at hand."

"Send her up to me," she said, not wanting to look him in the eye. "There are further items we need to discuss."

Looking over her shoulder, Margaret saw Maxwell bow before scurrying off to find her lady's maid. It was too soon to tell whether he could fill the void Billis left behind. Peter had said he was the most qualified, but his appropriateness for the house was yet to be seen.

Margaret did not need to wait long for Julia. A few moments after she entered her bedchamber Julia stepped in with an excited expression on her face.

"Well, Lady Margaret," the maid started happily. "What did he say?"

Margaret shook her head, at first having no idea what her maid meant, until her thoughts untangled themselves. She closed her eyes, and turned her head slightly, horrified at her own forgetfulness. She had gone to see Jonas to ask him to be the auctioneer for that evening. She had put off her request too long but truthfully the week had been so very busy she hadn't had a moment to stop by. She could have sent a note but she really needed an excuse to visit him in person. She never thought he would refuse, but she hadn't thought him to be so loose with his affections either.

"I'm sorry," Margaret breathed. "Something came up and I was unable to ask him."

Julia nodded, but Margaret could see the maid was trying to suppress hints of panic.

"Peter will do it," Margaret said quickly to allay her fears. "He'd do anything for me."

Julia nodded and walked the length of the room toward Margaret. "You look tired, Miss Margaret," she said softly.

Margaret slipped into the chair at her vanity table. Leaning into the table, Margaret brushed loose strands of hair from her forehead. "I don't know how I shall do it," Margaret said, thinking ahead to the evening in front of them. "Everyone will be looking to me as hostess but I haven't the faintest clue how to perform my task. Mother may not have enjoyed society but she had always been there for such things that were unavoidable. I don't know how I shall do it without her."

Julia drew near and began pulling the pins from Margaret's hair, knowing it would have to be restyled before the arrival of her guests. A young lady does not wear the same hairstyle in the evening as she would during daylight hours.

"You are not without her," Julia said solemnly. "She is with you. Always."

Margaret smiled at this and then wiped a threatening tear from her lower eyelid.

"Did you know your mother?" Margaret asked daringly.

"Yes, for a brief time," Julia explained, brushing Margaret's long brunette locks. "I only have a brother's love now."

"A brother? A real one?"

Julia chuckled. "Yes, Miss. His name is Robert. We were brought to the orphanage together. He has a wife and daughter now and they live in Aldsgate."

"Oh."

The pair grew silent as Julia concentrated and Margaret pondered her new discovery. It had never occurred to her that Julia should have a family.

"You know then about what's been happening," Margaret ventured to ask, unsure of how such a topic would upset her, "at the orphanage?"

"Yes ma'am," Julia answered quietly. "I know."

Margaret watched Julia's eyes close briefly, as if holding back tears, and decided to change the subject.

"How are you liking Mr. Maxwell?" Margaret asked, reaching across her toilette table for a canister of skin cream.

"He seems to be a nice man," Julia said. "An agreeable person. A fair butler."

"I believe he fancies you."

Julia nodded, but kept her attention on Margaret's hair. "I have noticed, ma'am." Julia retrieved the silver brush from Margaret's table and began to slowly run it through Margaret's hair.

"Do you think you could like him?" Margaret asked, trying hard to be nonchalant but fearing she was failing dreadfully. She'd like to think of herself as above such prattle but after her morning of heartbreak she was looking for something which would allow her to believe in love again.

"I don't think so," Julia answered, avoiding Margaret's gaze completely. "Besides, I am not sure if your father would like me entertaining such ideas." Julia gave Margaret a half-smile through the mirror.

There was a knock on the door and Violetta slipped in a moment later. "There is a gentleman here to see you," she said, standing just inside the entryway. "Dr. Davies, I believe."

Margaret's heart sank. She didn't believe she had the strength or courage to confront him so soon. Not enough time had passed for her to formulate her argument. Her tears had barely had enough time to dry and her resentment had only just begun to slip away.

"Show him into Father's study. I'd afraid all the other rooms are occupied for the auction," Margaret explained as she rubbed some cream into her cheeks. "I will be down momentarily."

Violetta nodded and left.

With a long exhale, Margaret squared her shoulders and looked determinedly at Julia through the glass. "Make me stunning, Julia," she said with a smile.

"Her ladyship does not need my help, in that regard," was Julia's flattering reply.

A short time later Margaret left her room and headed downstairs, all the while cursing Jonas's poor timing. She'd have to speak to him while dressed in her blue satin evening gown and elbow-length gloves while he very well could be wearing bloodstains on an otherwise unremarkable suit. It was not that she minded his trade. She rather admired him for it. Her discomfort stemmed from the fact that the division between their classes could not be ignored. Taking a meeting with him under such conditions only highlighted that reality all the more.

"Sorry for keeping you waiting," she said as she entered. "We are rather busy preparing for the charity auction."

Jonas had been leafing through one of her father's books when she entered. He looked up when she spoke and stood frozen for more than a moment, watching her as she crossed the room toward him.

"You wished to see me," Margaret said, attempting to end the silence.

"Well, yes," he stammered, replacing the book on the

shelf. "You look wonderful." He took a step toward her but she turned, taking a few paces from him before turning back to face him.

Miss Ivy's words trolled through her head, reminding her that her heart was to be broken, and so it had, but also that she would survive. Her anger toward Jonas thickened but her resolve to overcome the obstacle matched it.

"Like I said, we are very busy." Margaret raised her gaze with an air of challenge.

Jonas nodded and placed his hands in his pockets. "I only..." He let out a breath. "You didn't give me the chance to explain."

Margaret shrugged, trying hard to calm her heart, which roared inside her chest like a steam engine. "It's a bit self-explanatory, isn't it? The fault is entirely mine. Serves me right to disregard a reputation that has been rightfully earned. I should never have expected anything different from a rogue like you."

"I suppose I deserve that—"

"And a hell of a lot more!" Margaret took a few steps toward him. "I should have cast you out of here and told you never to come back."

Jonas looked up, his gaze unrelenting. "But you didn't."

Margaret lowered her shoulders. She could feel her emotions wavering between seething rage and irrepressible sadness. A single tear spilled out onto her cheek and Jonas took a step forward. Margaret put her hands up as if to prevent his touch and moved away toward the door.

"I'm asking you to leave," she said as she opened the door to the foyer.

Ainsley was pulling off his overcoat and handing it to Maxwell when Jonas begrudgingly exited the library.

"What brings you here, Jonas?" Ainsley asked as he approached them.

Margaret did her best to ignore her pain while she smiled at her brother. Jonas looked to her; she could feel his eyes on her, as if asking what to say, but Margaret refused to look at him.

"I wanted… Margaret asked if I could attend her event this evening," he lied, "but I'm afraid I haven't the appropriate attire." Jonas gestured to his standard day suit and gave an apologetic smile. "I'm afraid I should go." Jonas patted Ainsley on the arm and slipped past him for the door.

"Well, what about Father's closet? Or my own?" Ainsley called after him. "There's no reason you should miss out on that account. I'm sure between the two of us we can create something suitable."

Jonas looked to Margaret again, who was altogether too shocked to reply.

"I'd hate to impose." He looked to Margaret, imploring for guidance, but she could not bring herself to return his gaze. "Why not?" Jonas said suddenly.

Margaret could feel him looking to her as he followed Ainsley up the stairs.

"Are you all right, Lady Margaret?" Maxwell asked.

Pulled from her stunned silence, Margaret smiled and nodded. "Yes," she answered quietly, "Please go help Dr. Davies."

With the butler gone, Margaret turned, cursing herself for not speaking up and cursing Jonas even more for ruining what had started as an exciting day. Her guests were set to arrive within the hour and here she was fighting the urge to crumple into a heap on the floor.

There would be others, she told herself, as there always had been. Men more deserving would find her and seek her affection. Men who would honour their unspoken commitments even if they never said the words out loud. Jonas had made her feel as if there were some unspoken agreement, some promise that one day he would seek approval from her father. Margaret brushed her gloved hand over her forehead. She chuckled at her own folly. Her father would never have approved. It was bad enough Ainsley wished to work in trade; he'd be damned if his only daughter married a tradesman.

In the end, it is better this way, she told herself. At least only her heart was broken, and she needn't have bothered her father at all.

Margaret drifted into the library, where tables had been set up displaying the items that would be up for auction. Here, the guests could hold the items and look at them closely before bidding started. The room was a testament to her mother's life with an assortment of antique tables and vases, jewellery and hatpins. Between Margaret, Ainsley, and Daniel a few items had been claimed as sentimental but most, at least most of the items housed at Marshall House, were allowed to go up for auction. As Margaret surveyed the items, sometimes flipping over Julia's neatly written tags on each, she realized the monetary difference her event would make to the orphanage and she was so very glad of it.

In the dining room the silver trays sat polished and the china dishes stacked. All manner of delectable food was being prepared in the kitchen and would soon line the sides of the dining hall, which would allow guests to enjoy a bite or two while the auction progressed. Margaret had arranged to let chairs from a nearby hotel, and these had been lined up in rows in front of a podium set up at the back of the dining hall, where the auctioneer would stand.

All of the household staff, fluttering about with an air of anticipation, looked like toy soldiers in Margaret's army, all adorned in their best livery and smocks, freshly pressed and smelling sweetly of sandalwood or lavender. It had been some years since Marshall House played host to an event such as this and Margaret wondered if the staff had missed the excitement of it.

"Everything looks wonderful, Margaret dear."

Margaret turned to the sound of Lady Brant, who had entered the room.

"Your mother would be very proud."

It was rare for Lady Brant to offer compliments and so Margaret knew her words were genuine.

"Come now," Lady Brant said, offering the crook of her arm. "I saw some other carriages pulling up. We shall meet your guests at the door."

Chapter 22

Ideal sweetnesses shall over-glide you,
Resumed from ours.

Bethany Brundell completed her task exceedingly well. Margaret only recognized half of the people who stepped into the foyer but all seemed ready to share remembrances of her mother. Margaret greeted them gleefully, leaning into numerous kisses on the cheek and shaking countless hands. Every available staff member was on hand taking coats and hats while Margaret directed guests to the library, where they could survey the goods for auction.

There was a lull in the arrivals, long enough for Margaret to place a hand on her stomach and exhale. She looked behind her to Julia, who clapped her hands excitedly, though soundlessly, at the turnout.

"I shall make a few turns," Lady Brant said discreetly as she leaned into Margaret, "to remind everyone to loosen their purse strings for the charity."

Pleased she would not have Lady Brant attached to her side, Margaret nodded and Lady Brant followed a group as they filed into the library.

When Evelyn and Daniel walked in Margaret abandoned her proper composure and rushed toward them. "I am so glad to see you," Margaret said, pulling Evelyn in for a hug. When she pulled back she looked Evelyn over from head to toe. She did not bear any resemblance to a woman recovering from surgery, certainly not the invasive surgery Ainsley had been forced to perform on her. "I was not sure you were up to it yet," Margaret said, suddenly regretting her exuberant greeting.

Evelyn smiled, and gave a glance to Daniel. "I'm still not quite but I convinced him to come for your mother's sake." Daniel sneered at the mention of their mother and

Margaret thought it best if she pretended not to notice.

"I will instruct Cutter to retrieve a chair for you from the parlour, something more comfortable."

Evelyn nodded her thanks and turned to allow Daniel to pull her cloak from her.

"Evelyn. Daniel." Ainsley came down the stairs, dressed in a fine evening suit complete with coattails and a sleek top hat. Trailing behind him, Jonas as well was dressed smartly in a suit almost identical to what Ainsley wore. He held his hat in his gloved hands and looked nervously to Margaret, who could see how uncomfortable he was.

"Took a little bit of doing," Ainsley explained, gesturing to Jonas's new attire, "Father's shirt, my vest and jacket. Maxwell loosened the hem an inch or so but I'd say the finer things suit Dr. Davies rather well."

Jonas straightened his stance, as if suddenly realizing everyone was looking to him.

Margaret thought she ought to say something complimentary though she felt nothing but contempt for the man. He should have refused Ainsley's offer to dress him and left. Any other gentleman would have made an excuse on the spot, knowing how infuriated Margaret was with him. But then it occurred to her that any true gentleman would not all but take a solemn vow and then break faith by seeking the affections of another woman. It needled her greatly to have him there, reminding her how close she had come to aligning herself with the man. Even so she could not deny how becoming he was in coattails. Women flocked to him for a myriad of reasons, the most obvious of which was his devilishly good looks.

"You look rather handsome," Margaret said, unable to stop herself.

Jonas bowed in her direction, giving an unflinching stare, but Margaret quickly turned her gaze as another guest entered the doorway. Cutter held his hand out for his coat and hat but the stranger grabbed it in a handshake and shook it vigorously. "Good day, sir," the man said.

Margaret stepped forward to greet him with her hand outstretched. "Hello, I don't think we've met," she said, thankful for the diversion from Jonas.

"Theodore Fenton," Ainsley snarled from behind her.

Confused, Margaret looked from her brother to the man who just entered. A devilish smile spread over the stranger's face as he took in Ainsley. He tipped his hat. "Well, if it isn't Mr. *Specialist?*"

With guests continuing to mill about in the foyer, Margaret was not interested in creating a scene. Whatever Ainsley's issue was with the gentleman, it would have to wait until after the auction. "Mr. Fenton, you are most—"

"Unwelcome," Ainsley said as he pushed past his sister. "He works for the Daily Telegraph and Courier, Margaret."

"A journalist?" Margaret could not piece together how he had received an invitation to her auction.

"I heard tell of your contributions to the children and I want to cover it for our morning edition."

"My little auction?" Margaret was flattered, though the presence of the press made her more than a little uneasy. She had hoped to host the event without word reaching her father.

Theodore twisted his moustache between his thumb and forefinger. "Why not?"

"He's been writing garbage about the children, false speculations and fallacies," Ainsley said, his rising temper evident. "He's not here to publicize your charity event. He's here to gather salacious details."

Theodore feigned surprised, sucking in air quickly. "You wound me. My intentions are nothing of the sort."

"Out with you," Ainsley said taking the man under the arm. "This is a private event and you were not invited."

"Peter, is that really necessary?"

Ainsley shot Margaret a stern look, a look that reminded her of their father.

Within seconds, Theodore was flanked by Jonas on the opposite side of Ainsley. Together, the pair was an imposing force against Theodore, who raised his hands in surrender. "Very well," he said cheerfully. "Don't be frightened, my lady, 'tis not the first time." Theodore offered her a smile and turned at the increasing pressure from the men surrounding him. "Perhaps we shall speak another time."

Margaret retreated to where Evelyn stood, and glanced to the handful of guests still loitering in the lobby. She flashed them a defeated smile.

When the men returned, she saw Ainsley give Cutter explicit instructions not to let him through the doors and then Ainsley turned to Margaret. With a cock of his head he implored her to follow him into their father's study. Once inside, he closed the door and approached her with a hardened expression. "You will not speak to that man again."

"Who are you to say who I may and may not speak to?" Margaret challenged. She kept her voice light for the sake of the guests just beyond the door but her insides burned with anger. Her brother had never spoken commands to her and she was not about to let it become a habit.

"Margaret, do as I say," Ainsley said. His tone became hushed as he struggled for control.

"Who are you, my father?" she asked with contempt.

"You wouldn't listen to me if I were," Ainsley replied. Clearly agitated, Ainsley went for the door.

"This is about your true identity, isn't it?" Margaret said quickly, preventing him from leaving. "This Mr. Fenton has found out who you really are and now he's holding it over you."

His hand lingering on the doorknob, Ainsley avoided her gaze.

"Or you are afraid he'll try," Margaret pressed. "You could tell everyone of your own accord. He'd have no power over you if you did."

"And what of Father?" Ainsley asked. "Hasn't he suffered enough embarrassment?"

Margaret swallowed.

"Let me handle this, Margaret," Ainsley said, "in my own way."

Once beyond the door Ainsley donned a wide smile and eager handshake. Margaret dallied a moment longer, watching how her brother slipped into the crowd with ease. *All the world's a stage*, she reminded herself, *and we are but merely players in it.*

Chapter 23

In all your music, our pathetic minor
Your ears shall cross;

To Margaret's relief, Ainsley accepted his duty as auctioneer and if she did not know any better she'd think he was grateful for the tasking. "Anything for Mother," he said, when she asked. He meant it as a peace offering, she was sure. He had given her a kiss on the cheek before heading to the far end of the dining hall, where a podium had been set up. Cutter, Maxwell, and Julia were at the ready. They conferred briefly. It was Julia mostly who knew how the evening would be run. She and Margaret had already discussed that Cutter and Maxwell would bring in items from the library, in the order in which the tags dictated. Ainsley would encourage the crowd and announce finals bids while Julia would keep a record of each item's winning bid and collect the payment. A small desk had been placed to the side for her tasks and Margaret beamed at how refined her lady's maid looked while seated behind it.

With the food trays along the side wall plundered, everyone now filled the seats set in rows, eagerly murmuring to each other about items they had their eyes on.

Margaret felt a hand touch her elbow and turned to see Lady Brant. "Let us sit together, dear."

Margaret obliged, and slipped into a seat toward the back, where she could watch everything. At the podium, Ainsley sought her out from the crowd, and she gave the nod.

"Good evening, ladies and gentlemen. My sister, Lady Margaret Marshall, and I would like to welcome you to our auction to benefit the Limehouse Philanthropic Society Foundling Home. Margaret, would you please stand?" With his palm to the ceiling, his hand indicated where Margaret hid and in unison the room turned to look at her, some craning their necks to see.

Surprised, Margaret looked to Lady Brant, who encouraged her to do as he said. "Stand, my dear," she said.

Reluctantly, Margaret stood, gave a slight curtsey and secretly cursed her brother for making her the centre of attention. She slid back into her seat just before her cheeks turned crimson.

"My sister has been working tirelessly for this evening's event. Following in our departed mother's footsteps, Margaret has dedicated her time and energy to the children of Limehouse and this event, and the good that comes of it is entirely her doing."

Ainsley lowered his gaze, pausing briefly before continuing. "Recent events have shone a light on the everyday struggles of these children. I have no doubt you have read the papers and heard of the heinous atrocities being committed against these children." The room stirred as people spoke to their neighbours about what Ainsley had just said. "Without the orphanage, these children would starve. Mrs. Glendora Holliwell provides them with a safe haven, a place to find food, shelter, and if you have seen that woman with her wards, you would know she also gives them love. It is our duty to help her with the work she performs by opening our hearts and our pocketbooks. When you place your bids you are providing an orphaned child with a hot meal, a new dress, and renewed hope. Remember this and they will remember you."

Margaret beamed and then Lady Brant beside her began to clap ferociously. Margaret followed and soon the entire room roared with applause for Ainsley's dedication. Always a good orator, Ainsley continued to impress Margaret. She could never understand why he did not wish to follow their father into the House of Lords, as Ainsley seemed to take naturally to it.

"Let's get started, shall we?" Ainsley shouted to get over the dying fanfare. "Up first is a beautiful mantel clock..."

It had begun and Margaret was so proud. Hands flew up with each item and many times when the bidding began to stale a renewed competitiveness erupted, driving the bids higher and higher. Ainsley and his helpers moved items along as quickly as they could, a snail's pace compared to standard auctions, but no one seemed to care. As Margaret scanned the room, she saw that everyone appeared to be having a good time. Her eye caught Jonas, leaning against the wall at the back and she realized he had been looking at her. His expression solemn, almost apologetic. Margaret turned quickly, raising her chin slightly so he would see how unsympathetic she was.

"And now we have a hair comb."

Margaret's attention snapped to the front as her brother spoke.

"It's silver with some beautiful green and blue gems. I'm not sure if you can see it at the back." Margaret watched as he handed it to Maxwell, who proceeded down the aisle, displaying Lady Marshall's hair comb. Margaret gasped for air as he walked past and she placed her gloved hand over her chest. It was one of the items she had set aside. She had intended to keep it for herself. As a girl watching her mother preen in front of the looking glass, Margaret would hold that comb in her open palm until Violetta reached for it. It was her mother's favourite and Margaret had intended to keep it for her own.

"What is it, Margaret?" Lady Brant asked.

"I wished to keep that," Margaret answered softly. "It wasn't meant to be auctioned."

"Signal your brother then," Lady Brant said, shifting in her seat and waving her hand slightly to call Ainsley's attention.

"It's okay," Margaret said with resignation. "Bidding

has started. Not much I can do now."

"But should we bid on it at least?" Lady Brant asked.

Margaret searched the room and discovered three people bidding for the comb. Bethany Brundell, a man unknown to Margaret, and Jonas Davies. She groaned and turned away. She would have rather anyone else have it if she couldn't, but certainly not Jonas Davies, who most likely intended to take it to his new trollop.

Lady Brant's hand shot up. "Sixty pounds," she said determinedly. The room stirred, no doubt shocked at the large sum offered for such a small trinket.

"Please don't, Lady Brant," Margaret pleaded as she grabbed for her hand.

"Seventy pounds."

The attendees turned, looking over their shoulder toward Jonas, who stood smugly against the back wall, a few paces from where Margaret and Lady Brant sat.

"Does he not understand I am trying to win your mother's comb back?" Lady Brant hissed.

"Do stop," Margaret pleaded. "I dare say it's a sum he cannot afford."

"Then he should leave it to those of us who can," Lady Brant answered haughtily.

"Trust me, Lady Margaret," Jonas said, "I can afford it." He gave her a look of annoyance and his jaw tightened as he looked toward Ainsley at the front.

Suddenly, Margaret felt ashamed for what she had said. It had not been her intention to insult him and the guilt plagued her until she remembered how he had hurt her. By the time Margaret looked up the bidding had ended and Jonas strolled by her rather smugly to retrieve his item. Margaret's inside boiled and yet there was little she could do about it. The auction would soon be over and everyone had played witness to his obvious win. She willed herself to accept the loss of her mother's comb, convincing herself that it was the memories she held dear, not the object itself. From the corner of her eye, she saw Jonas slip the comb into his inside pocket before resuming his place along the wall.

Vases and side tables, gloves and gowns, made their way to the dining hall, each fetching eager bids. Eventually, Ainsley announced the last item of the night, a large armoire which took four men to usher in but only so far as the door. With the final knock of the gavel, the auction was over.

Guests began to say their good-byes, often bragging about their new treasures. Margaret felt little attachment to the items that had been auctioned off. There was no resentment toward anyone who had bid, or the prices they paid, except when it came to Jonas, who appeared to have only spent so much on the comb to prove that he could. Let the trollop have it, she told herself while trying to ignore his incessant stare. A comb could not give her any amount of class.

"Oh, Margaret, this has been such a nail-biting evening," Bethany squealed as she approached her. "Why, I haven't had this much fun in ages." Bethany pulled Margaret in for a hug.

"I'm so thankful for your help, Bethany," Margaret said. "I couldn't have contacted all these people on my own."

"Oh, it's a little thing," Bethany answered dismissively.

Margaret noticed her looking expectantly over her shoulder. The room had thinned somewhat, with only a few people lingering to nibble on the remaining food. "Looking for Peter?" Margaret asked.

Abashed, Bethany gave a half-smile. "He hasn't said two words to me this entire evening," she admitted, bringing her eyes back to Margaret. Her voice held a hint of shame mixed in with a generous helping of uncertainty. "We had a misunderstanding, you know."

Margaret nodded, remembering her brother's anger toward the event.

"I fear he has not forgiven my enthusiasm."

Suddenly feeling overwhelming pity for the girl,

Margaret placed a gloved hand on Bethany's arm. "I will speak to him," she said reassuringly. "Most likely he has just been preoccupied. I sprung the role of auctioneer on him at the last minute."

Bethany nodded but did not smile. Margaret wondered if her brother had broken her heart. She bore the look of a jilted bride recently reminded of the life she had been promised.

Margaret's eye caught a glimpse of Jonas nearby. He was alone and it looked as if he was waiting for an opportunity to speak with her. In an effort to avoid him, Margaret took Bethany's arm, in the same manner Lady Brant had often done with her, and began to lead Bethany from the room. "Come, let us find some interesting conversations." She dared not look over her shoulder. She knew Jonas would be looking after them.

In the foyer, Margaret and Bethany found some guests alongside the large items they had won. Julia was busy attaching tags to those items that would be collected later, most likely the next day during daylight hours. Cutter and Maxwell could be seen taking a large chest out the door while Ainsley stood alongside, shaking the hand of its new owner.

"Oh, Joseph!" Bethany led Margaret toward a group of guests standing closer to the library door. "Margaret, you remember my brother Joseph and his wife, Annabelle, don't you? And this is our dear friend Mr. Cyrus."

Margaret nodded and extended a hand in greeting. "I trust you enjoyed your evening."

"Oh, yes, Miss Margaret," Annabelle answered, looking to her husband as if nudging him to agree.

"Your brother is quite the auctioneer," Mr. Cyrus said with a laugh. "I can't say I have enjoyed an auction so much."

"He has developed a soft spot for the orphanage," Margaret explained. "For him, it's personal."

The group nodded. "My heart breaks thinking of those

children," Bethany said. "Especially with what all the papers are saying..."

Margaret was not listening. Her gaze found Jonas as he exited the dining hall, hands deep in his pockets as he strode over. Mesmerized by his movements, Margaret had forgotten she was supposed to be avoiding him and turned slightly toward him as he approached her.

He pulled her mother's comb from his pocket and slid it into her hand. Leaning into her ear his breath warmed her skin as he spoke. "I won this for you," he said. He glanced to the gathering and then back to Margaret's eyes. "I'm sorry." For a moment, she thought she saw tears threatening his lower lids, but he turned, straightening his stance, and headed for the door.

Shocked by the encounter, Margaret watched, the comb in her hands, as Jonas bid farewell to Ainsley and left. Margaret stroked the comb in her hands, relieved to have it back, while the realization dawned on her that had anyone else placed the winning bid it would have been gone forever.

Ainsley came over but Margaret hardly noticed. Her heart vacillated between anger at Jonas's early behaviour and relief that he would bid so high for a treasured memory of her mother.

"A gentleman is offering tours of the sites..." someone said, though Margaret was too busy fingering the precious keepsake in her hand.

"Would you like to join us, Margaret?" Mr. Cyrus asked, tilting his stance to catch Margaret's gaze.

"Oh, I beg your pardon," Margaret said, blinking back tears.

"Would you like to join us tomorrow night? On the tour?" Bethany asked.

Before Margaret realized what she was agreeing to, she nodded and offered a smile in apology. "Yes, that sounds lovely." Her gaze lifted to Ainsley, who stood over her, but her smile faded when she saw the anger in his eyes.

Chapter 24

And all good gifts shall mind you of diviner,

"How could you agree to go to such a thing?" Ainsley asked, his voice echoing in the dark, empty foyer. He had just closed the door to the last guest of the evening and was glad decorum no longer required his silence on the matter. "A murder tour? Margaret, of all the most ill-conceived ideas!" Ainsley marched past her heading for the library. His stride was so determined she could hardly keep up.

"I did not realize what I was agreeing to," Margaret pleaded as if searching for forgiveness.

"These children are not sideshow freaks," he growled over his shoulder.

The library looked empty save for the few tables that had been displaying items and the odd crate that remained from the cache of goods. Julia stood from her seat behind a table when Ainsley and Margaret entered. She smiled at him but her smile quickly faded when her eyes found Margaret. Hiding their liaison was proving difficult.

The maid held a large envelope and presented it to Margaret. "All the notes are here, Lady Margaret," she said, giving a quick glance to Ainsley. "Would you like me to take it to Mrs. Holliwell in the morning? I'm sure Mr. Maxwell or Mr. Cutter could escort me."

Ainsley grew nervous at the suggestion.

"That's okay," Margaret said, accepting the envelope Julia presented to her. "I will take it over."

"Without an escort?" Ainsley asked. "I daren't ask how much money is there but anyone can see it's a great deal."

Margaret grew hardened at the suggestion. Her jaw tightened and her eyes narrowed. "Maybe I would like to be more involved in things," she suggested harshly. "Perhaps I don't appreciate being held at arm's-length from anything that could prove difficult."

"Is this about the murder tour or the bank notes?" Ainsley asked, unable to hide his confusion.

Margaret glanced to the thick envelope she held before replying. "Both. You cannot treat me like a child forever, Peter. You are going to have to let me get my hands dirty." The severity of her words contrasted her tantrum like actions. She stormed out of the library and Ainsley could hear her marked steps as she stomped her way up the stairs.

Ainsley closed his eyes and ran a hand through his hair. The evening had been long but the hour on the clock was not nearly as late as he expected.

"Maxwell told the staff to head to bed. We will reassemble the rooms in the morning," Julia explained as she shifted her chair from one side of the table to the other.

As exhausted as he was Ainsley had no interest in going to sleep. The excitement of the evening and a terrible craving for a drink made him want to stay up to enjoy the quiet of the house. A part of him wished Julia would stay and keep him company. He opened his mouth to speak, his request there on the tip of his tongue, but he stopped himself.

Seeing his hesitation, Julia paused a moment and watched him. Transfixed on each other, the pair presented an interesting tableau for anyone who should enter. A foot from each other, both itching for contact, yet neither making the step that would bring them together.

"Good night, Mr. Marshall." Julia lowered her gaze and turned.

"Good night." Ainsley cursed himself when she left. Turning to look at the fire, Ainsley raked his hand through his hair again. Never before had he been so guarded with a woman. If he wanted someone he told them so, knowing often they felt the same. Most times girls were interested in a fling, a bit of excitement in their otherwise boring lives. Once or twice, though, he thought he may have broken a girl's heart, but that could not be helped. He expected and promised nothing, relying on his reputation to precede him. His feelings for Julia, however, were entirely different if terribly confusing.

The main halls of the hospital, normally congested with nurses, doctors, porters and surgeons, were stark and empty, with only the muffled wails of a patient filtering in from some of the wards. Before Ainsley reached the back stairs to the morgue, he stopped at one of the doorways and peered in. A gathering of hospital staff had their backs to him, facing something in the center of the room. Suddenly, the crowd burst into applause. Intrigued, Ainsley craned his neck to see what the fanfare was about.

A familiar voice grew from the wall of people. "I am indebted to you, Doctor Davies," the man said, "for now and for always."

Someone stepped away and Ainsley was able to see who spoke. Instantly, he recognized Sir Gilbert Radcliffe, a distinguished figure in the House of Lords, and personal friend to Ainsley's father. The gathering burst into applause again. Nurses rushed passed him, giggling and fanning themselves. Ainsley slipped into the hall, placing his back to the wall, and waited. He could not risk being recognized. When Sidney came from the room, Ainsley stepped alongside him and kept pace as they walked toward the back stairs.

"What was that about?" Ainsley asked, glancing over his shoulder to make sure Sir Radcliffe had not seen him.

"Doctor Davies saved the Lordship's life," Sidney explained.

Ainsley snorted. "Doctors save patients all the time," he said with a shrug.

"Doctor Davies was at the theatre when Sir Radcliffe collapsed. He restarted His Lordship's heart right there in the aisle."

The pair started their descent down to the colder

depths of the hospital. Ainsley grew quiet. He had tried to restart a heart once.

"I wish I could have been there," Sidney said gleefully. "Just to see how he had done it."

"Dr. Ainsley." The gruff voice of Dr. Crawford stopped both of them in their tracks. Ainsley turned and saw Crawford peering out from his office door. "A moment, before you get started, please."

Ainsley closed the door when he entered and prepared himself. There were innumerable things Dr. Crawford could admonish him for, the largest of which was the five bodies that remained in the morgue and that Ainsley refused to release.

"Yes, sir."

"Benjamin Catch. Where is he?"

"Pardon, sir."

"Where is he? He hasn't reported for work today." Crawford scowled at Ainsley, no doubt blaming him for convincing to take the boy on. "I am not running a charity here, Ainsley. If he doesn't work, he doesn't get paid."

"I don't understand," Ainsley said. "He should have been here."

"Well, he's not." Crawford fell back into his chair, huffing heavily as he did so. "I have held up my part of the bargain, so don't hold me liable on that account."

Ainsley shook his head though he hardly heard what the head morgue surgeon was saying. "What time did he leave yesterday?" Ainsley asked as he stood to look at the log sheets he knew Crawford kept on his desk.

Crawford looked at Ainsley doubtfully before glancing over the paper. "Says here he left at seven."

Ainsley himself had left early to prepare for Margaret's auction. He had not been here when Benjamin was finally dismissed for the day. Ben was a hard worker; Ainsley could see that already in the short time he had known him. Something about the kid endeared Ainsley to him.

"I have little care for what my workers do after they

leave those doors," Crawford explained. "I only care that they arrive on time, sober and not smelling like last week's soup."

Ainsley stood up suddenly. "Do I have your permission to search for him?" He wondered if Simms had gone back on his word. Perhaps he made an enticing offer to Benjamin to lure the killer forward. Not much of an offer was needed, though. Ben would have done anything to catch his friend's killer and like all adolescents he most likely thought he was invincible.

"Search for him? What in God's name for?" Crawford snarled and shook his head. "I only told you so you would keep your end of the bargain. I have kept mine, even though Benjamin has failed us both."

"I'm afraid—" Ainsley stopped himself. He doubted Crawford would have any sympathy for the child.

"Afraid of what?" Crawford asked.

Ainsley shook his head and turned to leave.

"Your commitment is not filled," Crawford yelled after him. "Do you hear me, Ainsley? Don't disappoint me now."

Ainsley could still hear the voice of his superior in his head as he made his way to the morgue. The chill of the room hit him suddenly as he walked in and then his brain registered the smell. Sidney was already prepped and waiting at the examination table, where a fresh corpse was laid out. Ainsley wondered how he could concentrate at all while knowing Benjamin was out there, possibly dead at the hands of the monster Ainsley had failed to track. He blamed Simms and would never forgive the detective if anything happened to the boy.

"Are you okay, Dr. Ainsley?" Sidney asked as Ainsley made his way down the aisle.

Ainsley waved his concern away and prepared himself for their first corpse. The morning dragged on, though tasks had become less tedious due to Sidney's growing knowledge. For the most part, Ainsley stood back while

Sidney asked questions and did as Ainsley said. The only consolation of the day was the knowledge that soon Ainsley would be rid of him. He wouldn't need Ainsley's tutelage for much longer.

Before midday, the morgue door opened and Ainsley turned. Seeing Inspector Simms, Ainsley stopped and crossed his arms over his chest. "How much money did you offer him?" Ainsley asked, trying to steel himself to the news.

"What do you mean?" Simms asked.

"Benjamin Catch has not come to work today," Ainsley explained. "You said you didn't need my permission but I thought you'd at least let me know before you set the snares."

Simms shook his head. "No. Ainsley, I have no idea what you are talking about."

Using the slab behind him to stabilize himself, Ainsley closed his eyes. The sun had risen and no new bodies had been reported and that should have alleviated his fears—but it didn't.

"You're worried."

Ainsley untied his leather apron and hung it on its hook.

"Doctor Ainsley, where are you going?" Sidney asked, paused over the body he had been instructed to dissect.

"The orphanage," he answered gruffly. "To check on Ben."

Simms followed him out the door, neither one stopping to give Sidney any further instructions.

The common room of the orphanage mirrored the gloom of the city streets outside. The air felt damp and the wide eyes that looked up at Ainsley and Simms as they entered looked equally miserable. When Ainsley looked to the stove he found no fire or means of warmth; even a small one would have done wonders to the feeling in that room.

After removing his soggy coat and hat, draping it over a

vacant chair at the door, Ainsley scanned the room for Mrs. Holliwell while Simms hovered at the door, hat in hand. The children, girls mostly, sat cross-legged on the floor, their hands clutching cords of frayed jute rope.

"Mrs. Holliwell is unwell today, sir," one of the older girls said. Three smaller girls seated beside her began to tug at her arm but she batted them away.

Ainsley's scowl deepened when he saw the girl's hands bleeding at the fingertips. Kneeling, he grabbed the hands of the girl nearest him. Small abrasions littered her palms but her fingertips suffered the most. He fingered the ropes and found the fibers coarse and unforgiving.

"Is this the entirety of your lessons today?" Ainsley asked.

No one seemed willing to answer and they all avoided his gaze as he surveyed the room. Ainsley looked to Simms at the door.

"Who is in charge today?" Simms asked.

The older one who had spoken to Ainsley earlier pointed a red finger toward the far door that Ainsley knew would take him to the office. "Ms. Green, sir."

Together, doctor and detective went for the office and found a rather stern-looking woman seated behind the desk. She was slender to the point of gauntness and her thin grey hair pulled taut into a bun betrayed her advanced age. Her expression did not alight at the sight of them, nor did she move to greet them. She glanced from her ledger in front of her, moving nothing but her eyes.

"Ms. Green?" Ainsley slipped into the room. "We are looking for a boy named Benjamin Catch. He did not report to work today. You may have kept him here unaware of his apprenticeship at the hospital."

"I am aware of everything, Mr. Marshall," Ms. Green said quickly. "He is not here."

"Where may he be?" Simms asked.

Only then did the woman behind the desk tilt her head to the side slightly, remarkably like a bird surveying a caterpillar before it strikes. "Am I to know the exact whereabouts of all my charges? If the boy has run away it cannot be my responsibility—"

"He is in your care!" Ainsley couldn't fight down the anger that rose inside him. He leaned into the desk, pressing his knuckles into the hard surface as his hands rolled into fists.

Without flinching, Ms. Green stood. She tightened her jaw and met Ainsley's gaze squarely. "He may be in our care but I cannot afford to take an interest in all the children who darken our doors."

"Isn't that what you are employed for?" Ainsley charged.

"My job is to ensure these books balance. That is all." Ms. Green pulled in her chair and sat. "Good day to you both." She reset her spectacles on her nose and returned her attention to the ledger.

Begrudgingly, Ainsley left the room, slipping into the bevy of children that worked steadily in the adjoining room. "I wonder if Mrs. Holliwell knows the children are subjected to this when she's not here," Ainsley said as they walked back through the common room. He stopped at a pile of oakum waiting to be unraveled.

"It must be part of her bookkeeping," Simms offered, turning over one of the knotted lumps with the toe of his boot.

"Mrs. Holliwell doesn't live far from here," Ainsley said, heading for his coat and hat at the door. "Let's see if she knows where Benjamin is."

The house Mrs. Holliwell shared with her son was a standard red brick row house, slender yet towering four storeys above Ainsley and Simms's heads as they stood on the stoop. The doorbell rang faintly and then they heard footsteps approaching the door.

"Mrs. Holliwell?" Ainsley said as the door creaked open slightly. He stepped forward trying to peek around the opening. "It's Peter Marshall and Inspector Simms."

Mrs. Holliwell appeared, peering around the edge of the door carefully. "My apologies, gentlemen," she said. "I am not feeling well today."

"We understand that, Mrs. Holliwell, but we're searching for a child and the matron left in charge at the orphanage is not being cooperative," Simms explained.

Mrs. Holliwell's gaze shot up from the floor. "Who is missing?" she asked, her voice shaking.

"Benjamin Catch, ma'am," Ainsley answered. "He has not shown up for his job at the hospital."

Mrs. Holliwell backed away from the door and as she did so raised a trembling hand to her mouth.
Ainsley pushed the door in and prevented her from collapsing to the floor. "Ma'am?"

Mrs. Holliwell looked up and revealed a deep purple bruise on her left cheek surrounding her eye, and a small cut to the corner of her mouth. She looked terrified, her spirit broken.

Ainsley clasped her with both hands, partly to keep her from recoiling in shame and partly to look over her wounds as a doctor.

"Who did this to you?" Simms asked from behind Ainsley. He shut the door, cutting off the light and noise from the outside.

"I'll wager a guess," Ainsley answered sharply. He could feel his back teeth grinding as he clenched his jaw.

"He's a good man," Mrs. Holliwell protested. "Just passionate, is all."

Simms stepped past them into the parlour, surveying the room with a detective's eye. Mrs. Holliwell wiped away some tears as Ainsley led her to one of the chairs. With her seated, he raised her chin with his fingers and looked over her wound. The wounds were fresh, the worst of it pooled just below the surface while the less damaged tissue looked as if it was already healing. He took her arm, pushing back the lace of her sleeves, and found a grouping of smaller bruises on her right arm. It looked like she had been pulled by the wrist, and the others told him she had raised her arms defensively.

"How often?" Ainsley asked, trying to keep a professional calm, all the while feeling nothing but a deep hatred for the man she called son.

"Please don't tell him you saw. He already apologized. I'd hate to embarrass him," Mrs. Holliwell explained, switching her gaze between Ainsley and Simms. She pulled a handkerchief from her pocket and used it to dry her eyes. "He's angry because I spend so much time at the orphanage, you see." Mrs. Holliwell glanced around the tattered room. "I'm afraid I'm not much of a housekeeper. I spend too much time with the children."

Ainsley hung his head and closed his eyes. There was something about Elliot he had never liked but he could not put his finger on it. Elliot held such contempt for his mother's chosen profession and, as man of the house, Ainsley supposed he felt entitled to express his displeasure.

"He wants me to resign, you see," she said with a sniffle, "with the papers writing such awful things about the orphanage. He's afraid for our reputation, that's all. I said no, of course."

"So he beat you," Ainsley said with a breath. He stood up from his crouching position, and began to pace the room, if only to expel the rage that was quickly gathering inside him.

"When did you have this discussion with you son?" Simms asked.

Mrs. Holliwell hesitated, so Ainsley spoke up. "Yesterday," he said to Mrs. Holliwell's surprise. "Your bruises," he said quickly. "Some are healing. He hit you hard, though, and the dark purple tinge indicates deep tissue damage."

The orphanage matron shook her head in disbelief before nodding when she looked to the detective. "He's right. It was last evening, at the dinner hour."

"Is that when Benjamin went missing?" Simms asked Ainsley, who nodded.

Mrs. Holliwell shifted forward in her chair. "Oh no," she said quickly, extending a hand to stop their line of thinking. "He's not capable of such... whatever it is you think he did. He couldn't have. Oh, dear me." She raised her hand to her mouth and began to cry again. It appeared as if she suddenly thought it possible.

"After he hurt you, did he stay here?" Ainsley asked.

"I can't remember," Mrs. Holliwell said. "No, wait, he did leave. It was very late. He knocked on my bedroom door and said he was going out. I was too scared to let him in." She pressed both hands to her face and wailed.

"What do you say we pay him a little surprise visit," Ainsley suggested.

"I was going to say the same thing," Simms answered.

"No, please, he'll know we talked," Mrs. Holliwell pleaded. She stood and walked to Ainsley, her handkerchief clenched in a fist. Ainsley held her shoulders and looked her in the eyes to comfort her. "I'm going to see to it he never hurts you again."

Chapter 25

With sense of loss.

Elliot Holliwell's accounting office was located within four blocks of the orphanage and the Holliwell home. Ainsley charged up a slender set of stairs and burst through the door at the top of the stairwell. A female secretary jumped in her chair at the sound of the door bounding open, but Ainsley blew right passed her.

"Sir, can I help you?" she asked. "Sir?"

"Mr. Holliwell!" he called as he marched down the hall. He peered in every door, and opened any closed ones. "Elliot!"

A clerk pressed himself against the wall as Ainsley passed, and others slipped into doorways to get out of his way. Finally, a man with a stack of envelopes in his hands pointed to a door.

Ainsley smiled slyly. "Thank you."

Inside, he found Elliot and a girl Ainsley recognized from the orphanage seated on his lap. The girl stood abruptly at the sound of the door and took a step away from Elliot, who seemed more disappointed than surprised.

"She's from your mother's school?" Ainsley asked, even more disgusted with the man seated in front of him.

"Yes," Elliot answered. "The arrangement is no different than what you have with Benjamin." Elliot smiled crookedly and winked at Ainsley.

Ainsley would have clocked him right there were he not concerned for the girl who stood timidly to the side. "Gather your things and head back to the orphanage. You will not return tomorrow." Ainsley cocked his head toward the door, signalling for the girl to leave.

The girl, who was no more than fourteen years old,

nodded and quickly left.

Elliot stood to protest but Ainsley pushed him back down in the chair. He was surprised how easily it was to push Elliot around. "What's the matter? You only hit women, I suppose."

Ainsley watched as Elliot's lips tightened and jaw clenched.

"We just paid a visit to your mother," Simms said from behind Ainsley. He slipped inside, though not too far, and crossed his arms over his chest while he leaned on the doorframe.

Elliot gave a sideways smile. "Oh, I see," he said as he leaned back in his chair as if a king on a throne. "You are trying to pretend to be all noble and such. That's fine, gentlemen, your secret is safe with me."

Ainsley pounced, grabbing Elliot by the collar and pulling him to his feet. "You are just a scared little boy, aren't you? You wouldn't dare raise your hand to someone who could knock you out, now would you?"

"He'd probably piss his pants," Simms said from the door.

Elliot batted at Ainsley's arms but it did nothing to loosen Ainsley's grip. "What would a toff like you know about beating up a man? Ah, yeah, some bruiser you are, huh?"

Ainsley punched him, landing his knuckle squarely on Elliot's jaw. Elliot staggered back, clumsily steadying himself on a teetering filing cabinet. Ainsley shook out his hand at his side and stretched his neck, sending a loud crack into the room. "A lot has changed since we were children, jackass."

Elliot stood and used the back of his hand to wipe some blood from the corner of his mouth. "You're mad."

Ainsley huffed. "Touch her again and I will hit harder."

Elliot slumped into his chair and propped his elbows on his knees. Ainsley leaned on the desk and stared down at him. "Benjamin Catch, where is he?"

"Haven't seen him for a while now," he answered with a disinterested shrug. "Has to be at least two days, maybe more. Why does it matter to you?"

Ainsley took a step closer, causing Elliot to flinch. He placed his arm over his head and turned away, as if expecting another blow.

"The boy hasn't been seen since late last night," Simms explained from the door.

Ainsley grabbed Elliot under his arm and pulled him clumsily to his feet. "You wouldn't know anything about that now, would you?" Ainsley asked threateningly. He pinched Elliot's arm and held him close. He was relying on every ounce of self-control he could muster to keep from pummelling the bloke.

"No, I haven't seen him," Elliot answered. Squirming, he tried to inch away from Ainsley's strong hold. "Ow, would you let me go?"

With a narrow gaze, Ainsley released him, letting him drop into his office chair. Elliot readjusted his collar and tie before feeling his lip once more. Already beginning to swell, there was no denying Ainsley's hit was going to leave a mark.

"Must I truly answer for his whereabouts?" Elliot said, glancing nervously from both Simms and Ainsley. His gaze dropped to his desk and he let out a panicked breath. "What more do you want from me?" He opened one of his desk drawers and reached inside. Before he could pull his hand out Ainsley leaned into the drawer.

The resounding yelp that escaped Elliot must have reached the other offices but no one came to his aid. Even Simms remained aloof and unaffected at the door. Elliot tried to stand but Ainsley shifted his stance without taking pressure from the drawer and forced Elliot to sit back down.

"I think you're lying...Where is he?" Ainsley asked with a marked growl.

"I don't"—Elliot scrunched up his face in pain—"know."

Ainsley pressed more forcefully on the drawer. "Think harder."

Elliot squealed again, and writhed in pain. "I don't know. I don't know!" he yelled in quick succession.

"Peter, that's enough," Simms said from the door.

Leaning in, Ainsley looked Elliot in the eye before he eased up the pressure on the drawer. Elliot drew his hand back quickly, cradling it against his body. Ainsley knew it wasn't broken, he hadn't applied enough pressure for that. Elliot glared at him from his seat. He'd probably have hit Ainsley by now had his hand not been injured. The thought made Ainsley smile.

"Where were you the night before last?" Simms asked.

"After you beat your mother," Ainsley clarified.

Elliot shrugged. "I went for a walk."

"So late at night?" Simms asked.

"I went to the public house for a bit of gin, no crime in that, is there?"

"What else?" Ainsley pressed as he crossed his arms over his chest.

Elliot looked up to him and swallowed nervously. "I met a woman and I paid her a little attention, is all."

"Engaging a prostitute is enough to send you to the clink," Simms said, tapping his pen on his notepad.

"Who said she was a prostitute?"

"You're lying," Ainsley charged. "No woman in London would lie with you. You'd have to pay her."

"Come now, that's enough." Elliot stood but Ainsley pushed him back down.

Leaning in, Ainsley forced Elliot to look him in the eye while he spoke. "I know you're lying. Stop playing games. The entire city is looking for someone to hang and my friend Simms here has more than enough evidence to bring before a jury, so start telling us the truth or we'll just arrest you here and now."

With a stern face, Simms pulled a small pair of manacles from his inside pocket. The sight of them nearly sent Elliot into a panic.

"You think I did something to those kids?" Elliot asked harshly. "Is that what this is about?"

"The thought crossed my mind," Ainsley said, glancing to Simms.

Elliot huffed. "I thought I was being followed. Bluebottles everywhere I turn, it seems nowadays. Tell me, detective, did your boys see me with the boy outside the orphanage? Will they corroborate your theory?"

"They don't need to. Your connection to the children is quite apparent," Simms said from the door.

"Some of the children. The others I would have no connection to." Elliot's voice began to falter and his tough exterior began to break down. "I never hurt those kids. I'll admit I cared nothing for them but it's not like the rest of the city neither. No one paid no nevermind to those foundlings."

Ainsley shook his head, disgusted.

"Oh, confess Peter, you had no interest in these children either until *The Surgeon* came along."

Ainsley shifted in place but his face remained hard.

"Now everyone is beating down our door to help. Even your own sister was quick to raise funds for our charity. Less than a year ago no one in the city noticed our little foundling school. Now all we hear about is the poor, dear children. I've been hearing it all my life and it makes me sick to think my mother cared more about them than she ever did for me." Elliot face scrunched up in disgust. "Give it time, gentlemen. You will either catch your man or he will fade away and then no one will give the children another thought. And you and your sister will live the rest of your smug lives believing you made a difference when it was *The Surgeon* who made the real difference. He got you and an entire city to see the children you once stepped over without a second glance. Admit it, Peter, you aren't angry with me or him. You're cross with yourself. I swear I had nothing to do with those kids who died."

Ainsley clenched a fist and took a step forward. "You expect us to believe that?"

Simms shifted his stance and kept his gaze on Elliot. When Ainsley looked over he saw the detective's demeanor soften. "He's telling the truth," Simms said at last, his mind made up.

"He beat his mother," Ainsley said.

"But he didn't kill her," Simms said in the man's defence, "and he didn't kill those children either." Short of pulling Ainsley from him, it was clear Simms wanted Ainsley to leave with him. "Let's go. We've heard enough."

Ainsley stood over Elliot, who licked his sore, fattening lip. Without a second thought, Ainsley delivered a sharp jab to Elliot's nose and watched as Elliot's face snapped back from the impact. "Lay another hand on your mother and I will come back."

Before Ainsley quitted the room he glanced back to Elliot, who sat with blood-soaked hands clenching his nose. "Put some ice on it," Ainsley said before leaving.

Chapter 26

We shall be near you in your poet-languors
And wild extremes,

She tried to back out of it, and even conjured up many possible excuses for her absence, but in the end Margaret relented. It would be rude, she told herself, since Bethany had invited her personally and Margaret had said herself that she hadn't a female friend in all of London. Too many years in the countryside left her with the curse of always being outside society, looking in like a child at a candy shop window.

She wasn't sure, though, if she could withstand Ainsley's resentment for long. He didn't understand this longing she had to be involved, to ask him about his cases. He viewed her probing as doubt in his abilities when it couldn't be further from the truth. She wanted to learn from him, to see a crime scene the way he and that detective saw it. He used to seek her counsel but perhaps he felt in this case it was too much, that she was too delicate to assist in tracking down a child killer. If anything, Margaret wanted to prove him wrong.

"Are you all right, Margaret?" Bethany asked from the other side of the trap, an open carriage with benches facing each other. It was a tight squeeze getting everyone in, but the excitement of the night helped everyone forget about the close quarters.

Margaret looked up from her tightly wrung hands and suddenly relaxed. "Oh, yes," she said with a smile. "Just picking daisies."

Margaret glanced to Bethany's mother, Mrs. Clarissa Brundell, who sat beside Bethany on the opposite side of the carriage. To Margaret's right sat Bethany's brother, Joseph, and his wife, Annabelle, but to Margaret's left sat an unfamiliar man.

The tour was being led by two men, a driver and a guide, both profiteers, in Margaret's view. She had no doubt they increased their price once they saw the caliber of their tourists. Margaret had tried to dress with austerity but as they rolled through the poorer neighbourhoods of London it became clear how overdressed she was.

"It gets quite dark in these parts," the man beside Margaret said. He was speaking to her directly, leaning as if sharing some private knowledge. Margaret gave a nervous smile.

"Is this your first time on the tour?" the stranger asked.

"Yes," she answered. She had meant to say more, even ask him how many times he had taken it but the words did not come. Instead, her mind questioned why someone would want to come more than once and when she looked to him he was already looking away to some fistfight that had broken out in the street.

Bethany shrieked and hid her face with her hand, and the upper-class tourists began shifting in their seats. Margaret took a deep breath and concentrated on her hands, so she did not have to see the brutality.

"Don't worry, Miss," the stranger beside her said with a smile. "They won't give you any trouble, I'll see to that."

Margaret felt obliged to nod her thanks but regretted it deeply when he inched closer to her on the bench. There was no further room for Margaret to move away. She looked to Bethany across the carriage, but she was engaged in conversation with her mother and did not notice Margaret's distress.

A little further down the lane the carriage stopped and the guide stood up and turned toward them as if it were a theatrical event.

"The first murder took place here," he said, making a grand sweep of his arms to the right of the carriage.

Between two buildings a brick archway framed a dark alley that appeared to go on forever. A pile of refuse was heaped along one wall and behind it Margaret could make out the form of a man, slumped to the ground, a smoking pipe in his hand. "A girl walked down this street at dusk when *The Surgeon* beckoned her to his side from this alley." The man spoke slowly, sweeping his arms above for greater effect. "The papers said it was here that she was *disemboweled* and laid to waste like the pile of rubbish she was found on."

Margaret searched the carriage for anyone as weary as she. In the failing light she could see most were enraptured by the man's tale, all except the man who sat next to her. When their gaze met he smiled on one side of his mouth. Margaret turned her gaze quickly but she was too late.

"His story changes with each telling," he said as he leaned into her. "I heard it was another place entirely where she was picked up. Lured by a warm crust of bread, so it's told."

Margaret nodded wearily. She tried to turn her attention back to the guide, who continued to speak at the front of the carriage. The guide sat when the carriage began to roll along again and Margaret looked to Bethany, who behaved as if she were attending an afternoon tea, not a murder tour highlighting the deaths of six defenceless children.

"Friends of yours?" the stranger asked.

Margaret nodded.

"To them, it's a game," he explained. "To figure out who did it, as if they could piece it together better than the police. Not like us. It's not a game to us."

Margaret agreed. It was amazing how her guilt-ridden conscience caused her to suffer while others seemed wholly unaffected.

After a time of rolling down the cobbled streets the stranger spoke again. "They are better off, you know," he said.

"You mean to say, they are in heaven," Margaret

suggested.

"Yes, that's right."

The carriage stopped at the site where the third victim was found. Margaret remembered reading about it in the papers the morning after her brother had been summoned to help investigate. It was a part of town Margaret had never been and it was interesting to see how her mind had conjured a different image of how everything looked. The wall of the building looked to be covered in a thick layer of filth, accentuated by the water that dripped down the bricks from the rooftop. A butcher, recognized only for his long white apron with speckles of blood down the front, stood before the shop door with his fist planted firmly on his hips.

Here the guide beckoned everyone to disembark before leading the small group in a single file line between the buildings to the back of the butcher shop. While Margaret stepped down from the carriage, she noticed the driver hand the butcher a small pouch of coins. The butcher nodded, slid the pouch into his breast pocket, and pulled the cigar out of his mouth to laugh shamelessly.

"Did you see that?" the stranger asked from behind Margaret. "The butcher gets paid two pounds, six farthings for each tour that comes through to his yard."

Margaret swallowed nervously. These heartless men profited from the deaths of these children and, what's worse, she had been a party to it. A portion of her admittance fee lay in that very pouch.

"Come this way then," the guide called from down the alley. It was clear he was targeting Margaret and the male stranger who lagged behind the rest of the group.

Once in the yard, Margaret lingered toward the back of the gathering. She had only a passing interest in the tale the guide was telling since she had realized early on that he was embellishing greatly and that his knowledge of the events only extended so far as what was printed in the papers.

"He was a fighter," the stranger said, so only Margaret could hear.

"I'm sorry, who?"

"The boy."

In the failing light, Margaret could see the man gesture toward the guide, who was explaining how Jonathon's body was found.

"Did you read that in the papers?" Margaret asked.

The man nodded.

"My brother said he was to be sent to Canada, as a farmhand," Margaret explained. She used her gloved hand to wipe a rogue tear from her eye.

"Your brother? A copper?"

Margaret shook her head. "Oh no, but he's helping them."

The stranger nodded and surveyed the yard. "The doctor? That Ainsley bloke?"

Margaret was about to nod when something inside her told her to be wary. She had already admitted too much and any further words could mean disaster.

"Margaret?" Bethany's voice grew over the gathering and then Bethany herself pushed her way through toward Margaret. "I had thought we lost you." She slipped her arm into Margaret's and led her away from the stranger. "Margaret, you look unwell. Is something the matter?" Bethany looked over Margaret's shoulder "Was it that man? Is he bothering you?"

Margaret shook her head, "No," she said feebly.

Chapter 27

What time ye vex the desert with vain angers,

The morgue was dark and still by the time Ainsley returned to the hospital. He searched the rooms methodically, calling out Benjamin's name in the faint hope the boy was hiding. Ainsley had known his search would be fruitless even before he started and with each empty basement room, hope grew dim. Nearly ready to leave, Ainsley saw a glow of light in Crawford's office. He had not looked there, assuming his superior would have locked the door before leaving for the day.

Ainsley rapped his knuckle on the window of the door and turned the knob when he heard a muffled sound. Inside, he found Crawford slumped over his desk, an empty bottle of Scotch in one hand, a half-drunk glass in the other. When the senior surgeon looked up to Ainsley he nearly smiled. "Care for a drink?" he slurred. He held out the empty bottle to Ainsley.

With a chuckle, Ainsley accepted it and read the label. Not a bad year. Pity it was wasted on someone who wouldn't remember in the morrow.

"Are you here alone?" Ainsley asked, placing the empty bottle back on the desk.

"Well, of course I am alone," Crawford barked.

Ainsley had never seen Crawford like this. Always stoic and exact, Ainsley often wondered if the man had ever done something that wasn't previously accounted. Stodgy, the other doctors called him, and Ainsley was forced to agree.

Reaching over the width of the desk, Ainsley slipped the nearly empty glass from Crawford's hand and downed the last mouthful.

"Hey, now," Crawford said, as he tried to stand. "I gave you some already." The doctor swayed slightly on his feet and finally sat back down in his chair. Clearly, he was in no condition to get himself home.

"Where's Sidney?" Ainsley asked, placing the bottle and glass on top of a cabinet.

Crawford sneered. "What do I care? Good for nothing—"

"His exam...was it that bad then?" Ainsley asked, fearing the worst. It was a mark against his tutoring if the man, who seemed to perform well in the morgue, couldn't pass a simple doctor's exam.

His mouth twisted into a deep scowl, Crawford shook his head. "He is worse than I thought," he said, looking to his empty hand as if expecting to find his glass. "My sister should have taken the switch to him early on," Crawford explained angrily. Suddenly, Crawford pounded his fist onto the table and began to cry into his hands. His entire body shook with each sob.

"Let's get you home," Ainsley said as he rounded the corner of the desk. He helped Crawford to his feet and began leading him out of the office and down the hall. On the stairs, Crawford staggered a bit but Ainsley kept him upright.

"You haven't seen Benjamin, have you?" Ainsley asked as they walked the dark hall to the hospital's front doors.

Crawford stopped suddenly and raised his gaze to meet Ainsley's. With wide eyes, Crawford searched Ainsley's face and gripped the sleeves of his shirt. The senior surgeon began to shake his head before he stopped suddenly and looked to the floor. Hearing the sound of drips, Ainsley looked down and saw a pool of liquid spreading out over the floor. Dr. Crawford had pissed his pants.

Startled, Ainsley jumped back and closed his eyes. "Nurse," he called out. "Nurse!" Within a minute a robust nurse came from one of the adjacent rooms. "Fetch a mop and bucket."

"Is that Dr. Crawford—?"

"Who he is isn't a concern of yours, now fetch the mop and bucket!" Ainsley snapped. He could not risk any of the staff seeing Crawford in such a state or they would run the risk of the Board of Directors finding out.

With the nurse gone to gather supplies to clean the mess Ainsley began to lead Crawford out the doors. The drunk surgeon began to lean on Ainsley more and more with each step. Ainsley expected they would find a hansom nearby and he hoped the driver would not notice the soggy state of Crawford's trousers.

"Peter?"

Nearly at the curb, Ainsley turned and saw Jonas walking quickly toward them.

"What's the matter?" He rounded Ainsley and sought a better look at the man slumped to the side. "Is that Crawford?"

"Not a word," Ainsley ordered with a pointed finger.

Jonas raised his hands in submission. "Have you found Ben?"

Ainsley's eyes widened. "No. How did you know he was missing?"

"I saw Frisker in the hall earlier," Jonas explained, "He looked distressed so I enquired. You don't think it's *The Surgeon*, do you?"

Ainsley exhaled. "I had been searching but I found him instead," he said, indicating Crawford.

"How much has he had?" Jonas asked, looking over Crawford. The old man appeared to have gone to sleep while they stood there.

"I found a bottle of Scotch, but I don't know how full it was when he started," Ainsley explained.

Jonas opened Crawford's jacket and undid his collar. "Can't hold his liquor, can he?" he asked, in an effort to make light of it. "Are you taking him home?"

Ainsley nodded.

"I'll help you," Jonas said as he held out his hand to stop them from leaving. "Wait here. I'll get my coat and we can look for Ben together."

Ainsley nodded and Jonas ran back into the hospital. A

snore escaped Crawford as he leaned into Ainsley's shoulder. Doctors, it seemed, could sleep anywhere.

An hour later, Crawford was heaved into bed, though neither Ainsley nor Jonas had an inclination to disrobe their superior and restore him to dignity.

"Where's a nurse when you need one?" Jonas asked.

Ainsley pulled a paper from Crawford's desk and began to write a note to Crawford's housekeeper, who would arrive the next morning. Jonas placed the chamber pot beside the bed but Ainsley held little hope for Crawford to use it appropriately.

"I feel bad just leaving him here," Jonas said.

Ainsley shrugged. "I haven't the time," he answered, folding the paper into an envelope. He scribbled the word *Housekeeper* on the outside of the folded paper and planned to leave it on the kitchen counter or another obvious place. "I have to look for Ben."

Crawford stirred on the bed and raised a hand as if to reach out to Ainsley. "Peter," he said quietly, "don't let him hurt that boy." Crawford's hand found Ainsley's sleeve and the senior doctor pulled Ainsley toward him. "Keep him away from that boy." Using his free hand, Crawford pointed a finger toward Jonas, who stood at the foot of Crawford's bed.

"All right, Dr. Crawford. I will." He patted Crawford's shoulder and placed his hand back on the bed. Within seconds, Crawford was asleep again, his laboured breathing turned to the rhythmic sound of sleep.

At Crawford's doorstep, Jonas turned to Ainsley as he drew the door shut. "What did he mean, don't let him hurt that boy?" Jonas asked.

Ainsley shrugged. Part of him wanted to believe the old man was merely drunk, perhaps rambling in a drunken and sleepy stupor, but he couldn't shake the fear in Crawford's eyes when Ainsley mentioned Benjamin. If there was one thing Simms had taught him, it was to keep his cards close, not revealing them until the moment when it was absolutely necessary.

"Peter! You can't think the old man meant me?" Jonas asked incredulously.

Ainsley shook off his friend's concern. "I need to find Benjamin, are you helping or not?"

Jonas nodded sourly but it could not be helped. Ainsley was more concerned for the welfare of the boy than he was for the status of his friendship with Jonas.

Chapter 28

Or mock with dreams.

Margaret could not concentrate on the second half of the tour. She could feel the strange man's eyes on her, even in the darkness, as they walked from site to site, even with Bethany keeping her close at hand. He had known there was a doctor working with Scotland Yard on the case, a detail she knew the papers never remarked on. In fact, he seemed to know quite a bit about the investigation and the facts of the case. This realization more than unnerved her and she found herself grateful for Bethany's incessant prattle.

"Besides," Bethany remarked dismissively, "as if I could ever agree to marry a Frenchman, not after Waterloo."

Margaret gave a half-smile, but kept her eyes low as they walked at pace with the rest of the group.

"Are you having fun, Margaret, dear?"

"Of course, what a question," Margaret said, wondering if she could sound convincing enough.

"You seem preoccupied," Bethany answered with a grave look to her face. "I'd say it was that man. He did something, didn't he?"

"No," Margaret answered, not wanting to alarm her friend. She had her suspicions of the man but Margaret thought there was no need to bring Bethany into it. "Tell me more about Sir Le Croix," she coaxed. "I am interested, truly."

Bethany eyed Margaret curiously, her hesitant gaze glinting in the gaslight over them. "Very well," Bethany said with a sigh. Her hesitation did not last long. Soon she was chattering away regarding all gossip from her yearlong stay in Provence. Assured her friend would not noticed, Margaret looked over her shoulder, wishing she hadn't the courage, and saw the stranger glaring at her from the back of the group. A muscle in his cheek twitched as his jaw tightened.

Margaret swallowed nervously and returned her gaze to the tour guide in front of them. She knew in that instant her suspicions held merit but her realization came with the knowledge that he knew her brother and could easily track her as well, if he had a mind to.

The five minutes that it took the group to walk the length of the dockyard were excruciating for Margaret, who felt like a fox being scurried into a corner by a bloodthirsty hound. Despite innumerable people around her, Margaret felt completely alone and vulnerable. She doubted anyone would be capable of coming to her aid, should it come to that. There was safety in the group, she decided, much like sheep. She'd have to be sure to stay in the middle of the herd, only breaking free at a time when she knew he would not notice.

"The girl was found here," the tour guide explained, stopping at the corner of a tall warehouse building. The group gathered in a semi-circle, fanning out around him to have a better look. Bethany guided Margaret to one of the sides, which gave the girls full view of the group. Margaret kept her stance straight but scanned her peripheral. She couldn't see the stranger anymore.

"Anyone know what was taken from her?" the guide asked when Margaret brought her attention back to the front. Margaret cringed at the line of questioning. The group was making a game of the child's murder, and there was nothing Margaret could do. So scandal-hungry, the city had become a place of macabre fascination for the middle and upper classes. The papers no longer told the story the way Londoners wanted to hear it. It had become far more fashionable to visit the sites where the murderer committed the deed.

Margaret raised her gaze just as the group began to

walk away. Left in near darkness, Margaret stepped forward, eager to find her safe place in the pack but felt a tug on her arm from behind. When she turned, she saw in the failing light a young boy shivering in the night's cold. She noticed his head was shaved recklessly with taller tufts of hair in patches. Margaret instinctively reached for her reticule in order to give the boy a coin of some sort.

"Lady Margaret, ma'am."

She started when the boy mentioned her by name and it was then that she realized who the boy was. "Ben?" She knelt down in front of him and looked him over. Without a sweater or boots, he shivered relentlessly. And then she remembered the stranger on the tour, the one she suspected had been more invested in the murders than as a simple tourist. "What are you doing here?" she said quickly.

"He'll find you."

Margaret scanned the darkness for any sign that the stranger was near. Bethany and her family had long since left with the tour group.

"Tell Dr. Ainsley—"

As Benjamin spoke Margaret was hit from behind and pinned to the ground. A heavy hand was placed tightly over her mouth as the stranger knelt over her. Margaret tried to push him away and began to scream, but her voice was muffled against the weight of the stranger's hand. She looked to where Benjamin stood and saw him step back into the shadows, fear punctuated on his grimy face.

Margaret could feel the cold cobbles through the back of her bodice and panic began to set in before the stranger began to soothe her like a mother would a child.

"Shhh," he said, releasing the most vile breath she could have ever imagined. In the dim light she could see him glance to the shadows where Benjamin hid. "You like this kind of thing? Walking the dark streets to the places were children lost their lives?"

Margaret dared not move. She was finding it hard to breathe through her nose against the tightness of his grip.

He smiled. "Like your brother, I see," he said laughing slightly. "Too curious." The sheen of a blade caught some light and she watched as he brought it to her cheek. "Me too. I've always wanted to know if we all look alike on the inside, if the high-born bleed red like the rest of us."

Margaret winced in pain as he pressed the blade to her shoulder. The blade burned hot and though she could not see, she knew he was sliding the edge down toward her chest. Margaret could see him smile as he concentrated on hurting her. His eyes fluttered toward her face, as if to check if she was in pain, and then darted back to his knife.

She clawed at him, and when her hand found his face she pushed him away. But he was stronger, and the pain was making it harder for her to move her arm.

Suddenly, his hand left her mouth and a scream escaped, piercing the mist that lingered between the buildings. Rolling to her side, she saw Ben standing over the stranger with a short piece of broken crate. He hit the stranger once while Margaret watched, but his makeshift weapon splintered on impact.

The stranger roared and lunged for the boy, who scurried away into the darkness between the buildings. Margaret grabbed the stranger's leg and tried to pull him to the ground but the man shook off her hands and grabbed for his knife, which he must have dropped in the scuffle. He held it to her throat and he pulled her up to stand.

"Margaret?" Bethany's voice could be heard at a distance.

Margaret saw the blade glint once more in the gaslight. She could see a line of blood colouring the edge, her blood. The man pushed her against the warehouse wall, out of breath, knife at her throat, and hushed her once more with his palm.

"Margaret, where are you?" Bethany's voice grew closer. An echo of voices began calling for Margaret. Any second they would turn the warehouse corner and discover them, but Margaret was also aware that any second he could drive the blade into her and end her life.

A tear, pooling on the rim of her eyelid, spilled over and slipped down the crest of her cheek, landing on his fingers, which were holding her mouth closed. Licking the tear, he pulled his hand away and winked. "Another time then," he said, before slipping between stacks of crates and further into complete darkness.

Margaret collapsed to the ground and raised a hand to her bleeding shoulder. Enough blood had gathered to cover her palm and she could feel it beginning to slip down toward her bodice. Without warning, she became very dizzy and struggled to keep her eyes open.

"Margaret!" Bethany rounded the corner and crouched in front of Margaret. "Margaret, wake up!"

Chapter 29

And when upon you, weary after roaming,

"Have you seen a boy, twelve years old, brown hair, brown eyes?" Ainsley asked a man walking past Jonas on the left. The man grunted, gave Jonas a shove, and continued on his way. Ainsley approached a woman who sat on her stoop. She rose to her feet as he approached and was closing the door before he could finish.

"We're looking for a boy," Jonas asked a pair of prostitutes as they paced the curb.

"No boys on this corner. Try the next block over," one said.

The other stepped in front of her and dropped her shawl, revealing bare mounds peeking provocatively out from her low bodice. "I can do ya better," she said, reaching for Jonas.

Ainsley grabbed Jonas and pulled him along down the road.

"No one is going to help us," Jonas said, frustrated with their lack of progress. "He looks like every other orphaned boy in East London."

In the span of an hour they had visited every public house and workhouse within the borough and no one had seen him. This wasn't a surprise. Most grown people paid little heed to children and would not take notice if they were in distress or otherwise.

"Maybe we should—"

A panicked scream interrupted Ainsley's suggestion. "Help! My friend!" The scream was undeniably female. Ainsley and Jonas crossed the road, following the calls as best they could and slipped down an alley toward the docks.

A group of people had gathered. A few stood back in

shock but most had knelt down as if seeing to someone on the ground.

"Send for a doctor!" a familiar voice yelled from the centre of the group. Ainsley saw Bethany crouched on the ground, her form blocking whoever it was in distress.

The man beside her stood up and turned, running for Ainsley and Jonas. "We are doctors!" Ainsley called out, pulling the running man back.

"Help us, please!" Bethany yelled. "It's my friend Margaret."

As they drew closer Margaret came into view and panic hit Ainsley like a sucker punch to the stomach. She was slumped to the ground, her body crumpled and bleeding, though Ainsley could not tell from where.

"Margaret." By the time Jonas's airy words dawned on Ainsley he was already at Margaret's side.

"Peter, I'm sorry," Bethany began. Her hands were covered in blood and had already soiled much of her dress.

"What happened?" Ainsley barked as he positioned himself at his sister's head. The gash on her upper collar was evident but in the dim light he could not see how deep the wound was. As he pulled her limp body from the wet ground her eyes fluttered.

"Margaret, can you hear me?" Jonas asked as he kneeled in front of her. He grabbed her hand, positioning his fingers to feel for a pulse. "She has a pulse. It's weak but I can feel it."

Nodding, Ainsley removed his jacket and noticed Jonas was doing the same. Padding the fabric into a pillow, he placed it behind her head while Jonas removed his shirt and pressed it to Margaret's wound to stop the bleeding.

"Do you have your bag?" Ainsley asked. Jonas shook his head. Just as well. Stitching her up in such soiled and contaminated conditions would invite infection.

"Does anyone have a carriage?" Jonas asked of the crowd.

Bethany stepped forward. "We do. Our driver is waiting

on Narrow Street."

"Send someone to fetch it," Ainsley ordered.

Bethany nodded anxiously and turned to the handful of people looking on.

"You are the only surgeon I trust," Ainsley said to Jonas. "We'll take her to Marshall House."

Jonas nodded.

Beginning to stir, Margaret reached for Ainsley. "I saw him," she breathed, before wincing in pain. She tried to roll over and stand but Ainsley held her down. "I saw him down the wharf." Her hand found Ainsley's shirt and she began pulling him down toward her.

"Who?" Jonas asked.

"I'm sorry, Peter," Bethany cried from the crowd. "There was a man... on the tour. She was out of my sight for but a minute."

Ainsley held up a hand in the hopes of silencing Bethany. "Who did you see, Margaret?" Ainsley asked, leaning in closer so he could hear amongst the murmur of the crowd.

"Ben. He ran to the water." With a shaky hand she pointed further down the dark alley.

"Benjamin?" Ainsley looked into the darkness, unable to discern crate from bricks or shadow from foe. "Take her home," Ainsley ordered Jonas. "I will meet you there." Knowing his sister was in good hands, Ainsley stood and charged into the darkness.

Recognizing Benjamin did not explain the origin of her wound or the person who did the deed but Ainsley could not let the boy slip from his fingers.

He could feel the mist on his face and sticking to his thin shirt as he made his way through the darkness. The world turned black when Ainsley turned a corner and the fog did nothing to help him delineate what was ahead of him.

"Benjamin!" He called out. "It's me, Peter! Don't hide. Don't be afraid!"

Ainsley tripped over a sack and stumbled in the darkness. Trying to keep himself from falling he reached out and found the brick wall. Using it to guide him in a straight line, he walked slowly until the alley led him out into the opening of the docks. A few dim lanterns creaked on the hooks above him but their glow merely illuminated the mist and little else.

"Ben!"

An animal, most likely a dog, brushed by Ainsley in the darkness. By the time Ainsley noticed the animal it had already passed by and disappeared into the mist.

"No one is going to hurt you!" Ainsley yelled out, his conviction faltering. Perhaps Margaret had been seeing things. What if the boy was already a victim of *The Surgeon*, his body discarded like the others just waiting to be found?

Ainsley brushed his damp hair, which had fallen to his face, and began to second-guess the wisdom of leaving Margaret's side. Deciding to retrace his steps to get back to her as soon as he could, Ainsley turned just as the sound of whimpering found his ears. He stopped.

"Benjamin?"

An eerie silence followed and Ainsley thought it was most likely the dog he had heard.

"Doctor?"

Ainsley froze. There was the sound of shuffling, feet scuffing along on the gravel lane. In the distance, Ainsley could just make out the bow of a moored ship bobbing slightly on the water. He squinted but saw nothing but grey.

"Ben?"

A small form came into view, a solid mass slightly darker than the grey of the fog. The boy walked hesitantly and Ainsley recognized him before the boy saw the doctor.

"I'm here," Ainsley called, taking a step forward. "I've been so worried about you."

The boy took one step closer and Ainsley stopped. He

squinted. He'd heard Ben's voice but the child in front of him could not have been him. The boy kept coming closer and it wasn't until the boy was directly in front of him that he recognized him.

"You shaved your head." Ainsley knelt down and touched Ben's hair, which had been cut short as well. The boy was shivering from the wet cold and Ainsley reached to remove his own jacket to give him but remembered he had left it with Margaret and Jonas.

"I had to," Ben explained. "He came for me."

Ainsley's heart skipped a beat. "Who?" Ainsley asked in a fierce tone.

"The one them papers callin' *The Surgeon*."

Chapter 30

Death's seal is put,

Margaret became aware of sound, odd shuffling, and hushed, aggravated voices, before she was able to force her eyes open to have a look around. The room was dark but she felt warm and dry. Groggy, she tried to move her arm but stopped the minute the searing pain swam through her torso. She hissed, clenching her teeth to suppress an eminent wail of pain.

She remembered then what the monster had done to her, how he cut in to her shoulder.

"Miss Margaret?"

A soft-toned female voice not far from her bedside forced Margaret to open her eyes, though it was harder to do than she expected.

"Lady Margaret." Jonas's familiar voice made Margaret smile.

"Her Ladyship should never have gone." Margaret soon recognized the voice of Julia and she realized she was at home. With her free hand she groped the threads of her bedclothes and felt an overwhelming sense of relief.

Turning her head slightly, Margaret saw the hazy outline of Jonas beside her. Julia crossed the room with the china basin and slipped from the room. Margaret reached out her good arm to Jonas and felt her hand touching his face.

"Jonas, I like it better when you call me Margaret," she said.

His hand grabbed her wrist and guided her fumbling grasp away from his eyes. Margaret could hear him laughing and then she could feel his hands cupping hers lovingly.

"I don't feel well," Margaret said, shifting slightly in her bed, mindful of her shoulder pain.

"You won't for a bit. I had to give you some laudanum. You kept hitting me."

Slowly, Jonas came into view, his hazy form sharpening to better resemble the man she knew.

"Am I so badly injured?" Margaret pulled her hand from his and reached for her injured shoulder. She could feel a thick bandage tied in place and she tried pulling it back.

"Don't do that." Jonas grabbed her hand and pulled it away. "Curiosity killed the cat," he said, half-jokingly. "I had to give you a number of stitches. We must look for infection now."

Margaret licked her lips and noticed they were dry and cracking.

"Peter!" Margaret tried to sit up but the pain only forced her back down. "I must talk to Peter."

"He ran off, looking for the boy," Jonas answered, keeping his hands in front of her, as if to keep her reclined. He only pulled them away when she made no attempts to sit up. "I sent your friend back with the carriage to look for him."

"Bethany?" Margaret's heart sank. Of all the people to witness such a thing, it had to be Bethany Brundell, society gossip and socialite.

The door burst opened and a stern Ainsley walked in.

"Did you find him?" A sharp pain came over Margaret as she tried to sit up in bed.

"Margaret, please," Jonas called out.

"Yes, he's in the kitchen. Cook and Violetta are tripping over themselves to feed him," Ainsley explained.

Silently, the door opened, and Julia returned with the empty, clean basin in her hands.

"How many stitches?" Ainsley asked, gesturing toward Margaret.

"Enough," answered Jonas. "She will be all right, Peter."

Rounding the opposite side of the bed, he came to Margaret's side. He leaned over her and tried to look under her bandage.

"Margaret, who was it?" Ainsley pressed, keeping his eyes squarely on hers.

"I don't know who it was...It was dark," she stammered.

"You must have seen something. Bethany tells me there was a man, on the tour. What did he say to you?"

Margaret swallowed nervously. She did not feel as sharp as she was used to and the words came slowly. "He talked about Scotland Yard. About Jonathon." The memory was sketchy. She remembered the man and remembered how he made her feel but the crux of their conversation eluded her. "He knew you by name," she said suddenly, licking her dry lips. "He called you Ainsley.

Chapter 31

By the foregone ye shall discern the coming,

A hardened glare took over Ainsley's features. He jerked his head toward the door, indicating for Jonas to follow him. At the door, Ainsley glanced back to see Julia take a seat on the edge of Margaret's bed and reach for his sister's hand. The look of worry on both the women's faces did not temper his anger.

Once in his room, Ainsley paced the floor like the devil was at his heels. "I'll kill him!" Ainsley turned and ran his hand through his hair while Jonas closed the door. "I swear to God I will kill him. And don't try to stop me. The little bastard has it coming."

"What is it?" Jonas asked. "Who has it coming?"

Ainsley confessed his firmly held suspicion, revealing the name of someone they were both acquainted with.

"Ben told me everything. He recognized him and wasn't afraid of him at first. He saw a rag in his hand and remembered when I told Simms *The Surgeon* used chloroform to subdue his victims." Ainsley closed his eyes. "He narrowly escaped with his life. God only knows what he wanted to do to Margaret."

Ainsley knew it would not take long for Jonas to back him. He knew Jonas well enough to know he would not back down from a fight, especially where Margaret was involved.

At the mention of Margaret, Jonas had his own hands curled into fists, his jaw clenched in obvious rage. "Let's get him."

Ainsley raised a hand. "Wait! I need to think," he said.

"What's there to think about? That son of a bitch doesn't deserve to draw another breath, not after what he did to those children! What he did to Margaret!"

Ainsley's face hardened "I want to confront him. I want him to believe there is nothing amiss."

Within ten minutes the two men had hatched their plan.

As Jonas went for the door, Ainsley went to his desk and opened the bottom drawer that hid the G. & J. Deane pistol. He placed his hand on it and closed his eyes. He remembered how much this case had consumed him, how much he carried the souls of those dead children around with him. Taking the gun would silence his mind and give those little souls peace at last.

The heavy haze of stagnant cigar smoke hung overhead like a blanket. The boxing ring was empty but remained lit, waiting for someone to yell out a challenge. Many seemed to be eyeing Ainsley, wondering who he'd call out. It was clear the young surgeon had blood in his eye and for a time Ainsley scanned the crowd as if searching for a worthy opponent. In truth, he had his eye out for one man that night, no one else would do.

"Mr. Specialist." Theodore Fenton approached, a thick cigar in his lanky fingers and a crooked smile on his lips. "Or should I address you as Mr. Marshall."

"I haven't the time for this," Ainsley answered impatiently. He scanned the room over Theodore's head.

Theodore raised an eyebrow in surprise. "I expected more courtesy coming from landed gentry. I've heard your father has gone to great pains to secure you a *private* education." Ainsley's hardened stare did not faze the reporter in the slightest. "I'm a collector of secrets, Mr. Marshall," Theodore explained. "One never knows when they may have need of them." Theodore tipped his hat toward Ainsley and walked past, leaving Ainsley with a heavy feeling in his stomach.

Jonas tapped Ainsley's chest and gestured toward the door as he slipped by. Sidney sauntered in, unaware that he was being watched closely. Ainsley snorted. If the man had any clue, he wouldn't have accepted Jonas's invite and stayed home that night.

"Hey, Sidney!" Ainsley approached him. "How 'bout that rematch?" Ainsley tried not to smile. Every part of him wished to rearrange the man's pretty face, perhaps exhumed some organs from him as he had done to the children.

Sidney hesitated. The kid looked to the men beside him, a buxom woman of ill-repute not too far away. It looked as if he would have refused had the men not nudged him forward with pats on the back and calls of encouragement. Sidney stumbled from an enthusiastic push and looked to Jonas. He must have known something was off but his pride prevented him from saying anything.

Smiling, Ainsley began to unbutton his shirt and turned to Jerry. "There another fight lined up?"

Jerry shook his head and raised a glass as if to give a toast. "Anything for you, Pete."

Everyone within hearing distance paused their drink-laced chatting and turned, some gathering in a semi-circle around Ainsley, Jonas, and the victim of their personal vendetta. When Ainsley lifted the thin rope and gestured for Sidney to go first, men rushed the bookmakers, hoping to place their wagers before the first punch was thrown.

In the ring, Ainsley removed his shoes and socks and tossed them aside. From the corner of his eye he saw self-assured Fenton amongst the crowd, watching the ring intensively. "Jonas, get him out of here!" Ainsley bellowed, giving a pointed finger toward the reporter.

From his place in the ring Ainsley could see Jonas escorting the man out, assisted by others who were loyal to Ainsley and willing to do anything if it meant a real and dirty fight.

For a moment, it looked as if Sidney would refuse Ainsley's challenge. He stood in his corner opposite Ainsley and eyed the crowd that had begun to gather around the platform.

"You said you wanted a rematch," Ainsley said, his arms out to the side and his bare chest poised for a hit. He wanted Sidney to get in the first punch. He wanted to see the look on Sidney's face when he realized his best could never unseat Ainsley. The bastard had watched Ainsley agonizing over the children, had probably enjoyed watching him cry silently as he leaned over their bodies, chiding himself for not stopping the monster sooner. All of this Sidney saw and felt nothing. The man felt no remorse or guilt and Ainsley knew if he wasn't stopped he would do it again, and again.

"I've already drank too much," Sidney lied.

Ainsley gave a sideways smile. "Didn't stop you before."

The crowd grew louder with cheers and chants. They leaned on the ropes, raising their arms in the ring, some pulling at Sidney's shirt to encourage him to prepare. The room seemed to swell with extra bodies and five times as much smoke. Ainsley looked to Jonas, who had returned and now stood behind him in his corner. "Get me a couple pints," he ordered.

Sidney watched as Jonas slipped into the crowd.

"We can make this a fair match," Ainsley said. "How many have you had?"

"Too many."

"Then I shall have that too."

Jonas presented Ainsley with two mugs. He hadn't the patience to nurse them. He wanted the night over. He wanted revenge.

"Careful, Peter," Jonas warned. "I doubt he would have downed them so fast."

Ainsley handed him the empty mugs and wiped his mouth with the back of his arm. The ale tasted bitter and stale. Jerry stood behind Jonas, another two pints in his hands. Ainsley took one and gestured toward Sidney.

"One for my friend here," Ainsley said with great showmanship.

Jerry handed the mug to Sidney, who eyed it

suspiciously.

"Drink up," Ainsley ordered.

Sidney shook his head and tried to hand it back. Ainsley took it as an insult. He stepped forward and placed himself between Jerry and Sidney. "Drink the damn ale," Ainsley hissed. "We'll have ourselves some fun tonight."

Begrudgingly, Sidney put the mug to his lips and took some gulps but Ainsley was finished before he had drunk half.

"Let's go," Ainsley said, snatching Sidney's drink from his hand and giving both mugs to Jonas. Sidney smiled and began to unbutton his shirt. Once he was dressed in trousers and nothing else, Ainsley invited Sidney over with a quick flutter of his fingers. The crowd roared with anticipation and Ainsley took his stance, hopping toward Sidney, who also stood ready.

Ainsley noticed Sidney's demeanor was much changed. He had obviously been studying more than just anatomy. The men circled each other, tracing the outline of the square boxing ring, their fists poised and their muscles flexed. Ainsley circled and waited, staring at Sidney over his knuckles with the most hatred he had ever felt for a single man. It wasn't about the children anymore. The betrayal Ainsley felt fuelled his hatred. Not only had Sidney's murderous deeds marred his profession but his invasion of Ainsley's examination room, his sanctuary, was unforgivable. There was no way around it, the man deserved to die.

Suddenly, Sidney pounced. He snapped his right fist forward and Ainsley blocked it but he did not anticipate the sharp swing of Sidney's left hand that caught him on the jaw. The pain stretched from his face down his neck but Ainsley pushed through. He rushed toward Sidney, who appeared to hesitate as he came. He landed multiple punches, all in quick succession, before Sidney fell back into the ropes and Ainsley retreated. Enjoying himself too much, Ainsley was not interested in such a clean end.

"How does it feel?" Ainsley asked, noticing the tightness of his jaw as he spoke. "Would you like me to fetch some chloroform?"

Sidney licked the corner of his mouth where blood had begun to pool and eyed Ainsley suspiciously.

"You have some in your bag, do you not?" Ainsley pressed. "And a cloth."

Sidney took his stance and again the men circled. The crowd grew impatient. They couldn't have known what Ainsley was about or that Sidney was the man which the entire city of London had been fearful of. All they knew was they wanted a fight, a bloody good one, and with Ainsley in the ring they were sure they would get one.

Giving away his next move, Sidney's shoulder slouched back and Ainsley rushed him. With bare knuckles burning, Ainsley gave two quick jabs to Sidney's face and sent his left fist into Sidney's side, just below the ribs. Sidney staggered back, coughing.

"I think I just cracked your twelfth rib," Ainsley explained. "That's the pain you're feeling."

Sidney began to laugh despite the obvious pain he was in. He nodded and wiped his upper lip with his hands and shook his shoulders, readying himself for the next round of punches. "Another anatomy lesson?" he asked.

Suddenly, Ainsley began to feel the ale making its way through his bloodstream. He had fought drunk a number of times before, always with the expectation he would lose and always grateful for the drinks that dulled his pain. This day, however, he could not afford to lose. He shook his hands at his sides in an effort to retrieve feeling and readied himself for another bout. There were no rounds, no bells, no referee. In this club, you fought until someone couldn't walk away.

Ainsley blocked a right hook with his elbow but felt a sharp pain sear up his arm. He threw a right-handed jab toward Sidney and caught him next to his eye. The skin turned red almost immediately and a small trickle of blood began to seep out of a cut before turning into a noticeable gash. Sidney raised a hand to his face, brushing the stream of blood from his cheek, and recollected himself.

He looked so smug, Ainsley noticed, somehow assured that he would triumph. He wondered if that's why he targeted children, easily overthrown victims who could scarcely match his strength, given their size and age. As Ainsley circled him, his stomach turned until he found the man absolutely repugnant. No more games, Ainsley decided.

Rushing forward, Ainsley hit Sidney on the left then right, grazing his jaw, and then landed a near perfect blow to his already injured eye. Sidney staggered back and the room grew quiet.

Ainsley charged, hitting him multiple times in the ribs, ensuring he broke at least two before aiming a left hook to Sidney's face. Sidney dodged the last blow and Ainsley lost his balance. Falling forward slightly, Sidney caught him in the ribs with his knee, hitting him in such a way Ainsley fell instantly to the floor. The pain nearly knocked Ainsley out of his senses and as he tried to get up he had to pause to catch his breath. Starting at the point of impact, the pain spread throughout his torso, preventing him from moving from his crouched position.

Sidney pushed Ainsley from the back with his foot, tossing him to the floor like a discarded animal.

Coughing on his side, Ainsley tried to get up and saw blood pooling on the ground. Either his nose was bleeding or he had punctured a lung. He raised his hand to his mouth and nose but still could not tell where the blood was coming from.

Ainsley rolled over and looked up to Sidney, who stood over him. Sidney had his fists at his side.

"Is this what the children saw?" Ainsley yelled up to Sidney. "The ones you butchered?" Ainsley coughed again and realized his lungs were filling with blood.

Sidney came toward him, reaching out a hand as if to

grab Ainsley's hair, but Ainsley wrapped his leg around Sidney's and twisted his body, bringing the man down to the floor with him. At first, Ainsley was on top, hitting the man relentlessly, but somehow Sidney was able to push him off and they were scrambling for dominance.

And then Sidney had his hands on Ainsley's throat, choking the life out of him.

Ainsley began jabbing Sidney in the ribs as hard as he could despite the struggle to get air. He could feel his windpipe instinctively wanting to cough but Sidney's thumbs dug into his esophagus. The world around them fell into an indecipherable haze. Ainsley kept hitting and even tried reaching for Sidney's eyes and face, but the man had the upper hand and was able to stay just out of reach.

He was going to die.

Chapter 32

Through eyelids shut.

There was a flash of black and then an explosion of white before Ainsley was able to open his eyes. The roar of the room returned, growing louder with each of Ainsley's heartbeats. Suddenly, Ainsley rolled on his side, coughing up blood, gasping for air, and cursing the agonizing pain that pulled at his throat.

As the room came into focus once more, Ainsley could not tell where the boxing ring ended and the crowd began. Spectators had stormed the ring and he could hear the heart of the ruckus behind him.

"Peter!" Jonas was at his side. "Peter, get up!"

With a strange heat burning at his eye, Ainsley looked to his friend, who held his coat over the crook of his arm. He pushed himself from the floor, each muscle in his arms and chest screaming against the pain of it, and crawled to his feet.

A few men from the crowd held Sidney back on the other side of the ring, pinning him against the abrasive rope, looking to Ainsley as if waiting further instruction.

"He's *The Surgeon!*" someone yelled to Jerry as he tried to keep the spectators at bay. "He tried to kill Peter! You saw what he did!"

The mob was growing impatient but it was clear Jerry wasn't sure what to do. Summoning the police would put his entire operation in jeopardy. But, clearly, no one was willing to let the man just walk out of there.

Ainsley saw a bloody smile crawl to the corners of Sidney's face as he took in the confusion. Their eyes met and for the first time Ainsley saw the darkness that existed within Sidney's soul. What Ainsley first saw as hardened anger in the man morphed into lunacy.

"It's me," Sidney said suddenly through clenched teeth. "I'm *The Surgeon.*"

Jonas slipped through the ropes and began guiding Ainsley away, perhaps hoping he would get out of the ring entirely but Ainsley stood his ground against Jonas's strong guidance and even began pushing toward Sidney, ready to spar again.

"It's me!" Sidney called again, almost laughing at the ruckus his confession stirred. His smile taunted Ainsley from the opposite side of the ring.

"Shut him up!" Jonas yelled over his shoulder. "Peter, let's go. Let the crowd take care of him. He won't make it to the gallows."

Ainsley pushed at his friend's arm, digging his feet into the floor. "He killed them," Ainsley said through gritted teeth. "He killed them all."

"I know," Jonas said calmly. "I know."

Propelled forward by rage alone, Ainsley grabbed the jacket in Jonas's arms and after three steps he crossed the ring, the G. & J. Deane pistol pulled from the pocket and now pointed at Sidney.

A single shot rent the air and the room slipped into a haze as Sidney's body fell over with a pronounced thud. Blood poured uninhibited from the fresh wound in *The Surgeon's* skull, spilling out over the grey pad that made up the flooring of the ring.

Suddenly the pistol was taken from Ainsley's hand. He turned, taking in the scene, the people, the shouts, the chaos, but the room spun wickedly. Held on his feet by Jonas, who had rushed to his side, Ainsley swayed as the shock of what he had just done rushed over him. The noise grew into a roar and anarchy ensued as the smoke from the powder dissipated over their heads.

"Peter, we have to go," Jonas whispered into his ear. "Peter!"

Ainsley raised his hands to his hair, disbelieving the final outcome that he had orchestrated. He felt a shove from Jonas, who forced Ainsley to look at him.

"Think of Margaret. We have to run. Let's go!"

Ainsley nodded and found himself guided by Jerry through the ropes and toward the back of the hall. Jonas remained close at their heels. An easy path through the crowd, which parted as they approached, led them to a long hallway with a slanted floor. Finally, after being dragged along, stumbling against the screaming pain of his body, Jerry punched open a door to the back alley. A torrential rain pounded on them as they exited the building.

"Jerry, I—" Ainsley stammered as he turned to his coach.

The man shook off Ainsley's attempt to speak. "Just go," he said harshly. "The boys and I will take care of it." He pushed Ainsley further into the rain. Jonas followed, tossing Ainsley his coat. "Go you two!"

Grateful, Ainsley nodded his thanks and turned. Together, they limped down the alley into the welcoming darkness.

The morning sun crept up over the city and eventually the windows in the morgue began to show its light. Ainsley had not dared head home that night, knowing if Simms came for him his arrest wouldn't be in front of Margaret or Julia. Jonas saw to his wounds in the basement of the hospital, stitching up his knuckles and a gash on his cheek. They sat around the vacant examination table, a bottle of whiskey between them.

Jonas and Ainsley, who fought and loved like brothers, waited for dawn quietly, neither one certain what the day would bring. "What do you suppose Jerry meant when he said he and the boys would take care of it?" Jonas asked.

Ainsley gave a half-smile. "I don't know." Ainsley could only guess to what the club owner would do with the mess Ainsley had left for him. Ainsley mentally prepared himself for the confession he would have to make, feeling no remorse except that which his actions would have on his family.

"I've decided something about you and Margaret," Ainsley said suddenly. He swallowed and avoided his friend's gaze.

"I know you disapprove," Jonas interjected.

Ainsley winced at the sadness that laced his friend's words. "I do not," Ainsley corrected him. "Not anymore." Ainsley slipped from his stool, hissing against the tightness in his joints. "You will have a time of it convincing my father, but you will not hear another peep from me."

"Do you mean that?" Jonas asked as Ainsley shuffled toward the trough sink.

Ainsley nodded. "Margaret will need you now that I—" Ainsley choked on his own words, regretting his previous night's actions for the first time. "There's someone else," Ainsley added suddenly, "someone I care for deeply—" But Ainsley was denied the opportunity to finish.

The far door to the morgue opened and Simms walked in, a lanky, bald man trailing behind him, and Frisker following further behind. "Dr. Ainsley."

Ainsley closed his eyes. The time had come. The young doctor waited at the trough sink, his back turned to the detective and his eyes closed, resigned to what was to follow. He wished he could say he had done it for the children but, in truth, he had done it to free himself. He could not live in a world where men such as Sidney roamed free.

"We caught our man," Simms said, forgoing any excitement.

Jonas and Ainsley remained silent. Ainsley turned, crossing his hands over his chest and leaning back into the sink. If the detective noticed Ainsley's injuries, and there was little doubt he did, he made no mention of them.

"Our *Surgeon*," Simms explained as he stood next to the examination table. "There was a ruckus last night at an illegal boxing match. Someone dispatched our man upon hearing a drunken confession." The detective's face was stern and unforgiving. He eyed Ainsley from across the table. "Don't you want to know who it was?" Simms turned to the lanky bald man behind him and then back to Ainsley.

Ainsley studied Simms intensely while the detective spoke, his mind unable to comprehend the tale he was hearing.

Ainsley nodded, suddenly unable to form syllables.

"Lionel Sidney."

Ainsley swallowed, unsure what would come next. Jonas raised his gaze from the table, his eyes exhibiting a certain degree of hope. Perhaps Jerry and the boys had pulled off the unimaginable.

"This may be a shock to you, Dr. Ainsley," the detective continued, "being as you worked so closely with him."

"Yes," Ainsley said with a forced nod, "definitely a shock."

For a moment, Simms and Ainsley stood looking at each other, saying nothing until Simms finally spoke again. "We found a pair of boots in Mr. Sidney's room," he said. "We believe they match the ones Jonathon would have been wearing."

"Was there a washtub?" Ainsley asked, remembering his theory that Alice had been bathed.

Simms nodded. "And we found this." Simms held up a long string of red rosary beads, a crucifix charm fixed to the end of the chain. The detective handed it to Ainsley, who fingered the beads as they dangled from his hand. Made of an unremarkable metal with the beads clearly glass, the trinket held little worth in the wider market.

"This was Jonathon's," Ainsley said suddenly. "This was what he thought the carpenter stole."

Simms nodded. "We can put their bodies to rest now," Simms said. "Mr. Dell here has come to take them." Simms turned to the man behind him and gestured to the bodies. Frisker followed the man into the adjoining room.

"Where are they going?" Ainsley asked. "I can send a

note to Vicar Thompson ahead of the carriage. He's done me many favours in the past."

The detective stood to the side as Frisker and the gravedigger pulled one of the stretchers from the room. It was Jonathon's body. Ainsley brushed passed Simms and went to the body. Pulling back the sheet from Jonathon's face Ainsley placed the string of rosary beads over Jonathon's head, careful to lay the crucifix charm over the boy's chest.

Ainsley directed a pointed finger at the gravedigger. "Anyone touches that and I will personally see to it they never touch anything again."

The man nodded vehemently with wide eyes, no doubt believing any man who looked as mangled as Ainsley imagined he did deserved to be taken seriously.

One by one, the bodies of the children were removed, taken to a waiting police carriage. It was assured they would be buried by the end of the day. Once alone, Simms turned to Ainsley, who still couldn't look the detective directly in the eyes.

"Dr. Ainsley, the pistol, the G. & J. Deane, you still have it, haven't you?" Up until that point the exchange had been cold and impersonal, marking the new reality of the detective's and surgeon's relationship.

Ainsley shook his head steadily. "I threw it in the Thames," he lied, "days ago."

The detective regarded Ainsley sternly, his expression unforgiving and his gaze unrelenting. Suddenly, the detective lurched and pushed Ainsley into the wall. A debilitating pain cascaded down Ainsley's back, causing him to cry out.

"I know what you did," Simms snarled, as he held Ainsley by the collar. From over the detective's shoulder Ainsley could see Jonas stepping forward, intending to break them apart, but an outstretched hand from Simms kept Jonas back. "You may think you fooled everyone but you haven't fooled me, you arrogant arse." Simms eased his grip before pushing Ainsley back into the wall once again. "People like you make me sick."

Attempting to loosen the detective's grip at his throat, Ainsley swallowed. There was a fury in Simms's eyes that Ainsley had never seen before. "Don't you ever stop by my office again, do you understand me?" The detective's scowl depended when Ainsley didn't respond straight away. "Do you?"

Ainsley nodded. "Yes, sir," he answered calmly.

Simms gave a huff before releasing his grip from Ainsley's throat. He adjusted his jacket, pulling the fabric squarely on his shoulders, as he stepped away. The detective glanced to Jonas and then back to Ainsley before softening his tone. "You should take care of yourself better, Peter," Simms said, gesturing to his own face. "You look a fright."

Ainsley watched as the detective walked down the aisle between the other bodies, his gait determined and slow, as if laden with a heavy burden. Clearly, Simms had been torn between two possibilities: prosecuting Ainsley as the law prescribed or congratulating him for doing what the police force could not do. As he watched the man leave, Ainsley decided he was deeply indebted to Simms and the detective's decision not to enquire further. However, Ainsley's actions the night prior had come at a price. Scotland Yard would not be contacting the young surgeon in the future.

Jonas appeared just as surprised as Ainsley. Both had been certain Simms had come to arrest him.

Ainsley took a drink straight from the bottle of whiskey on the table, emptying it completely, and savoured the feeling of the alcohol burning his throat as it went down. He inched across the room, feeling every step through his swollen limbs and joints.

"Will you be all right?" Jonas asked as he watched Ainsley lean over the examination table.

Ainsley nodded contemplatively. He would be all right,

eventually. But the case had made an undeniable mark on him. It cost him an injury to his soul that would never fully heal. The ghosts of the children would never leave him, he knew this already, just as the memory of his own mother's murder haunted him still. The alcohol, once reliable and foolproof, did little to quench his thirst for freedom.

"I will be," Ainsley answered solemnly. "I just need another drink."

Chorus of Eden Spirits
By Elizabeth Barrett Browning (1806-1861)

HEARKEN, oh hearken! let your souls behind you
Turn, gently moved!
Our voices feel along the Dread to find you,
O lost, beloved!
Through the thick-shielded and strong-marshalled angels,
They press and pierce:
Our requiems follow fast on our evangels,—
Voice throbs in verse.
We are but orphaned spirits left in Eden
A time ago:
God gave us golden cups, and we were bidden
To feed you so.
But now our right hand hath no cup remaining,
No work to do
The mystic hydromel is spilt, and staining
The whole earth through.
Most ineradicable stains, for showing
(Not interfused!)
That brighter colours were the world's foregoing,
Than shall be used.
Hearken, oh hearken! ye shall hearken surely
For years and years,
The noise beside you, dripping coldly, purely,
Of spirits' tears.
The yearning to a beautiful denied you,
Shall strain your powers.
Ideal sweetnesses shall over-glide you,
Resumed from ours.

In all your music, our pathetic minor
Your ears shall cross;
And all good gifts shall mind you of diviner,
With sense of loss.
We shall be near you in your poet-languors
And wild extremes,
What time ye vex the desert with vain angers,
Or mock with dreams.
And when upon you, weary after roaming,
Death's seal is put,
By the foregone ye shall discern the coming,
Through eyelids shut.

The Marshall House Mystery Series

CHORUS OF THE DEAD
DEAD SILENT
THE DEAD AMONG US
SWEET ASYLUM
PRAYERS FOR THE DYING
SHADOWS OF MADNESS

About the Author

Tracy L. Ward lives near Toronto, Canada with her husband, two kids and an intellectually-challenged dog named Watson. THE DEAD AMONG US is the third novel in the Marshall House Mystery Series. Her website can be found at www.gothicmysterywriter.blogspot.com or you can follow her on Facebook at www.facebook.com/TracyWard.Author

www.ingramcontent.com/pod-product-compliance
Lightning Source LLC
Chambersburg PA
CBHW051104030726
47504CB00006B/1780